P9-BYB-974

"NATO SAYS A SEAKING SANK ONE OF OUR NUCLEAR-CLASS BOOMERS."

Brognola jerked his head forward. "Now let me get this straight," he demanded. "A goddamn pleasure yacht took out a nuclear submarine? You sure about that?"

The VP tossed a red computer disk onto the desk. "The information has been confirmed by our Keyhole spy satellites and the NSA. One guess how they did it."

"Shkval," the President muttered, clenching his fist. "Goddamn it, another Shkval!"

Pulling out his cell phone, Brognola hit a programmed button and immediately placed an order for a Bell JetRanger helicopter to meet him in five minutes on the White House lawn. The big Fed wouldn't wait for the results of the CIA wet team. He would activate the Farm right now, today, within the hour. The clock was already ticking on a race that America couldn't afford to lose.

If the hammer fell on civilization, Stony Man would already be there, waiting to strike back hard.

DON PENDLETON'S

STONY

AMERICA'S ULTRA-COVERT INTELLIGENCE AGENCY

MAN®

DEEP
RAMPAGE

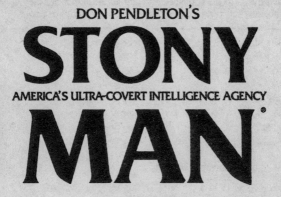

A GOLD EAGLE BOOK FROM
WORLDWIDE®

TORONTO • NEW YORK • LONDON
AMSTERDAM • PARIS • SYDNEY • HAMBURG
STOCKHOLM • ATHENS • TOKYO • MILAN
MADRID • WARSAW • BUDAPEST • AUCKLAND

If you purchased this book without a cover you should be aware that this book is stolen property. It was reported as "unsold and destroyed" to the publisher, and neither the author nor the publisher has received any payment for this "stripped book."

First edition December 2002

ISBN 0-373-61946-4

DEEP RAMPAGE

Special thanks and acknowledgment to
Nick Pollotta for his contribution to this work.

Copyright © 2002 by Worldwide Library.

All rights reserved. Except for use in any review, the reproduction or utilization of this work in whole or in part in any form by any electronic, mechanical or other means, now known or hereafter invented, including xerography, photocopying and recording, or in any information storage or retrieval system, is forbidden without the written permission of the publisher, Worldwide Library, 225 Duncan Mill Road, Don Mills, Ontario, Canada M3B 3K9.

All characters in this book have no existence outside the imagination of the author and have no relation whatsoever to anyone bearing the same name or names. They are not even distantly inspired by any individual known or unknown to the author, and all incidents are pure invention.

® and TM are trademarks of Harlequin Enterprises Limited. Trademarks indicated with ® are registered in the United States Patent and Trademark Office, the Canadian Trade Marks Office and in other countries.

Printed in U.S.A.

DEEP
RAMPAGE

PROLOGUE

Thames River, Connecticut

Nobody paid attention to the ship as it chugged up the river.

Badly in need of a good scraping and fresh paint, the ancient tugboat slowly sputtered along the greasy Thames, heading inland. High above the murky waters, the sky was clear, with only a few puffs of clouds drifting leisurely about.

The tug's badly tuned engines were thumping noisily as the old boat was heavily overloaded with pressurized air cylinders. The decks were jammed full, and the craft struggled to make speed against the gentle current of the river.

Sleek leisure craft, crewed by the rich and barely dressed, skimmed by the tug, and trawlers with full holds ponderously lumbered past. The bearded captain gave way to the others, the crew working the ropes as the engines fought to keep the tug in motion.

After only a few miles, the boat was chugging past the high-security expanse of the New London submarine pens at the Grouton Naval Yard. Unseen chemical sensors hidden in the shoals along the rocky shoreline showed that the vessel wasn't carrying plastique, viable biotoxins or nerve gas, and the underwater sensors showed it wasn't laden with nuclear material. The sensor buoys were chained to concrete slabs resting on the bottom of the river, extending for thirty miles upriver and out into the Atlantic Ocean.

Set at different levels to avoid a silent penetration by enemy scuba divers, the buoys were mixed with an impressive array of Navy mines, each carrying enough chemical explosives to rip open the armored hull of a Russian aircraft carrier, much less an enemy submarine. Titanium nets could be raised to block the passage of enemy ships, or to preemptively detonate enemy torpedoes. There were even hidden batteries of Phalanx 40 mm electric cannons and HAWK missile bunkers to defend the base. Radar swept the sky, and keen-eyed men watched from the shores, keeping the base secure in its business of building and repairing nuclear submarines.

Fighting back a yawn, a bored ensign standing sentry duty in a Civil War brick tower marked the approach of the battered tugboat, duly noting that it was staying on the west side of the river where it belonged. Civilian traffic wasn't allowed closer than fifty yards from the naval base. Drunk fools often challenged that invisible boundary, and always seemed surprised when gunships forced them to shore and they were obliged to spend a cold and uncomfortable night in a concrete brig. But then, life was a learning experience and a hard taskmaster.

From across the top room of the two-hundred-year-old guard tower, the ensign glanced at the glowing screen of the low-level Doppler radar and saw that the craft was packed with cylindrical objects from stem to stern. She was overloaded for a tug of her age, the sailor decided. The owner had to be in desperate financial straits to risk sinking his craft on a single cargo run, poor bastard.

"Want a cup?" a sailor called out, lifting a steaming pot of coffee from a hot plate. The sonar screen behind the man showed clean and clear, a small school of fry darting about in the depths but nothing more.

"No, thanks, but thanks," the ensign said, studying the deck of the tug through field glasses. There was little else to do on sentry duty. This was more of a punishment tour than actually working. At least walking a shore patrol beat, he could grab a beer from the barracks and chat with the new girl in the commissary. Here he had only the placid river and a stale coffee.

Sweeping the deck of the craft, the ensign noted the professionalism of the crew, constantly checking the ropes and chains holding tanks in place. Each was color coded for contents, but he couldn't recall what each color stood for. Six to eight feet in length and some as thick as a man, the damn things resembled torpedo shadows on the glowing radar screen. Funny thing. But then radar wasn't as precise as they showed it in the movies, and often innocuous objects appeared to resemble dangerous weapons on the fuzzy radar screen.

Laying aside the binoculars, the ensign started to light a cigarette when something important occurred to him. He clawed for the glasses again to check the surface of the river.

Damnation, there it was. The rainbow wake of the tiny boat shimmered in the pale afternoon sunshine. Now, there was no way an old commercial tug would have gasoline engines. The fuel was much too expensive. Tugs only used diesel. All of them. And with a cargo as heavy as these pressurized tanks, how could the captain make any profit using expensive gasoline engines? It made no sense.

"Hey, Barton, something's weird here."

"What's up, sir?" the sailor asked, laying aside the novel he had been reading. "Surprise inspection again?"

The ensign started to answer when a tremendous explosion blossomed in the middle of the river, the roiling fireball engulfing the tugboat and blowing chunks of the hull and crew into the sky, along with dozens and dozens of the big cylinders.

"Man overboard!" the ensign shouted, as the tug exploded again, spilling more of its cargo into the drink.

The sailor grabbed the intercom and hit the transit button to relay the distress call as a shower of debris rained onto the river. Less than a minute later, the emergency siren started to howl and rescue teams rushed into power launches. There were a lot of warships moored along the northern shore, but it would take those sailors forever to get a skiff in the water. By then the rescue team would have any survivors from the explosion safely in the base hospital. It had to have been those gasoline engines. The captain was an idiot.

Watching for any sign of swimmers amid the bobbing wreckage, the ensign blinked as he noticed something moving fast just below the surface of the river.

Instantly the P-3 sonar began to beep wildly, and the radar keened a single long warning.

"What's going on?" the ensign muttered, adjusting the focus on the binoculars. Damn him for a fool, but that looked like the wake of a torpedo in the water and heading straight for the base. "Barton, get security on the blower. Raise the nets! Four through twelve. No, raise all of them!"

"Why, sir?" the sailor asked, frowning at the wildly flashing bank of monitors on the console. "There's nothing out there but that burning tug."

"Look at the sonar, man! Those are live fish in the water!"

The sailor rolled his eyes. Officers! "Sir, that's just the P-3 reacting to those air tanks sinking. That's all. If we raise the nets, the rescue team won't be able to get back ashore with any wounded from the tug."

"Jesus, that must be what the bastards are counting on!" the ensign snarled in sudden realization. Striding to the corner, he smashed his fist through the locked glass doors of the weapons cabinet and pulled out a an M-16/M-203 combination assault rifle. The NCO had a 9 mm automatic pistol at his hip, but he knew the side arm would be as useless as spit against a torpedo. Those babies carried enough solid armor to smash through the hull of an aircraft carrier. He needed big punch and this was the best available.

"Forget the nets! Detonate the shore mines!" the ensign shouted, thumbing a fat 40 mm round into the grenade launcher. "Nine through thirty-seven. That is a direct order!"

"Sir, detonating the mines requires authorization from the base CO," the sailor stated firmly, "and you're not him. I refuse."

"Do it, man. There's no time!" the ensign snarled, snapping the breech shut on the grenade launcher and stepping to the window. Using the barrel to smash out the glass, he aimed at the telltale wakes streaming past the rescue teams and aimed just ahead of the underwater disturbances, then fired. The 40 mm round arched through the air and hit the river in an explosion of steam and smoke that completely obscured the view.

"Sir, have you gone insane?" the sailor demanded, loosening the flap of his holstered side arm.

"Shut up!" Quickly reloading, the ensign waited impatiently until the river breeze cleared away the fumes, then he loudly cursed. All four, no six, of the wakes were still moving, and a hell of a lot closer to the base than he ever imagined. Christ, they were fast.

That was when the torpedoes spread out in a fan pattern and one started directly for the watchtower.

Instantly, the ensign tried to lay down a wall of lead into the water to prematurely detonate the warhead of the incoming weapon. Privately, he sent a prayer to whoever might be listening that those weren't armed with nuclear warheads. If they were, the base and most of the city of Grouton would be radioactive vapor in about twenty seconds unless he stopped them here and now. But he just couldn't seem to track the damn thing. How could anything underwater move so fast? It was impossible!

Dropping the spent clip, he reloaded and tried again, this time aiming at the other five dangerously close to the docked ships. This longer angle was better. He may already be dead, but there were thousands of sailors on board those parked ships, and the only thing standing between them and the incoming torpedoes was his M-16.

The heat of the chattering weapon seemed to fill his world as he pounded the water trying to get ahead of the wakes. He could do this. No problem. He could do this!

"Hello, Watch Commander?" the sailor said into the hand mike. "Sir, we have a problem in tower nineteen. Ensign Hutching has started firing a weapon into the river, claiming to see incoming torpedoes. Yes, that's what I said, sir, torpedoes.''

A split second later the first torpedo hit, and the guard tower vanished in a column of fire, the granite blocks shotgunning across the five square miles of the submarine base to tumble from the sky like meteors.

Instantly, the base fire alarm began to howl as another blast ripped the battered tugboat apart, disgorging more air tanks into the churning river.

The blast capsized the launch of the rescue team, and the men actually felt the passage of something under the water, something large and red-hot, closely followed by the familiar churning wake of foamy bubbles from a charging torpedo.

Men and women were running everywhere along the dock when the second torpedo reached its target and punched straight through the armored hull of a Ticonderoga-class cruiser moored at slip 8. Cocooned in scaffolding and rigging, the warship was receiving a fresh coat of gray paint.

The USS *Lincolnshire* actually trembled from the impact as the live fish didn't explode at first, but plowed deep into the warship. Paint-smeared sailors on the scaffolding tumbled into the river just as the *Lincolnshire* blew apart in a deafening concussion. The hull yawned open wide and was lifted from the water by the sheer force of the explosion, the hull literally breaking in two.

Smashed bodies and flaming debris were hurtled across the repair docks for hundreds of yards.

Staggering away from the destruction of the dock, a bosun in the shore patrol lurched to the imagined safety behind a truck and used his belt to tie off the flow of blood from his thigh. A sliver of metal was sticking completely through his leg, but that could wait for the moment. As the blood eased its pumping, he checked the radio on his belt for damage and thumbed the transmit switch.

"Base, this is Harrison," he shouted into the hand mike. If there was a response, he couldn't be sure. Everything was strangely quiet, and the man was starting to get terrified that he might be deaf from the concussion of the blast. "The *Lincoln* is gone! Blown to pieces!"

Stepping from behind the truck, he tried to give an estimate of the damage when he spotted two more foaming wakes streaking away from the sinking tug, even as the first batch of four went past the line of helpless warships and arced around the breakers to head into the slip heading straight into the submarine dry dock. The bosun could not believe their speed; it was like something out of a nightmare!

Unexpectedly, a series of underwater light flashes came from the river, and the water boiled as the mines detonated, discharging a firewall of DU fléchettes. The superdense slivers of depleted uranium, more than ten times denser than ordinary lead, boiled the river as they reached the surface. But there were no explosions from the depths marking a kill. The desperate had been too little, too late. The last two torpedoes were already past the mines and seeking targets.

"They're heading for the submarine pens. Do you read me? The submarine pens! Close the doors. For the love of God, close the doors!"

Unable to hear any response, Harrison ran through the smoky silence, continuing to make reports of damage and wounded. Running along the growing inferno of the smashed dock, he reached a vantage point where he could see the submarine pens. The doors were wide-open, the river water sloshing against the sides of the nuclear attack subs.

Rising to foam the surface with its frothing wake, a torpedo angled sharply past another launch and slammed directly into the side of a Seawolf-class attack sub. The torpedo almost exited the other side before cutting loose, and the hull of the great vessel writhed as if it were in pain from the fiery detonation. Hatches blew off, vents bellowed smoke and a lance of flame rose from the conning tower, and then the boat ripped apart lengthwise as its stores of ammo, reserve generator fuel and torpedoes ignited. The explosion slammed back the dry dock doors, smashing a launch into kindling, its crew pulped beyond recognition.

The next submarine hit was a Los Angeles–class boomer, and it received two of the torpedoes, fore and aft. Both punched through the reactive armor of the submersible and blew off the ends, igniting the solid-fuel propellant for the sixteen ICBMs in the launch silos. The resulting fireball engulfed most of the dock-yard, trucks and corpses sent hurtling toward the distant city of Grouton.

Then from the inferno, two of the damaged missiles rose into view on fiery contrails, the attack activating their launch protocol. But after only a hundred feet the onboard computers automatically canceled the unauthorized launch and blew the ICBMs apart, the resulting shower of flame and shrapnel barely noticeable in the spreading hell zone that had once been the pride of the U.S. Navy.

Suddenly the canvas sheets covering the Phalanx cannons were ripped away by a gun crew and the weapons instantly started spewing a maelstrom of steel-jacketed lead into the water. But as fast as the cannons responded, the blurred wakes were already past them. The antimissile cannons simply weren't equipped to handle underwater targets moving at air-missile speeds.

The last salvo of the enemy torpedo slammed into the only closed dry dock door, ripping through and exploding amid the metal lattice of supports of the Virginia-class submarine under construction. With a terrible groaning noise, the support structure crumbled under the shifted weight of the colossal vessel, and the Virginia slowly toppled over sideways, the conning tower crumpling flat as the boat rolled along the dock, crushing men and flattening machinery in an unstoppable rampage of destruction until reaching the side of the dock.

Rising above the fiery destruction, a wing of Apache Longbow gunships rose from the northern airfield, moving through the billowing black clouds covering the naval base. Reaching the river, they unleashed their full complement of rockets, missiles and electric Gatling guns into the remains of the tugboat, chewing the craft apart, even while placing the shots carefully to try to allow the frantically swimming rescue team to reach the far shore alive.

Then a flight of Harrier jets streaked through the sky overhead, doing a recon flight before banking slowly and using their belly jets to hover over the river to add their own considerable arsenal of Sidewinder and Hellfire missiles to the attack on the rickety tugboat.

The ancient craft nearly disintegrated from the combination attack, the cargo of pressurized tanks bursting and going airborne as their brass valves snapped off and the compressed air shot out to shove the steel bottles into the sky like rockets.

Resting on the dented barrel of a 160 mm deck gun from the obliterated USS *Lincolnshire,* the bosun massaged his aching leg and watched while helicopters delivered teams of SEALs who jumped into the turbulent river to search for any survivors. To the west, the never-ending flash of civilian photographers from the Route 95 bridge soon started to resemble sheet lightning.

Even after the blitzkrieg strike was long over, more and more secondary fires spread across the decimated base as stores of munitions in the smashed vessels began to cook off from the growing heat. Within an hour, the black plume of thick smoke rising from the annihilated base resembled the mushroom cloud of a nuclear explosion. Military and civilian fire crews converged on the base to fight the out-of-control blaze while battalions of medics tried to aid the countless wounded and dying. Soon the news media arrived and the ''exploding gasoline storage tank'' story was splashed across the TV screens of the free world. A terrible tragedy to be sure, but just a freak accident. Nothing more.

By midnight, a Naval intelligence team had a preliminary forensic report before the Joint Chiefs of Staff in the Pentagon. NI knew exactly who had attacked the base and how.

The report received a Beyond Top Secret seal and was immediately hand delivered to the President of the United States at four o'clock in the morning. Fifteen minutes later the entire White House staff was wide-awake and telephones began ringing across the capital.

The first call placed was to the vice president. The second was to the Arlington, Virginia home of Hal Brognola, director of the Sensitive Operations Group.

CHAPTER ONE

White House, Washington, D.C.

The Secret Service agent on hallway duty nodded at Hal Brognola and waved the Justice man into the office. The Man was waiting for him. Inside, the private office was cool in spite of the sunshine streaming in through the tall windows. The trees along the Jefferson Mounds outside completely blocked any possible view of the city below. The decorations were sparse, the walls covered with corkboard coated with handwritten notes and colorful pie charts. Stacks of books leaned against bulging file cabinets, and the wastebasket was filled to overflowing with the confetti remains of shredded reports.

No staff meetings were held in here. This was the true nerve center of America, and it was off-limits to nearly everybody. Not even the Secret Service agents assigned to guard the President could enter without his direct permission. Most of the general public didn't even know the President had a private office.

"Good to see you, Hal," the President said, standing from behind the wide oak desk. The man was alert, but seemed drawn and tired.

"Morning, sir," Brognola replied, shaking the President's hand.

"You've heard about New London," the Man said, resuming his chair and leaning backward. The springs squeaked slightly.

"Couldn't miss it, sir," Brognola said, taking the only other chair in the room. "What was the damage?"

"Heavy," the elected official said with a sigh. "Luckily the *Culpepper* had most of its crew on liberty so there was only a skeleton crew on board. Twenty men. However, the *Lincoln* was ready to heave anchor on the tide and had a full crew. One hundred and twenty-seven officers and crew. That brief battle cost dozens of American lives and over four billion dollars of military hardware. It is the worst naval disaster since the sinking of the USS *Scorpion!*"

"We make anybody angry lately?"

"Always," the Man said dryly. "But Navy intelligence found the bodies of the terrorists who did the job. Iranian nationals. It was a straight terrorist attack."

"There's something else," Brognola said after a moment. He could hear it in the other man's voice. "Has there been another attack?"

"Of the worst kind. The Russian ambassador

stopped by less than an hour ago and dropped off this video disk."

Brognola frowned. "Russia is behind the attack?" He guessed, then shifted mental gears. "No, they got hit, too!"

"See for yourself." The President slid the disk into a slot on his desk. A section of the wall disengaged and broke apart to reveal a flat screen monitor.

"According to the Russian ambassador, this was assembled from a hundred security cameras," he said, resting both arms on the littered desktop. "Apparently, the entire attack lasted less than five minutes."

There was a muted hum from the desk that changed into a sharp whine and the monitor brightened into a view of a choppy gray sea. Hal Brognola leaned forward in the chair and watched as the television screen flickered into life showing numerous Most Secret, and Authorized Eyes Only seals, which was as about as far as he could read Cyrillic.

A voice-over started talking in Russian, and Brognola caught the mention of Murmansk, which was Russia's top submarine base. The big Fed took a guess that this originally was going to be some kind of a promotional video, maybe for recruitment centers. But he was already getting a sick feeling in his stomach that he wasn't going to like what he was about to see.

On the monitor, the cheerful voice was chopped off in the middle of a word and the scene abruptly cut to a telescopic view of the ocean, the picture edged with numbers like the ranger finder of a weapon scope.

Sputtering and clanking loudly, a dilapidated old Soviet diesel submarine was struggling past the jagged fjords of the Baltic Sea and into the calm harbor waters of the Murmansk submarine base.

Brognola recognized the model as an older Soviet diesel. Russia had been selling those like hotcakes for years to help balance the national economy. Oddly, there were no markings, but then many of the owners didn't wish to advertise their country of origin.

There was a crackle of static and then a voice spoke over the picture. The words were in Russian, but there was a scroll along the bottom of the screen with the English translation.

"Lieutenant?" a man asked. "The sub is ignoring our hails."

"No wonder," a second voice replied. "Look at them! Busted all to hell. The radio must be out. Send out a powerboat to hail the fools. This is restricted water. Tell them to leave or—"

Brognola wasn't surprised when the choppy Baltic Sea was suddenly alive with the wakes of incoming torpedoes. What did surprise him was the speed of the things.

"Sir, is this on fast-forward?" he asked scowling.

"I wish it were, Hal," the President said. "But this is standard time."

The torpedoes crossed the expanse of the bay in only seconds and hit the dock in a double thunderclap.

The view went wild and immediately cut to another angle from high atop a building of some kind. Pieces of the dock were still raining down as more of the ultrafast torpedoes struck a gunboat at the dock and blew it out of the water. Sirens started to howl and men began to shout, with no translation showing on the bottom of the screen. None was needed. Pain was a universal language.

A smaller picture appeared in the main picture showing a sonar screen. More shapes appeared from the approaching submarine and darted away at incredible speed, the pings from the TTRL sonar nearly merging into a keen. Then underwater explosions showed on the sonar screen.

"Clearing away mines," Brognola guessed, without taking his eyes away from the monitor.

"Removing a torpedo bunker," the President corrected him. "The Russians arm their major ports with crippled submarines buried under tons of concrete. Makes a hell of a deterrent to invading forces."

"Damn good idea. But it didn't appear to work with these guys."

"No, Hal, not these."

Dressed in only fatigues, some without shoes, soldiers rushed through the snow on the ground to reach the shore and start loading an RPG-7 antitank launcher. Just then a fuel tanker sitting at the dock erupted like a nuclear blast, sending a tidal wave of burning diesel fuel over half the dockyard. A pair of legs without a torso was thrown past the screen, and the view shifted to a warehouse. A fire truck started to race by, and a line of fire reached out to strike the vehicle and blow it into pieces. In the background Brognola could hear machine guns firing, the sharp staccato of the AK-47 well-known.

Somebody in a radiation-proof full bodysuit stepped in front of the camera, raised a gun at the lens and the scene shifted to a rooftop view looking down on the same warehouse. The air was cloudy with smoke, the alarms and screams muted to a murmur as the door to the warehouse was blown off its hinges by another rocket attack. There was another huge explosion off-camera, and the view shook as flaming debris flew past.

From the interior of the warehouse a group of soldiers came charging out, firing AK-47 assault rifles. The people in the radiation suits jerked at the impact of the rounds, but didn't fall. Obviously, they were wearing bulletproof vests under the rad suits. Then the strangers fired back. The defenders were slaughtered, and the invaders entered the warehouse.

A few moments later, the same group raced through the doorway carrying an attaché case, bloody handcuffs dangling from the handle. A few moments later, a flatbed truck appeared, its rear filled with huge oddly shaped torpedoes. Or at least that's what the big Fed thought they might be.

The view shifted several more times, tracking the escape of the thieves and the final state of the naval base. It was horribly reminiscent of the New London disaster. The gutted hulks of submarines lay on the beach, their interiors exposed to the sky and filled with flames. The view switched several times to show the widespread destruction of the Murmansk base, then went dark and a sequence of numbers appeared, followed by more Most Secret seals and then black.

"Two hundred and seventy seconds from start to finish," the President said as the disk cycled up from the desk. He held it in his hand for a moment, then placed the DVD aside. "Four and a half damn minutes. The city of Murmansk burned for a day from the fallout, and they still don't have an accurate death toll."

"Was there any radiation leakage?" Brognola asked, rubbing his chin.

"None. We assume the rad suits were used primarily to hide their identities, or perhaps only to disguise the fact they were wearing bulletproof vests. The Russians aren't very good sailors, but they are good shots. If the troops had seen vests, they would have gone for the head."

"The suits also made the soldiers nervous thinking there might be a radiation spill and they were already dead. Damn clever trick," Brognola said in grudging admiration. "These boys were pros, not just hired muscle."

The President waited, allowing the man to sort through the influx of information.

"What was it the invaders took from the warehouse? I've never seen a torpedo with a flat warhead,'' he said, watching the screen. "Are those rocket vectors on the rear? Must be. So they're some sort of missile, not a torpedo."

"They're both. It's called a Shkval," the Man said, passing over a sheet of paper. "That means 'squall' in Russian. Those weren't torpedoes, but rockets. Supersonic underwater rockets."

"That isn't possible," Brognola said in disbelief, starting to read the Top Secret document.

"Unfortunately, it is. They operate using cavitation waves," the President said. "The principle stumped us for a decade, but now we know how they work. Fairly simple once you understand the approach. The data is all there on the next sheet. Some of which came from the Internet."

Brognola flipped over the page to briefly glance at the sine-wave charts and heavily numbered graphics on plasma-wave formations. According to the CIA report, Shkvals operated on an unknown principle and moved at almost two hundred knots.

"What is the speed of the best torpedo we have?" Brognola asked, still reading the material.

"Forty-seven knots, but we only admit to forty," the President said, then paused as a light appeared on his desk phone. He hit the button to kill the call and continued. "However, the data in those reports is old. Our P-3 sonar correlates with the Russian TTRL sonar. These Shkvals were moving at closer to 300 knots. Must be the new, improved version."

"How can anybody stop them?" Brognola asked,

then saw the expression on the President's face. "There is no way. We can't stop them, can we?"

"Nobody can, not even the Russians. And we can't get cavitation torpedoes to last for longer than a few seconds. They keep blowing up from the thermal back-blast of their own jets. The only possible defense might have been the Vandal antitorpedo missile, but the project was canceled to save money.

"The Russian government has done its best to cover up the Murmansk disaster. But when we got hit, they sent this disk to us. I'll give them that. They didn't dick around when it was clear what was happening."

"One question, sir. Murmansk was attacked with Shkvals so the terrorists could steal more," he said slowly. "But unless I counted wrong, they used eight and stole four."

"You are correct. And then six more were used by the Iranians at New London."

"Oh, hell," Brognola said softly. "The briefcase. That contained the blueprints. The bastards are making more of them."

"That is the official belief of the TDT. And the Pentagon's Theoretical Danger Team is rarely wrong."

Brognola rose from the chair. "Sir, this is bad. If these unknown thieves start manufacturing the Shkvals in bulk and selling them on the black market, then every terrorist group and hate fringe in the world will suddenly become major players. A single suicide with money and a speedboat could successfully challenge a billion-dollar aircraft carrier.''

The President nodded. ''Yes, that is the heart of the matter. At present, I have our bases on full alert, ready to respond instantly. But how can we maintain that posture? Men get tired, get sick. And even with their fingers on the triggers, can anybody react to a surprise attack and retaliate in under a minute?''

The Man rose and walked around the desk to sit on the edge. ''The Joint Chiefs say yes, but I disagree. I consider this the thin edge of the wedge. These have to be stopped right now, before real trouble starts.''

''There's no way we could evacuate any target in time,'' Brognola said gruffly, looking at a picture on the wall of the USS *Kitty Hawk* moored at Tokyo harbor. ''Once we spot a Shkval coming, it's already too late.''

''It's not the military bases that I'm worried about,'' the President stated. ''That's their job. I'm more concerned about civilian targets, tunnels during rush hour, bridges, even coastal buildings.''

''What do you want us to do, sir?'' Brognola asked. ''Name it. My people are ready to go.''

''Brief them on the situation, and have the Farm prepare alternative means to tracking the sale of these illegal weapons. The CIA found a possible lead in New London and already has a wet team on the job tracking the thieves. I want your people up-to-date and ready in case the CIA fails. How long do you think it will take your people to—''

"Hello. Hello, in there," a voice said as the intercom crackled. "I'm coming in. Emergency-access code Archimedes."

The President stood at the interruption, and Brognola recognized the voice as that of the vice president. He turned just as the door to the office swung open and the VP hurried inside. His face was a storm cloud waiting to break.

"Sorry to interrupt," the vice president said quickly, "but NATO just reported that a gang of German Volksfrie terrorists in a SeaKing yacht just sunk one of our Seawolf boomers off the coast of Norway."

"Damages," the President demanded gruffly.

"All hands lost."

"Damn!"

Brognola bent his head forward. "Now, let me get this straight," he demanded. "A goddamn pleasure yacht took out a nuclear submarine? You sure about that?"

The VP tossed a red computer disk onto the desk. "The information has been confirmed by our Keyhole spy satellites and the NSA. One guess how they did it."

"Shkval," the president muttered, clenching a fist. "Goddamn it, another Shkval!"

Pulling out his cell phone, Brognola hit a programmed button and immediately placed an order for a Bell JetRanger helicopter to meet him in five minutes on the White House lawn. The CIA was good, but occasionally got overconfident believing its own propaganda. If the Agency dropped the ball on this mess, the whole world would be in trouble, the cost in human life incalculable.

In his mind, an important decision was already made. Hal Brognola wouldn't wait for the results of the CIA wet team. He would activate the Farm right now, today, within the hour. The clock was already ticking on a race that America couldn't afford to lose.

Stony Man Farm, Virginia

"SO THERE YOU ARE," Barbara Price said, waving Carl Lyons into the Annex conference room. "Grab a seat. We have a problem." Lyons was the last member of the Able Team to amble in from the firing range.

Dressed in a red flannel shirt, faded denim jeans and work boots, Price resembled a farmer in spite of her ample curves. However, to a trained observer her hands were too smooth, those of an executive not a laborer, and her eyes held a fiery intelligence that daunted most men. A former NSA agent, Price was now the mission controller for Stony Man Farm and ran the base with the competence of a Marine gunnery sergeant.

Lyons grunted a greeting at his partners.

"Want some coffee?" Price asked, making a help-yourself gesture at the bubbling pot of brew.

"Did Kurtzman make it?" Lyons asked, sniffing

carefully. The coffee smelled okay, not the usual corrosive sludge Aaron "the Bear" Kurtzman and the rest of the cybernetic experts of the Farm computer team seemed to savor.

She smiled. "Actually, yes, he did."

"Pass," Lyons said, taking a seat at the long table.

He turned to Price. "What's the situation? I've heard about New London. Something along that line?"

"Yes and no," the woman replied and passed out copies of the top secret report delivered here by Brognola.

The team spent a few minutes in silence reading the data sheets, their expressions grim.

"So somebody has cracked the secret of the Shkvals," Gadgets Schwarz said, putting down the report. "Well, it had to happen sooner or later. I had hoped it would be us, or a friendly nation, who did it first."

Rosario Blancanales raised an eyebrow. "You knew about these things?"

"I know people, I hear things," Schwarz replied. "I just wasn't sure the damn things really existed."

"Any clues, data found, any traces?" Lyons asked, getting to the heart of the matter.

"According to Aaron and Akira, the Internet is clear," Price said. "Lots of reports on the attacks, of course, many claiming to be responsible for it, but all were posted after the news was on television, nothing before."

Then she added, "Although some damn shutterbug with a digital camera was on Route 95 when the attack occurred and got several very good pictures of the destruction, clearly showing it was no gasoline-tank explosion. Fortunately for us, he then posted them on the Net. Akira burned them off, crashed his hard drive, and the FBI has confiscated all of the photos under national security. New London is, after all, a top secret facility."

The matter solved, Lyons moved on to the next topic. "Anything we can use? How about cell phone calls from the area prior to the attack?"

Price shook her head. "Nothing. Hunt and Carmen are still checking the records for the area, along with any suspicious e-mail, but that's probably a dead end. The Iranians who operated the tugboat are all dead. The people we want are the ones who raided Murmansk and are now selling the Shkvals on the open market."

"They've already shown how smart they are," Blancanales stated, stirring his cup of coffee thoughtfully. He took another sip, grimaced at the flavor and continued. "Or at least, how smart their leader is. It's gonna make them a bitch to find the usual ways."

"And time is against us," Schwarz agreed, leaning back in his chair. "No way to burn the rope of this problem, without first some place to start."

"Russia," Lyons stated. "Could be radical extremists. Lots of those loose in Europe these days. Or else maybe the SUR has finally grown some balls and think they're the new KGB.''

"Possible," Price admitted hesitantly. "But if the Russian secret service has gone hardcase, that means we're facing a whole new war. And why would they blow up their own naval yard to steal something openly they could have smuggled out with false paperwork? It doesn't make sense.

"Then again…" Price added slowly, standing to walk to a wall intercom.

"Greene here," a gruff voice answered.

"Buck, this is Barbara. I want the Farm to go on alert status. There could be trouble coming our way."

"On it," the chief of security replied. "Any idea who it might be? Or how?"

"Unknown, just stay alert and keep the missile banks ready to take down anything unauthorized coming our way."

"Roger that." The connection was terminated with a soft snap.

"Okay, so undercover seems our best bet here," Lyons said. "We can be ready to go as soon as Bear works up our profiles. Maybe ex-cons looking for weapons for a big revenge hit."

"Good," Schwarz said. "We better be already in motion when the blood hits the fan."

"You mean the other stuff," Price said in correction. "When the shit hits the fan."

"Lady, we're already in deep shit," Ironman stated grimly, cracking the knuckles of both hands. "It's blood that's coming next, and lots of it."

CHAPTER TWO

Barcelona, Spain

The setting sun was just descending behind the majestic Mount Tibidado, silhouetting the ancient Church of the Black Madonna in the glorious colors of a dying rose. The light cascading through the stained-glass windows of the church sent a glorious rainbow across the sleepy shadows of the Spanish capital city.

Riding in a rental car, the CIA wet team, code name Inferno, was maneuvering through the beautiful stucco homes, with their wrought-iron second-story balconies and red tile roofs. Here and there a modern building of steel and glass rose above the older structures. But even then the new offices were edged in mosaic tiles and granite walks with curved arches. The grace of the old aristocrats mixed with the efficiency of the new financiers, forming a city unlike any other in the world. The people filling the busy streets called out and sang in a dozen different languages, and the air was rich with the aromas of the decorative lemon trees combining with exotic spices and the salty aroma of the nearby ocean. Barcelona was more like a work of art that people lived in, rather than a mere city of commerce.

Checking their silenced weapons, Inferno team watched the bustling throngs through the tinted windows of the sedan, looking for familiar faces or people suddenly alert as the sedan drove by. The wetwork squad was zeroing in on the Shkval thieves and fully expected to encounter some level of resistance before terminating the terrorists with extreme prejudice. Political soldiers—the words *kill* or *murder* weren't used by them—but it was exactly what they did, and they were experts at the job.

Reaching the smaller streets outside the downtown hub, the driver make a left at the world-famous Picasso Museum. There the driver locked the doors as the sedan rolled into El Raval, the worst slum in Spain.

"In America this would be simply called the inner city," one of the agents said, checking the fast-draw derringer tucked up his sleeve. He then extended his arm as if in handshake, and the derringer shot out on a plastic assembly, the hammer dropping with a loud click. Satisfied, he began loading the weapon with .44 Glaser rounds.

"Americans lie to themselves more than Spaniards," the local driver said. "We are basically an honest people and like to call a rock a rock, not something else to pretend it is less hard. This is where the people with no money live. It is a slum, no more, no less."

"And you are sure the foreigners aren't Spanish," the leader of the CIA team asked again, tucking a radio transmitter into his ear. The man tapped his multifunctional watch. There was a crackle of static in the earphone, and then he heard the regular breathing of the rest of the team.

"Links are live," another man said, touching his ear.

"Foreign? *Sí, sí,* the newcomers are very pale, with blond hair. I would think them German, but others think not."

The leader narrowed his eyes and cracked his knuckles. "Germans, eh? Interesting."

The driver shrugged. "Just my opinion. I could be wrong."

Angling into an alley dark with shadows, the car slowed to allow the passage of an old woman walking a pack of tiny yipping dogs. Lounging in a doorway, a thin man swilling red wine from a bottle with a broken neck stared at them without interest, never pausing in his careful drinking.

In this section of Barcelona, there were no tourists. Some drove by on a bus, but the rest stayed away. There were wonders to see here, but the locals disliked the flashing cameras, as if their misery was something to be saved and treasured by the rich for their amusement. Occasionally, pompous fools from other countries got drunk at the little bars clustered on almost every corner, and in the morning there was always a corpse lying on the side, stripped of all its belongings, and often its very clothing. With a million suspects for each crime, the federal police did little on such matters. They knew the simple truth that there was no law among the truly poor, only survival.

As they reached a spacious piazza, the tall spires of the Gothic cathedral could be seen reaching high above the golden city. But the walls of the sagging local buildings were garishly painted with some small touches of actual skill here and there scattered among the vulgarities and smears.

"I hate Spain," one of the CIA killers grumbled, screwing a sound suppressor onto a 10 mm Falcon pistol. "Too hot."

A bald man frowned at his companion. "Yeah, and Sweden was too cold. Stop complaining."

"Spain is fine by me," another added with a grin. "I like Latina women."

"Now for me, I prefer a plump and juicy Georgia peach to any of these tiny Latin dishes," said the fourth man in a thick Southern accent. "Way too small. Barely more than a mouthful."

"What?" The other man snorted. "I wasn't talking about food, you damn hillbilly."

Sliding a stiletto into a sheath on his belt, the big CIA assassin grinned widely. "Neither was I, Yankee boy."

The lone woman of the wet team scowled at her male counterparts but kept her own counsel. She didn't like any of them but the CIA often teamed people together who didn't get along. They said it created synergy. She just considered it a pain in the ass.

"This is it," the driver said, easing the rental car to a gentle stop at the granite curbstones. A lounging group of old men looked up from their game of checkers at the arrival of the luxury car, then returned to the game with the slow grace of old bones brittle enough to break from their own weight.

"Get hard, people," the leader commanded, performing a final check on the satellite uplink that would connect them with the secret war room of the Agency back in D.C. The director may not want to get his hands dirty, but he always wanted to know what was happening.

The tugboat that attacked New London had been stolen from a small shipping company in Maine. Video cameras from the local bank had caught the license plates of the cars used by the thieves, which sent an FBI recon team to the owners' apartments in Rhode Island. There soil samples and a single coin found under a sofa cushion led the SID to believe the terrorists had purchased their Shkval torpedoes in Barcelona, Spain.

A local contact from the cold war days had tipped the CIA to a group of European men hidden at an old apartment complex in the middle of the sprawling slum. The strangers didn't speak Spanish very well, or Italian, German or any other language that the locals knew, but had tremendous amounts of cash and were ruthlessly efficient with anybody who cheated them on giving change for their groceries, drinks or even the whores they used. With the proper induce-ment, the streetwalkers reported that the men were heavily muscled, covered with scars, many of them the pale, puckered starfish patterns of bullet wounds, and some odd military-style tattoos. Good enough.

The strangers also killed a drug dealer who tried to sell them some cocaine, yet they purchased a large quantity of revolvers and new ammunition. More than good enough. This information fit the textbook profile of a new weapons dealer, which made the CIA wet-team leader very nervous. When anything seemed to be perfect, that usually meant it wasn't and that some-thing important had been missed. The CIA couldn't identify the strangers from that limited amount of data, but clearly they were pros in hiding. That was good enough for a hard probe and, if necessary, wet work.

None of the team's weapons were traceable back to America, not even the ammunition or the clothes they wore.

After watching the neighborhood for a few minutes, the team climbed from the sedan and the driver quietly drove away. He would return at irreg-ular times to disguise the fact that he was on a circular route.

Clicking their empty cameras at the people and the buildings, the team strolled along a few blocks and then casually entered the enclosed piazza of the crumbling apartment complex through an arched tunnel that went through the ground level. There was an iron grating to close off the tunnel, but it hung impotently against the wall, its rusty hinges no longer attached to the dirty red bricks. Reaching the piazza they saw ropes of drying wash hanging across the courtyard. A child's red ball lay on the cobblestones, but not a soul was in sight. The numbered doors of the apartments lined the courtyard, most of them patched and in desperate need of paint.

"Routine six," the leader subvocalized into his throat mike, and the team spread out in a standard search pattern formation.

Moving swiftly across the courtyard, the team saw that every balcony was closed in spite of the afternoon heat, and that each apartment door was missing a latch and doorknob. Some even had white marble benches placed in front to bar entrance.

"To keep out thieves?" one of the men asked, adjusting his designer sunglasses.

"More likely to keep us in the courtyard," the leader said, feeling the hairs rise on the back of his neck. He flexed his hand, and the Colt derringer snapped into his palm. "Delta three, secure the tunnel. We are leaving and right goddamn now."

"Roger, Delta One. Hey—" the Southern agent said in surprise as the mouth of the tunnel was suddenly closed off by a truck moving across the opening. There was no sound of a running engine, only the squeak of brakes locking into place.

"Alert," he reported quickly, drawing his pistol from a shoulder holster. "The tunnel is closed off. This is a trap."

"Routine nine," the woman ordered over her throat mike, pulling an Ingram machine pistol from her black leather purse and jacking the arming bolt.

But even as the wet team drew its weapons, a swarm of shiny objects came arching over the red tile rooftops of the surrounding complex to crash on the cobblestones and whoof into pools of flame. Molotov cocktails! One of the agents was standing directly alongside a hit and was instantly covered with gasoline.

As he began to shriek piercingly, the big team member pumped half a dozen rounds from his 10 mm pistol into the parked truck. The big rounds punched through the sheet of canvas draping over the side of the vehicle, and there was a rush of pink fluid from the line. The air became thick with a pungent chemical stench. Mother of God, it was a tanker full of gasoline!

As the fuel washed through the tunnel, the woman and the Southern agent both got badly splashed and quickly starting stripping off the flammable clothing.

The other assassins quickly backed away from their drenched teammate and the spreading pink flood on the ground as even more Molotovs came crashing down from above. The woman burst into flames as a spark from the now burning laundry landed in her hair. She screamed hideously as the flames covered her entire body, then turned the machine pistol around and died in a chattering stream of her own bullets.

"Gamma Four to Omega, we are under attack," one of the man said aloud, touching his earphone, then he cursed and threw it to the ground. "The transmission is being jammed!"

Pulling a pin on a grenade, the leader flipped off the spoon and threw the charge at a marble bench blocking a doorway. The delicately carved stone was blown apart, the heavy door ripped off its hinges to expose the room beyond. The apartment was jammed completely full busted pieces of wood, and again there came the strong smell of gasoline.

The leader backed away, his weapon searching for a target. Sweet Jesus, this whole place was a killing box, and they had walked in like rank amateurs.

"This way, sir!" one of the men shouted over the growing crackle of the spreading fire.

As the agent crouched against the plaster wall and cupped his hands, the leader raced across the cobblestones and placed a shoe in the other man's hand as he leaped upward, and the first man heaved with all his might. They may be trapped, but one of them would escape to finish the job!

The boost was enough, and the CIA operative reached the iron railing of the balcony and made it over. He landed in a crouch and threw himself at the closed louvered doors. The wood veneer shattered, and he rammed into the brick wall filling the doorway. Twisting sideways, he kicked at the bricks in a martial-arts move that achieved nothing.

"Next balcony!" he shouted, pulling out his last grenade and removing the pin. His team was trapped, but not dead yet. When they got hold of these bastards, it would take them a week to die. Sons of bitches were going to pay!

Priming the charge, the CIA operative threw the bomb at the other balcony, clearing away the false doors and blowing open the stacked bricks. More firewood tumbled from the smoking gap.

As sweat began trickling off his face from the stifling heat of the enclosed courtyard, the man couldn't believe what was happening. How could anybody have filled an entire building this way on such short notice? As the pungent fumes of the heat of the mounting fire swept across the piazza, the truth hit him like a bullet in the guts. The enemy hadn't done this on short notice. This was a trap established long before the terrorist attacks had begun. They knew there would be an investigation and had prepared an elaborate trap to eliminate their future hunters.

"Relay!" he ordered frantically, and the men on the ground threw grenades up to him. There was yet a small chance he could blow open a passage through the firewood with a grenade and possibly escape.

But even as he flipped off the arming lever, the loosened bolts of the balcony began to creak, and it ripped free from the stucco wall to plummet to the cobblestones. The team leader felt both of his legs shatter from the landing, and he lost his grip on the grenade. The military charge rolled only a few feet away, and the man desperately clawed for the grenades when there was a loud crack. The CIA team leader was flipped over, blood spreading from a huge hole in his chest to mix with the expanding pool of gasoline still pouring from the tanker blocking the tunnel.

Triggering their handguns blindly into the smoke, the CIA wet team hit only open sky and stucco as the hidden sniper shot three more times, wounding each agent in the hip. Then the big blond man departed, leaving the Americans alive and at the mercy of the flames.

As the heat and smoke of the conflagration steadily increased, there were three more pistol shots from within the center of the apartment complex, and then nothing but the strident crackle of the horrible inferno.

CHAPTER THREE

Reno, Nevada

Four wet tires whispered on the smooth new road as a freshly polished Excalibur limousine hummed along the empty Nevada road through the outskirts of Reno.

Far to the southeast, Las Vegas was alive with lights and sounds, music and laughter. But Reno was a more subdued town, and the northern section was under heavy construction in another major push for expansion by the city council.

The passengers of the limo were pleased with the news; they knew that construction sites were always good locations for clandestine meetings. The civilian population was at a minimum, which meant fewer witnesses to remove if things went wrong, and virtually no police. What was there to steal—bricks and planks? Oh, there would be hired security, old men with fat bellies and guns unfired for twenty years. A handful of cash sent them away. If there was a hero who refused to do business, then a knife thrust into that soft belly removed the troublemaker and there were unlimited places to dump a corpse in a construction zone. Yet another plus for choosing this locale.

The passengers in the heavy vehicle sat silently as the driver expertly maneuvered his way through the maze of gigantic trash bins and piles of bricks filling the gravel streets. Naked steel frames rose from pale concrete foundations, wires and aluminum conduits snaking through the metal skeletons like metallic ivy, and acres of plastic sheeting draped over the buildings too protect the work crews from the ravages of the desert heat.

"Air-conditioned construction sites," one of the men muttered. "America is wonderful."

"Decadent," another said, scowling.

The first shrugged. "Same thing. Decadence is wonderful."

"Yes, Comrade," one of the men said into a telephone receiver. "Thank you. The payment will be made to the Swiss account as usual. Goodbye." He placed the receiver into a recessed compartment of the rear seat, which closed automatically.

Sitting alone near the silent DVD player, a huge man in a trench coat waited for a report. The British-made garment seemed to be specifically designed for hiding weapons. Pure coincidence, or more brilliant designing from the always clever Brits, there was no way of ever knowing. But the conclusion was the same. And this early in the morning, it would still be reasonable for them to be wearing the coats. Deserts were only hot in the day, but often bitterly cold at night.

British clothes, American limousines, German guns, Japanese women, Scotch whiskey. With their new millions from selling arms, the world was fast becoming quite an enjoyable place for the retired soldiers. But there was a little business to conduct this night, and thus this long trip into the desert of Nevada.

"Spain went off without a hitch, Sarge," the man who had taken the report stated. "Everybody is dead, and our mercs laid a false trail to the IRA in Dublin for the idiot CIA to follow."

The limousine paused before entering the abandoned parking garage, and a bum shivering on the corner gave the driver an odd hand signal before returning to his bottle of wine hidden inside a brown paper bag.

"Something's wrong," the driver announced as the bulletproof sheet of Armorlite glass slid down, opening the interior of the luxury vehicle into a single area. "Our sentry reports more men waiting for us than expected."

The five men in impeccably tailored business suits immediately drew weapons. Their shoes were of the finest Italian leather, their ties made of raw Chinese silk. Yet somehow they wore these trappings of wealth as if they were a uniform, stiffly formal. Their hands were heavily scarred and looked more suitable for a stevedore, and their eyes were those of professional killers, hard and calm, without mercy or remorse.

"We expected as much," former Lieutenant-Colonel Sergei Zofchak rumbled deep in his throat as he drew a sleek KEDR subgun from underneath his trench coat. The angular weapon was twice as long as normal with the addition of a curved clip and slim sound suppressor. One of the first lessons they had learned here in America was always do business at night. It was the perfect excuse for wearing flowing coats that could be used to hide so many things from the sight of the enemy.

The other members of the squad prepared their own weapons and worked the bolts arming the rapid-fire Russian KEDR subguns.

"Better than our old Skorpions, eh?" a man with thick curly hair said with a smile, glancing out the tinted window of the limo. "Much less jamming."

"More money, better guns," rumbled a bald man sporting a full beard, while flicking off the safety of his subgun with an oddly pink thumb. The nail was gone, leaving only the bare flesh. A gift from the KGB that had been paid back a thousandfold.

"God bless America," one of the others said with a chuckle, loosening the belt of thermite canisters strapped across his wide chest. "More money means better everything here, isn't that right, Boris?"

The curly haired man nodded agreement.

"I still prefer hills of Moravia to Beverly Hills,"

Solomon, the tallest man, said, using each hand to jack the slide of the other's Glock 20.

The guns were a perfect match, and were jokingly referred to as the twins by the rest of the assault team. It was only common sense for them to all use the same model of subgun, as ammunition could be shared in case of trouble. But a man's handgun was a personal choice, and each carried his own personal favorite. Every weapon was top of the line and absolutely brand-new.

"Sergeant?" Zofchak asked, leaning forward slightly. "Do you think the fools plan to rob us, or have they cut a deal with the American government?"

The limousine gave only the smallest jounce as it rolled into the garage in near pitch darkness.

Sitting in the rear seat, former Master Sergeant Jozsef Vadas raised his head in a saurian manner. A long jagged scar ran across his entire face, down his throat and disappeared into his freshly laundered shirt, going all the way to his groin. It had been the first cut from the women of Afghanistan. They had planned to do much more, but a Soviet gunship arrived just in time to kill them all and destroy their village afterward. If the women had struck fast, Vadas would have been killed, or at least horribly mutilated. But since they had chosen torture first, he lived. As a courtesy to all women, he never raped again, and simply executed them with a single round to the temple. The sergeant always paid his debts, especially to his enemies.

"We are safe from collusion. This street trash

would not deal with the American government,'' Vadas growled, his voice distorted from the old wound. His face was bad enough, but his voice was something to frighten children. Away from his troops, Vadas rarely spoke to avoid seeing the horror in their eyes at his broken words.

"If they were assisting the FBI, there would be many cameras for their courts," the sergeant continued, looking at a briefcase. Inside was an array of surveillance equipment, the screens and meters clear. There was no working electrical equipment in the immediate vicinity of the parking garage.

"There might be chemical film cameras," Boris Bezdek suggested, brushing a hand over his wild crop of curly hair. As a child his parents had tied silk bows in his long curly hair, then as a teen he killed them both with an ax. When a sniper for the Soviet army, he kept it short enough to fit under a combat helmet, but now he kept his hair wild and as long as he wished. A fitting memento of his foolish parents and the blessed ax.

"Then be sure to smile a lot," Zofchak said, nodding at his commander.

Vadas merely grunted in acknowledgment. In the service Zofchak had been his superior officer, but now as fellow businessmen, the wise colonel accepted the sergeant's orders. This confused many outsiders listening to their conversations, and this also pleased the Czech soldiers. The less an enemy knew, the more helpless he was.

"Stop here," Vadas rumbled, checking the clip in his American .44 AutoMag. Small women, large guns, as his father always used to say. A very smart man indeed.

As the vehicle gently rolled to a full stop, the sergeant slid the massive handcannon into the pocket of his trench coat and openly carried another KEDR subgun. The weapons may have been named for the majestic cedar trees of Minsk where they were manufactured, but soldiers joked they were as silent as the wind and as deadly as the winter snow. After so many years of being forced to use the poorly designed Skorpion, it was a true pleasure to have a reliable weapon. In spite of his great hatred for the filthy Russians and what they had done to the Czechs during their Communist occupation, as a soldier he had to admit it was a well-designed gun.

"Infrared shows five in front," Davida Pran said from the driver's compartment of the limo. A small monitor built into the dashboard showed a thermal graphic of the garage. "Four behind, but there are six warm cars parked across the lot, near the portable generator."

So the worksite was using its own electricity? That was good to know. "Far too many cars for so few men," Vadas said, glancing upward. "Watch the ceiling for snipers."

The members of the crew nodded assent, and on cue they opened their doors in unison. It was a small thing, designed to rattle civilians, and always seemed to work.

Vadas stood still with Zofchak by his side while the rest spread out in a defensive pattern and took positions behind the thick concrete pillars supporting the concrete ceiling of the Reno garage. Only Pran stayed in the limo, both of his hands prominently in view on the steering wheel assuring his innocence and good faith.

The headlights from the different vehicles crisscrossed the dark interior of the garage, forming a crazy pattern of overlapping shadows. Then from across the wide expanse of concrete came five figures walking toward the Czech soldiers. The young Oriental men were barely out of their teens, wearing white linen suits with their bulging shoulder holsters clearly visible.

"Amateurs," Vadas said under his breath.

"Hold it right there," Zofchak ordered, laying on a Russian accent. Americans had no opinions of Czechs, but they respected Russians, so for this current business venture, they pretended to be Russian. Often he claimed to be a former KGB agent; that really impressed many of the customers they sold weapons to. More Yankee foolishness. The KGB had been ruthless, but completely without honor.

The gang stopped a few yards away from the gently idling limousine.

"Nice ride," one the teenagers said in appreciation.

"Shut up," the man in front snapped.

He then turned to face the hulking Czechs. "Alcatraz."

The soldiers kept their expressions neutral, but could barely believe what they were seeing. This boy was covered with crude prison tattoos, diamonds sparkled in his ear, cuffs and rings. He reeked of some kind of perfume, and his watch looked capable of launching a space shuttle. There was a beeper, a pager and a cell phone on his tooled leather belt, the buckle a gold dollar sign. Each of the others was similarly decorated, with coiffured hair and woven leather sandals.

Vadas did his best to hide the disdain he was feeling. The whores in Prague wore less jewelry than this Oriental. Was this a so-called street soldier that the American television seemed to fear so highly? Ridiculous. They were no more than children playing games. But children with guns, so he stayed alert and ready for betrayal.

"Shawshank," Zofchak said, giving the countersign. "Where is Mr. Alvarez? We were expecting to meet him here."

"He is busy. We're his representatives. I'm Charlie Wu. Mr. Wu to you," the slim Oriental snarled, then pointed a manicured finger. "And you're in big trouble. The tong takes crap from nobody."

Ah, Chinese street punks. Interesting. "Do not speak that way to me again, Wu," Zofchak said in a low and dangerous voice. The men standing behind this peacock were trying to appear as threatening as possible, but were coming off as nervous. This was already starting to feel less like a meeting and more like an ambush.

Wu looked backward at his companions, sneering. "You hear that shit?" He turned and spit on the concrete floor. "Yeah, well, fuck you, bitch. Those fancy torpedoes didn't work, man. My goddamn boss is furious. Half a million bucks for jack shit. Damn things exploded as soon as they hit the water! Half of my people were killed from the blast, and the Colombian shipment got through without getting scratched. We were ripped off!"

"Impossible," Zolchak stated forcibly.

"No, merely unlikely," Vadas spoke, his gravel voice drawing all attention to himself. "Did you launch the Shkvals into the water at the proper speed?"

"Cut the shit," Wu snapped, waving that aside. "They're torpedoes, man. I seen the movies. You put them in the water and they take off. We didn't waste any time with that 'hard-launching' bull you were feeding us. We want our money back for those five duds!"

"Ah," Zolchak said, taking a half step to the right to open his stance for better balance. "Then you are not here to purchase more of our product?"

"More?" The laughing teenager turned to his associates. "The man wants to sell me more. Russians! Un-fucking-believable."

The Czech soldiers didn't correct the American criminal.

Now Wu jerked his wrist and a switchblade knife sprang into life, the blade shining mirror bright in the mixed beams of the headlights.

"Look, asshole," he growled menacingly, "we will get paid, and your pet Frankenstein over there doesn't scare us worth shit. So cut the hype and—"

"Enough!" Vadas shouted, and there was a muffled explosion from the pocket of his trench coat.

Charlie Wu flew backward, blood spraying into the air. The thunder of the shot was still echoing throughout the garage when the dead man hit the concrete floor hard with most of his throat missing.

Two of the Chinese street soldiers gasped in horror at the sight, but the others swung mini-Uzi machine pistols from behind their backs and opened fire. A burst of rounds stitched across the chests of Vadas and Zofchak, forcing the big men to stumble. But neither fell, and there was no sign of red on their clothing.

"Now!" Zofchak shouted, and the limousine's headlights blazed into life, momentarily blinding the others.

The street gang fired back randomly while the Czech soldiers cut them down in a withering cross fire from the humming KEDR subguns, the modified 9 mm Makarov rounds finishing the job with brutal efficiency.

"Above!" Vadas commanded in Czech, shrugging

off his tattered coat and pulling free the big .44. His silk shirt was torn into pieces, exposing the NATO bulletproof armor underneath.

Streaks of flame stretched from the muzzles of the machine pistols, spent brass flying everywhere, the incendiary rounds burning lines of fire across the garage and then exploding into miniature fireballs wherever they hit. In the hellish light, four gunmen were exposed above, crouching amid the bare steel beams. Two were killed instantly, but the others rallied and fired steady streams of lead at the Czech soldiers.

Then more gunfire came from the parked cars across the garage, shotguns mixing with handguns. The Czechs ignored those gunners for a moment. The range was too great for such weapons to have any accuracy. Only the snipers mattered.

Stepping out of the light of the high beams, Vadas threw thunder into the darkness above, the bursts of lead peppering the floor around the man. Reloading, he winced as a 9 mm slug slapped his arm, blood spraying from the wound. But his scarred face registered no pain as he calmly continued to trigger the big-bore weapon at the overhead rafters.

A cable snapped and whipped away, smashing a cluster of light bulbs. Then one of the snipers was hit and died instantly. The other gunner tried to dodge and lost his footing. As the yelling man fell, the Czech soldiers tore the man apart with concentrated gunfire before he impacted with a meaty whump onto the concrete floor.

Reloading quickly, Vadas whistled sharply and motioned with his hand. Now the Czechs started forward, darting from pillar to pillar, constantly firing their weapons and covering one another in a nonstop advance.

Hiding behind their cars, the surviving members of the Chinese street gang were shooting their weapons wildly, near panic.

Then the Czech soldiers stopped firing and began to retreat.

"They're out of ammo!" a beefy Chinese youth cried, and started forward only to freeze in his tracks as a line of grenades bounced into the bright beams of their headlights.

A teenager cursed and turned to run, but it was too late. The military ordnance cut loose, filling that section of the garage with thunderous flame. The line of explosions flipped over the vehicles and threw the gunners against the walls even as the wave of shrapnel tore them apart.

"Kill them all!" a stocky man with facial tattoos ordered from the second group of cars, lifting an Ingram SMG from the truck of a sky-blue convertible.

The rapid-fire weapon laid down a deadly wreath of copper-jacketed lead toward the soldiers, a rain of bullets hitting the hood and windshield of their limousine. But the hot slugs stayed exactly where they hit, stuck like flies in amber in the resilient Plexiglas window.

Diving for distance, Vadas rolled along the ground

and slammed into the wall, wincing as he hurt his wounded arm. The pain was like fire in his blood, but he blanked the sensation from his mind. Kneeling to offer as small a target as possible, he carefully picked his targets, emptying the .44's clip at the street gang. A teenager spun as his left arm was torn away. Sprayed with his blood, his teammate broke and ran for cover behind their vehicles as the massive booming slugs continued to slam into the cars, blowing off the hubcaps and deflating the tires. Perfect.

That was when the door to the limo swung aside and out stepped Pran, holding an RPG-7.

"Clear!" he shouted, and waited two full seconds for the other soldiers to reach cover, then pulled the trigger.

The massive 40mm rocket thumped from the launcher and streaked fifty yards across the garage to strike the middle car. The BMW sedan leaped into the air from the blast, the expanding fireball engulfing the other cars and men.

Shrieking in mindless pain, the burning teenagers lurched across the littered concrete floor, shooting blindly.

Vadas waited a few moments for them to run out of ammunition, then snapped off an order in Czech. Now the soldiers moved forward fast and low, taking out the tong street punks with merciful head shots until no one was left alive.

"Enough," Vadas said, dropping the spent clip and reloading the pistol. Instinctively, he jacked the slide to chamber a round for immediate use and then holstered the monster handgun.

"Agreed. We have wasted enough time and effort here," Zofchak said with a frown, working the bolt on his subgun to clear a jammed round. "The fools do not use the torpedoes properly and blame us? Madness."

"They worked perfectly," Vadas muttered angrily, the words so distorted to be almost indecipherable. "I believe they wanted more, but at a cheaper price, and so staged this foolishness to try and bargain with us like a haggler in the market."

Removing a silk handkerchief from his shirt pocket, Vadas pressed it against the wound in his arm and added, "Soon Alvarez will contact us again and apologize for his stupid men. Offer to make amends and to buy even more weapons than before, if we can cut him a deal. Yet another trick to lower our price."

"We would allow this, sir?" Bezdek asked, sounding puzzled.

Returning to the limo, the big former sergeant knelt to examine the wound in the headlights. Ah, just a flesh wound, nothing of importance. Repairs could wait until they got back on the road for home.

"Do not be foolish. Of course we would not allow that," Vadas said with a growl, reapplying the handkerchief. "We will ambush them next time and crucify Alvarez alive to be found by the local police. Then fewer people will attempt to rob us, and our price can go up again."

"I dislike torture," Pran stated.

"As do I, my friend. Revenge is bad business, but this is no longer business between us and Alvarez. Now it is a matter of honor."

CHAPTER FOUR

Ford Island, Pearl Harbor

"Well, that's just in damn bad taste," Commander Edward Glenn said aloud with a deep frown, staring at the sky.

Wearing his Class A dress Navy uniform, Glenn was standing at the podium on a review stand waiting to make a speech, when the antique planes in the sky caught his attention.

Ahead of him, the base band was marching by in perfect lockstep. Out on the silver waters of the harbor, the USS *Kitty Hawk* aircraft carrier was moored alongside the Ford Island Bridge, fireworks shooting high from her launch deck. The floating bridge was jam-packed with locals, along with a lot of veterans, actual survivors on the day back in 1941 when the Pearl got lambasted by the Imperial Japanese navy and America entered WWII with the bloody cry for revenge.

Watching the tiny specks get closer, he had to admit it was the strangest damn thing. If the man hadn't known better, he would have sworn those were World War II–era Japanese Zeros. But at Pearl Harbor? Who the bloody hell would be that much of a moron?

"Sir, do you see that?" Lieutenant Johnson said from his folding chair on the stand. The man had to speak loud to be heard over the band's rousing rendition of "Over There!"

"Goddamn Zeros over my base," Glenn muttered out of the side of his mouth. "Makes my skin itch just to think about them."

"Don't recall that any Japanese airplane of the time period could carry torpedoes," the lieutenant said with a growing sense of unease. "Damn realistic how they are coming with the sun right behind. Almost as if it was a bomb run."

"Think it's part of the Blue Angel show?" an adjutant asked nervously, checking his clipboard. "I have nothing on the program about a dogfight simulation."

Glenn frowned. "Could be some sort of surprise," he admitted slowly. "Have the Japanese pilots land with a garland of flowers for the veterans, or something. Crazy public-relations men from D.C. come up with the most senseless notions…. Hey."

The lead Zero had suddenly banked and was starting into a screaming dive for the shimmering blue ocean below. The noise steadily rose until the band stopped playing and the crowd turned to see the chilling sight.

"Wow, really looks like he can't pull out, doesn't

it?'' the adjutant said hesitantly. ''Damn, those Angels are good.''

''Hell bells, man, are you an idiot!'' the commander roared, pulling out his cell phone and hitting a programmed button for sea-air rescue. ''No Angel would pull a stunt like that without prior authorization from the CO. Look at the crowd, they're terrified! This must be real, and the stunt pilot is out of control!''

''Rescue emergency line,'' a voice said on the cell phone.

Watching the plane knife for the sea, the commander spoke quickly. ''This is Commander Glenn. We have a plane going down in the harbor. Looks like a Japanese Zero. I want rescue choppers airborne in two minutes. Now, move!''

''Zeros? What are you drunk or something?'' the voice said in exasperation. ''Listen, buddy, do you know that impersonating a superior officer is a serious charge in the Navy? The CO will toast your ass on the fires of hell over a gag like this.''

''I am the CO!'' Glenn roared, ''and if you don't— Christ!''

At full speed the old plane slammed into the ocean and blew apart into a million pieces, the broken propeller spinning away across the surface of the harbor.

''Plane down!'' Glenn shouted over the screams of the crowd in the reviewing stand. ''Get those choppers airborne now, or you're a snipe for the rest of your damn hitch!''

Hundreds of people were rushing to the chain fence strung along the shoreline to point and stare at the crash site. The other Zeros skimmed low over the area just as sirens started howling across the Pacific Island base.

"Crash site is one hundred yards off the south-southeast section of Ford Island," Glenn continued, walking closer himself. "Alert the hospital and get a scuba team here pronto!"

"Y-yes, s-sir!" the sailor stammered, and the line disconnected.

The lieutenant removed his hat and placed it on his chest. "The poor son of a bitch never had a chance. Must have completely lost control."

The feel of danger was getting stronger every second for the base CO as he watched ocean cease to roil at the crash site, the wound already closed and healed. "I've never seen a plane do that before, dive straight down," he muttered, loosening his tie. "Almost as if he did it deliberately."

"Maybe he did," the adjutant suggested, frowning. "Could be some sort of bizarre stunt to proclaim how awful war is."

"As if combat veterans need that news update."

"Lots of civilians here, too, sir."

"Sir, Commander," the lieutenant said quickly, touching his earphone. "Sir, sonar reports a hot noise in the water. Sounds like a sustained explosion, or maybe a torpedo. They can't be sure."

"Sustained explosion?" Glenn said, looking over

his shoulder. "More like a rushing noise, a deep thrum? Or more like a Jacuzzi?"

The description sounded ridiculous, but according to the top secret reports he had read, a Shkval torpedo did sound vaguely like a working Jacuzzi. Far enough away, gunfire often sounded like bacon frying, just one of the oddities of life.

Quickly, the officer relayed the query and turned the CO with a pale face. "Yes, sir," he reported. "Sonar reports that is exactly what it sounds like."

"Red alert!" the CO bellowed, striding from the review stand. "Raise the nets and arm the mines! Get the dry dock doors closed and the Phalanx guns in operation immediately!"

"Shkvals?" the lieutenant asked. "On a Japanese Zero?"

"Why not? Who would suspect such a thing? And the crash is perfect cover for hand-launching the frigging things! Now raise the nets, mister!"

The lieutenant didn't reply; he just did as he was ordered and hoped to God the CO was right. Or else they were about to slaughter half a dozen U.S. Navy pilots for no reason but paranoia.

"Shit loves?" the adjutant demanded in confusion.

Glenn glowered down at the man. "Didn't you read the security report?"

"Well, I can't read them all."

"Hope you like civilian life because that's what you are now, idiot."

"Hot fish!" an ensign cried, pointing at the water.

A line of disturbance sliced the calm surface of the harbor, moving at incredible speed, and streaked past the review stand faster than a speeding car, the spray forming a rainbow in the air as it drifted down and moistened the sailors and their families.

"Christ, those things were fast!"

"The nets will hold," Glenn said, more as a prayer than a state of fact.

Bypassing the dozens of pleasure boats dotting the harbor, the Shkval dived deep and arced around the inlet of the sub dock to strike the first titanium net rigged underwater. The resilient nets held firm and didn't break, but the links snapped off the concrete moorings from the incredible pressure and only slightly slowed the Russian rocket-torpedo as it dragged a half ton of titanium along behind.

Unstoppable, the Shkval lanced past the rows of docked warships on display and angled about to strike the side of a Los Angeles–class submarine, where a picnic lunch for visiting dignitaries was being held. The billion-dollar boat rose from the sheer force of the strident explosion, and most of the sub pen was engulfed in a fiery tidal wave as the propellants of the ICBM missiles also detonated. Chunks of metal were thrown far and wide, smashing into buildings and other vessels.

"We've been nuked!" a young sailor yelled in terror, turning dead white.

"Worse than that," the officer said, then turned to the sky and saw the other six Zeros swinging around

Ford Island to start an attack run. "Lieutenant, arm the surface-to-air missiles! Blow those things out of the sky!"

"Already done, sir," the lieutenant said breathlessly, watching the foaming wake streak through the harbor.

Way ahead of the others, the lead Zero screamed for the sea and slammed itself into kindling against the ocean. At those speeds the water would be like a rock wall. But moments later, there was motion below the surface and a wake cut across the harbor moving for the *Kitty Hawk.*

"You didn't wait for my commands?" Glenn demanded.

The officer went stiff. "No, sir. My own initiative."

"Good man!"

"Just hope it was fast enough."

"You and me both, mister."

Suddenly, missiles launched from the SAM bunker on the far side of the base, the flaming darts shooting across the sky as four more Zeros angled straight down and started a death run toward the Pacific.

"Come on, boys!" a bosun urged, raising both clenched fists. "Go get 'em!"

But the high-tech missiles flashed past the wooden planes and detonated a hundred feet behind the antiques. The modern-day warheads simply weren't able to automatically compensate for the severe lack of metal in the planes to trigger a proximity blast. Then a second salvo dotted the sky and as a Zero fireballed, the attending crowd cheered in victory.

"Brilliant! Those were antimissiles!" the lieutenant cried. "Those locked on the Shkvals, not the wooden planes!"

"It's not over yet," Glenn growled, clenching and unclenching his fists. The commander was furious over his inability to do anything direct about the matter. The cell phone was his best link to air defense and the security patrol, and at least here he had a clear field of vision to direct the attack and rescue operations. He was a sitting target for the Shkvals himself, but he was betting his life a single man was too small a target to waste the million-dollar weapon system on. If he was wrong, so be it, but this was his post and here he would stay.

From the inland airfield, Apache gunships lifted into view above the chaos of the base and started forward with their 30 mm chainguns spitting fire at the descending planes. A cascade of debris tumbled over the side of the *Kitty Hawk* as a Hummer with a plow blade pushed the working fireworks display overboard, then steam lines hissed white geysers as the carrier cleared the top decks to launch fighters.

But Commander Glenn knew that any help from the aircraft carrier was minutes away, and half of his base was already on fire from the debris of the destroyed sub.

Tossing their musical instruments aside, the Marine band members lined the shore and started emptying their decorative handguns at the plummeting planes, but if the firing line achieved any hits it made no difference.

More antimissile SAMs were fired, then the salvo ceased as the Apaches entered the aerial strike zone. Their chain guns audibly chattered now. A third Zero was blown apart by the Navy gunships, but the rest successfully impacted on the harbor water same as before. Promptly, the Apaches started to pound the crash areas with their rockets, the barrage of explosions boiling the sea.

"Sonar reports three more fish!" the lieutenant reported, licking dry lips. "And base radar reports six more Zeros incoming from the west!"

"Shoot them down!" the CO roared. "Have our planes crash into them if nothing else works, but not one of the fucking bastards is to hit the ocean intact!"

"Aye, aye, sir!" The orders were relayed, and another salvo of SAMs streaked away from a hidden missile bunker to the extreme southern tip of the base.

Alarms were howling everywhere, and the destroyed sub roared again when its diesel supply ignited, throwing more wreckage skyward. Sailors were running about madly. A squad of SPs arrived and started passing out Stinger missile launchers to the band members.

The civilians were screaming in panic, pushing one another aside and fighting to reach their parked cars. Standing alone in the melee, an old veteran stood with tears on his face as he stared with raw hatred at the diving planes, the hand holding his cane shaking from suppressed fury.

Flashing across the open water of the harbor, one of the Shkvals turned toward the white marble memorial to the north of Ford Island, then disappeared as it dived deep underwater. Commander Glenn felt his heart stop beating for a second. Then there was a submerged flash of light, and the waters rose in an exhalation of steam and rusted machine parts.

"They blew up the *Arizona!*" the lieutenant snarled. "I'll kill them with my bare hands!"

"We have to catch them first," Glenn said as a Harrier lifted from the *Kitty Hawk* and rose high, the disturbance from its belly jets visible in the clear air.

The jet headed toward the incoming planes, then it neatly pirouetted about and launched a full salvo of Sidewinder missiles into the water near the Ford Island Bridge.

With the island museum in his way, Glenn couldn't see from that angle, but he could guess the reason why. Dear God, no, not that.

A split second later the middle span of the bridge lifted from the harbor, the pontoons flying into pieces as civilian cars were thrown high, parents and children shotgunning through the smoky sky.

Now all of the Phalanx cannons of the *Kitty Hawk* blew flame at the water, then three abruptly stopped, the drowning civilians in the way of the 20 mm rounds. The last cannon continued hosing lead and steel into the water, throwing a wall of metal at the incoming death dealer. But even the computerized guns had trouble tracking the aquatic missile. The software wasn't designed to track an incoming object underwater moving at air-missile speed.

Incredibly, the Shkval detonated only yards from the bare hull of the aircraft carrier, throwing a column of water thirty yards high.

"Those rounds were nowhere near the Shkval," the lieutenant said in a wooden tone. "It must have hit something."

"Or somebody," Glenn said, watching his peaceful training base being destroyed. "Saved by our own dead."

Swinging about hard, the Harrier launched its last missile, and a distant Zero was smashed apart as the Sidewinder punched completely through the antique plane, the warhead exploding yards beyond the fuselage. Instantly, the other Japanese bombers banked sharply and started toward Honolulu.

Oh, hell. Glenn realized they were planning on using the homes of the civilians as cover. If the fighters blew them out of the sky, the burning planes would fall on the city and kill hundreds of people. The terrorists were smart and ruthless. He had no idea what the naval aviators could do, but he trusted their ingenuity. However, as far as he could see, it was an impossible situation until the fighters reached open sea once more.

More SAMs streaked across the blue sky, randomly exploding, filling the sky with shrapnel. Bleeding red hydraulic fluid and black smoke, one of the Zeros started down in a spin, then began to straighten as the pilot fought his dying craft into its last task, to hit the water square on and launch the Shkval.

Out of missiles, the Harrier hit its afterburners and streaked toward the diving plane on a collision course. Only yards away, the Harrier pilot dropped his airfoils, blew the belly jets and banked hard, the roiling wash flipping the enemy craft and tearing off a wing. Out of control, the Zero went into a tailspin and hit the ocean sideways in a dozen pieces. The crowd seemed to hold its breath, but as seconds passed and there was no motion below the water the civilians cheered again even louder.

Just then an F-18 SuperHornet launched from the deck of the *Kitty Hawk,* its afterburners reminiscent of the thrust vectors of the Shkvals. The antique planes sputtered about in a circle, firing their .50-caliber machine guns at the massively larger jet fighter. Folding back its wings, the F-18 went Mach and blew straight past the prop planes, its wash hitting them like a controlled tornado. The wooden planes were tossed about helplessly, and tumbled away from Honolulu to splash harmlessly onto the golden beach, two of them exploding into flames.

Civilians and sailors both shouted themselves hoarse as the SuperHornet skimmed over the crash site, strafing the area with its bow guns. Now another F-18 launched from the *Kitty Hawk,* and two more Harriers lifted from the Pearl Harbor airfield to the north. Within a minute, the sky was full of Navy fighters spreading outward in a protective umbrella, searching for any more of the disguised killers.

"We got them, sir," the lieutenant said with a tremor in his words. "Dirty sons of bitchs aren't going to be hitting any more U.S. Navy targets. That's for damn sure."

"Too bad." The CO sighed bitterly. "Because that means now the terrorists will go after civilian targets with no chance in hell of surviving."

As the crowds continued to cheer, the Navy officers went grimly silent, their thoughts dark with the somber realization that the dire situation had just gotten worse.

North Atlantic Ocean

"FIRE!" THE CAPTAIN ordered, and the fishing trawler bucked as a Shkval torpedo was launched hard and fast into the choppy ocean.

The foaming wake of the aquatic missile went straight past the civilian ship full of news reporters and Greenpeace members to slam directly into the side of the male humpback whale. The creature rotated onto its back from the sheer force of the blow, pale blood gushing from the ghastly wound. The people of the Greenpeace ship screamed in horror and rushed about uncertain what they should or could do. Then the warhead detonated, and the whale burst apart, organs and flesh spraying across the ocean in a grisly explosion. The rest of the pod of whales submerged and rose below their dying friend, terrified at the blood, frightened and unsure. But the animal was dead, its backbone clearly visible through the titanic cavity that completely penetrated its giant body.

The deck of the civilian ship became ablaze with flashing cameras, and the captain of the trawler flipped them the finger as he laughed at their antics.

"Again!" he ordered, into the intercom on the bridge. "Again and again!"

The remaining two Shkvals were launched and the terrified whales tried to dive for safety, but it was hopeless. The Russian rocket torpedoes tracked down the humpbacks in seconds and killed the largest two deep underwater, the corpses rising to the surface in a spreading array of ragged gobbets and hundreds of gallons of warm blood. The international crew of the Greenpeace vessel was going insane at the slaughter, more than one person actually jumping into the water to try to reach the dead animals, while others were using knives to cut through the rigging and lower the longboats.

"Are they trying to attack us?" the captain asked in amusement, opening his coat to reveal the .44 Webley revolver holster alongside his belt buckle.

A crewmen pointed. "See there, sir? The big one we killed with the gray patch seems to have been pregnant. They're trying to rescue the baby."

"Excellent." The captain chuckled in delight. "We killed an expectant mother in front of hundreds of witnesses? This could not have been better if we planned it. Well done!"

"Too bad we don't have another Shkval," another sailor growled, slamming a fist into his palm. "Killing the newborn would drive the liberal press out of their minds."

"Yes, it is a shame," the captain agreed in his native language. "But we have done enough. Proceed, full steam ahead."

The navigator replied in Algerian and the trawler started moving straight through the grisly floating remains of the great whales so the photographers would have a perfect shot for their televisions and newspapers.

Although the flag flying from the mast was American, the ship was actually Algerian. But the name painted on the bow was *Yankee Clipper,* and the sturdy vessel held the falsified registration of a fishing boat from Maine.

"Be sure to let them see the name," the captain warned. "The stinking Americans must be blamed for this."

"Aye, aye, skipper!" the pilot called, turning the wheel to give the reporters on the Greenpeace ship a perfect view.

The captain nodded in satisfaction as the cameras turned their way, and a sailor standing at the gunwale on the foredeck unzipped and relieved himself onto the ragged carcass of the annihilated whales. Death threats were called from the Greenpeace ship, raised fists shaking in outrage.

Perfect. Now let the Great Power reap the rewards of their crushing strangulation of his nation's economy. The liberals of the world would denounce America for the senseless slaughter of the pretty whales and cause endless political problems for the fat and foolish United States. The million dollars spent on the three Shkval torpedoes had been well spent. Nothing else could have done the job quite so spectacularly for the television cameras.

"What now, skipper?" the navigator asked as the vessel cleared the kill zone and reached clean salt water once more.

Lighting a pipe, the captain drew in a deep lungful of rich, dark smoke. "Home," he declared with a grin, the pipe jutting from the corner of his mouth. "We have done our job well. It's time to go home and get warm."

"Yes, sir!"

Continuing to build speed, the disguised trawler steamed away in triumph, the mission of revenge completed.

ON BOARD THE GREENPEACE vessel, the crowd of scientists and ecologists openly wept over the senseless slaughter, unable to fathom why anybody would do such a thing. The efforts to save the infant from its mother's ruptured body were close to hopeless, and there really was no doubt that the baby would never live the day. Meanwhile, the video cameras of a dozen nations caught every heartbreaking detail in full color.

"Damn the Americans!" a German woman wailed, pounding on the railing. "Damn them all to hell!"

"But why did they do it?" a Frenchman asked, his face contorted in complete puzzlement. "In the name of God, why?"

Nobody had an answer for that, not even speculation. But they had all seen the crime committed before their very eyes and knew exactly whom to blame, even if the reason behind it was unknown.

The United States would be made to pay for this bloody act of barbarism, and pay dearly.

CHAPTER FIVE

Folkestone, England

A British Harrier jump jet was streaking low across the clear sky as the Porsche 911 entered the tunnel at Folkestone. Not bothering to wait for the signal to fade, Trevor Curtis turned off the radio and switched on his CD player. A sweet jazz riff flowed from the eighteen hidden speakers and filled the car so that the driver felt as if the band were in the car.

The walls of the channel tunnel were so thick radio waves couldn't reach inside so a driver either got a CD player or drove in silence for the next forty-nine and a half kilometers until reaching Calais, France. Sometimes that took two hours depending on the traffic. Curtis had no idea why they didn't build the mouth of the tunnel closer to the water. It was only barely possible to see the channel from here. Something about safety procedures, but Curtis assumed it was really about cheap land. England had only so much beachfront property, and losing a large chunk of it was bad business for everybody.

After paying an exorbitantly high toll to the smiling Euro-Tunnel Corporation employee, Curtis settled in for his long boring drive. The chunnel, as the wags liked to call, was a modern marvel of boring efficiency. Bland tiled walls for kilometer after kilometer, only the gentle curve of the tunnel itself giving any respite from mind-numbing boredom. Yet whenever business forced him into Paris, he took the chunnel. It was much faster than fighting the traffic at Heathrow International Airport, and a hell of a lot cheaper. Safer, too. Sometimes planes crashed. That couldn't happen when you were already fifty meters underground.

The jazz combo finished its set and the CD player clicked and clacked softly to itself as the next disk started playing something old from the Irish rock band U2, when the Porsche trembled. For a horrified moment Curtis braced himself for the steering wheel to become loose, positive that he had just lost a tie rod somehow. Then the vibration came again, stronger this time, and several of the recessed ceiling lights in the tunnel winked out, throwing most of the highway into darkness for long stretches.

The cars streaming along the enclosed roadway lost their formation for a few moments as panic swept the drivers. What the hell was going on here? This couldn't be an earthquake. This region of the sea was as solid as the Rock of Gibraltar. No quakes here. Then a horrible possibility came to mind, and Curtis glanced at the wall to his left. My God, could the passenger train in the middle tunnel have crashed? That was a relatively new addition. That was the answer. This was just the rumble of a heavy freight train passing close by the car tunnel. How embarrassing, here he was getting all frightened over a little noise. What an absolute tit he was. A damn fool.

Vaguely, he remembered reading the articles while the chunnel was being built, the endless financial troubles, and the modifications necessary to meet British safety regulations. Three separated tunnels instead of one large divided tunnel to prevent any single disaster from closing off the entire length. Set a good fifteen meters away from each other, each tunnel was buried in solid limestone far below the bottom of the sea, with an additional ten meters of steel-reinforced concrete as a protective sleeve. The thing was impregnable. According to the London *Times,* the royal war bunker in 10 Downing Street wasn't this well built.

Then Curtis frowned. But if the tunnels were so far apart, how could he be feeling the passing of a freight train? Now he truly became nervous, his hands becoming damp with sweat in their monogrammed driving gloves.

Suddenly, the tunnel shook again, harder, the vibrations lasting longer, and cracked tiles began falling off the curved walls like autumn leaves. Steering fast, Curtis avoided a flurry of the ceramic squares, then another batch dropped onto his trunk, denting it.

More and more tiles fell off the wall like some

terrible disease exposing the bare concrete. A Volvo lost control and spun to crash into a BMW. That instantly formed a traffic jam, and horns began to blare loudly. Then the noise stopped as another tremor shook the tunnel hard, the pavement buckling in spots like a rumpled sheet. Lord love him, it was an earthquake!

Just ahead of him, the wall got dark, moisture forming in a spreading pool as the concrete sleeve loudly cracked and rods of water shot across the roadway to impact on the side, blowing more tiles off the wall. This far down the water pressure had to be enough to punch through his car like a cannonball! Acting on impulse, Curtis hit the gas and the turbo roared into life, hurtling the sleek sports car ever faster.

As he approached the roaring bars of water, Curtis saw a VW minivan try to get across, and the stream shattered the windows and pushed the crumpled vehicle across the roadway, pinning it against the opposite wall.

Curtis reached for the gearshift, then removed his hand. Anybody in that van was already dead. Nothing he could do to help them now.

The engine revving to the max, he automatically ducked as his Porsche shot under the widening streams of ocean water, and he emerged alive on the other side. Yes!

Now alarms were howling, and red emergency lights were flashing at steel hatchways showing the escape routes out of the damaged tunnel. More tiles hit the hood of the Porsche, and Curtis ignored the damage. Pushing the engine to the red line, he raced for his life toward nearby France and open air. The sooner he was out of this bloody underwater coffin the better.

Following the curve, Curtis froze at the sight of an entire wall of water cutting across the highway at waist level. Bloody hell! Praying to God, Trevor charged into the stream and was instantly flipped over sideways to slam into the wall of the cracking tunnel. He registered a single heartbeat of confusion and pain and then utter blackness forever.

Scotland Yard, London

"MOTHER OF GOD," the chief inspector said, reading the computer printout in horror. "And you got this over the Internet?"

The young duty officer nodded quickly. "Yes, sir. I checked with the Chunnel Authority first, and got only a busy signal. Bad sign that. So I checked with the Royal Coast Guard and was told to push off."

"Damn thing must be true, then," the inspector muttered, barely able to believe what he was reading. Some crazed group of mad Highland nationals calling themselves the Sons of Scotland were claiming they had just smashed open the transatlantic chunnel with something called a Shkval. Whatever the hell that was. Plus, they threatened to do more, and worse, unless Parliament granted immediate independence to

Scotland from the iron yoke of England. Bloody morons, half of Parliament was Scottish and perfectly happy to be there. What in God's name were they yammering about? Iron yoke? Ridiculous!

"What I can't understand," the young officer said tersely, "is why they sent this manifesto to us, and not 10 Downing Street, or the palace? What are coppers supposed to do about it?"

"Our name," the chief inspector said, reaching for the phone and punching the number for the antiterrorist division of MI-5. The line was busy. "Damnation!"

"Sir?" the duty officer asked in confusion. "Our name?"

"This is where the old kings used to humble the Scottish lords to break their spirit. That's what our bloody name means, Scotland Yard. Real old-time Black Museum stuff. Very nasty."

"You're daft," the officer chided in disbelief. "Go one, pull the other one."

"No, it's true.

"Bloody hell. I never knew."

"Not something we brag about these days, lad," the chief inspector said, trying MI-5 again and still getting no reply. "Any more than the Americans do their infamous disappearing treaties with the Indians. There's a skeleton in the closet of every nation."

The inspector realized that the ATD had to be seriously occupied not to answer the danger line. This was starting to look very bad indeed. If these madmen had somehow smuggled bombs into the chunnel, thousands could be dead or dying. This was a nightmare!

"Scottish terrorists," he growled. "This could be Dublin all over again!"

"Only with better weapons," the duty officer said angrily.

Just then the telephone double rang and the young constable lifted the receiver.

"Chief inspector's office," he said, then grew pale. "It's for you, sir. Number 10 Downing Street. It's the PM."

The prime minister? The inspector took the receiver and listened for a few minutes to the man on the other end of line, then set the receiver back into its cradle.

"Well, it's real," he said, running a hand across his face. "Some sort of Russian underwater rocket. They pounded the seabed with them exactly above the east tunnel until the walls cracked. Thankfully, some Royal Marines were on nearby aerial maneuvers, got the call and blew the terrorists out of the water before they could finish the job. The eastern chunnel is leaking like a sieve, but the walls are holding for the moment and the pumps are handling the flooding."

"Damn lucky, sir. How many dead, sir?"

"Too many," the inspector snapped, swiveling his chair to look out the office window. The city of London spread before him in all of its majesty and might.

"However, lad, I have a very bad feeling that the next time we'll need more than luck. We'll need a bloody miracle to stop these things."

New Orleans, Louisiana

WITH A SQUEAL of rusted metal, the door to the old warehouse was forcibly shoved aside, admitting a wealth of early-morning sunshine.

Careful of where they stepped, the trio of men entered the building. Sewer rats scuttled away from the invasion of light. Their shoes splashing in the puddles of dirty water dotting the concrete floor, the strangers crossed the vast expanse of the warehouse and surveyed their new domain. The floor was covered with a carpet of trash and broken bottles, the air reeking of human waste and mold. Broken pieces of furniture decayed in the corners, and vulgar graffiti covered the steel beams supporting the high ceiling, the metal red with layers of rust. Softly in the background came a slow, steady drip of falling water.

Not a word was spoken as the dismal state of the building was observed and considered. In stark contrast to the crumbling structure, the men were nattily dressed in expensive clothing, their fingernails manicured and shiny with polish. The air about them was heavy with expensive musk, and each man carried a Glock 20 pistol and an Uzi submachine gun in a fancy double rig holster strapped under his tailored pinstriped suit.

On the deed to the abandoned warehouse, they were listed simply as ABH Industries.

"This'll do," Gadgets Schwarz said, dropping his equipment bag onto a relatively dry section of the floor. The canvas hit with a heavy thump and the soft clatter of metallic items.

"Place was earmarked for demolition next week by the planning board," Rosario Blancanales said, removing his designer sunglasses to see better in the gloom. "But now it's ours for the next month."

"Sure hope this doesn't take that long," Carl Lyons said, opening a metal locker. The corroded door handle came off in his grip, and then the door itself fell to the floor with a loud crash.

"And somebody is going to make this craphole livable?" Schwarz demanded with a scowl. "I've seen more attractive POW camps than this dump."

"Better be presentable by this afternoon. We have our first clients coming in six hours," Blancanales said, checking his gold Rolex watch. With Carmen Delahunt riding the Internet and setting up Able Team's covers, and Brognola spreading the word on the street through his contacts and stool pigeons in the Louisiana crime underworld, every crook and thug in the state would soon know there were new players in New Orleans and that they were looking to make some major-league weapons purchases. Soon enough, the sellers would come to them. All they needed was a "store" to deal in, a good story and lots of cash. This Able Team had in abundance. Whether Russians would be among the sellers was the gamble, but the plan was still their best bet to find the weapons makers quickly. Every Shkval sold equaled hundreds dead. They had to be found and stopped as fast as possible. The big question for Gadgets Schwarz was how had the enemy gotten their initial six Shkvals and been able to steal the blueprints to make more? Unfortunately, nobody had an answer for that, but speculation ran high.

"After we settle in tonight, I'll set up AutoSentries in the rafters, there and over there," Schwarz said, gesturing at the beams supporting the high ceiling. Birds' nests and other refuse draped the steel in a profusion of neglect and decay.

"Rubber bullets only," Lyons directed. "The cops may try for a raid and we don't want to kill them."

"Or any spies," Blancanales added, drawing his Glock as a particularly bold rat scuttled out from underneath a collection of rusted oil drums. As if sensing danger, the rat slunk away again, but stayed just out of sight amid the yellowed newspapers and crack pipes.

"We could get a lot from a spy with the proper inducement," he added, holstering his piece but not putting on the restraining strap.

Schwarz chuckled and Lyons shrugged. Their teammate didn't actually torture anybody, but he always seemed to be able to get even the toughest hardcase to talk. He just had a way of instantly becoming a person's friend, and suddenly the person was spilling his guts. It was the damnedest thing Lyons had ever seen.

From outside came the sound of vehicles rolling to a stop, and the Able Team leader turned to see six identical vans all bearing the logo of a corporate cleaning service.

"Here comes our crew," he said.

A dozen men dressed in full-body biohazard suits with sealed hoods, heavy gloves and boots that reached to the knees exited the vehicles.

"They going to scrub the place," Schwarz asked, "or burn it down?"

"They normally clean up the blood and brains from crime scenes after the forensic team is done looking for clues," Lyons explained, waving the crew inside. "They're fast, very expensive and can clean anything."

"Toni recommended them highly," Blancanales said, wrinkling his nose at the stench of the chemical spray. "And if they're good enough for my sister, then they're the best in the business."

The members of the crew looked like something from a biological-weapons lab, but then considering the condition of the warehouse, that was about right.

"Have to be miracle workers if they can do this armpit," Schwarz added, stepping out of the way of the cleaners as they laid flexible steam hoses along the floor. A different group was already piling trash into a wheeled cart and uncovering a wide variety of vermin.

Lyons grunted. "Better be. Furniture is coming at noon."

"Midday? No problem, Mr. Smith," a man said through a voice vent in the biosuit. "We'll be ready, sir. But you gentlemen might wish to step outside now. We'll be fumigating the establishment while we hose it down."

"Use a double dose of poison," Schwarz muttered, retrieving his bag of weapons.

Locking his equipment bag into the truck of their new Cadillac, Schwarz joined his friends as they watched the cleaners step up for a few minutes. Then as the beeping tanker trucks of cleaning solution backed into the warehouse, Able Team moved to the sidewalk and watched from a safer distance.

A few people on the streets stopped to stare, then hurried off whispering. The activity would also help spread the word they were rich and here to stay. Who would do this much work if this was only a temporary accommodation? Lies within lies, wheels within wheels, that was the very heart of deep cover.

Then Schwarz snapped his fingers. "Damn," he said in annoyance. "We forgot something. Hookers. We better get some whores today. Our cover says we just got out of prison, and that would be one of the first things we'd want."

"You mean, call girls, absolute top of the line, best the city has," Lyons corrected grimly. "What did we used to like? A man's taste in such matters rarely changes."

"I have no idea," Blancanales admitted, spreading his hands. "That was something I simply didn't check."

"Wing it," Schwarz suggested. "Get a dozen assorted. That should cover the lapse."

"They're women, not doughnuts."

"I still like mine sweet and cream-filled."

Suddenly, a violent cloud of steam erupted from the open doorway, followed by the squeaks of rats dying, and years of thick filth began to dissolve off the long array of brown windows edging the roof. Clean spots began to appear.

Retreating across the street to a vantage point between a billiard parlor and a massage studio, Able Team became alert as a cop strolled into view. Blancanales rubbed a thumb across the tips of his fingers, and the cop nodded, touching a baton to his cap in reply, then strolled on whistling softly.

"How did you know he was on the take?" Schwarz asked, jerking his head at the patrolman.

"A lot of cops in the slums are. Just a fact of life."

"Lots aren't," Lyons growled, feeling a rush of anger at the crooked cop. All the time he was on the Los Angeles police force, he kept slamming into the stone wall of blues on the green. The silent crime, as they said. The graft had eventually been mostly stopped, but by then Lyons was long gone and a member of the Stony Man team. But every cop on the take that he met flooded the man with a terrible anger.

"Hey, there!"

Trying to appear casual, Able Team turned as a slim, well-dressed man walked toward them beaming a friendly smile. But his hands were scarred, ears flat and crumpled, and the cartilage was built up around his nose from frequent fights. They identified the man as an enforcer before he said his second word.

"Good morning!" the stranger said, ambling closer. "Wow, quite a job these guys are doing. Look at that! Are you the new owners of the building?"

"ABH Industries," Blancanales said, offering a hand. It was accepted and they shook. "Imports and exports of farm machinery. What can we do you for?"

"Good one." The stranger chuckled at the ancient play on words. "And actually, I'm here to offer you a unique and special service."

"Oh, really," Schwarz said, crossing his arms so that his fingers were touching the grip of his hidden Uzi.

"Yes, sir. I'm the local independent fire inspector," he stated, glancing at the busy warehouse. "And even from here I can tell that your company is woefully lacking sufficient insurance."

"Yeah? Tell me more," Lyons urged, feeling the rush of battle fury building inside. He already knew where this was going, but wanted to let the man say the words and condemn himself before reacting. There was always a one-in-a-million shot he was a legitimate insurance salesman with the worst pitch in history. Nothing should ever be attributed to evil if it could be easily explained by simple stupidity.

"Happy to! Look at all this money you're spending fixing the old place up, and what guarantee do you have it won't burn down tomorrow?" The stranger grinned. "Now, I'm in the position to absolutely guarantee the safety of your establishment. That is, of course, if you purchase some insurance right now.

"And continue to purchase more every week for a hundred bucks," the man added gruffly. "Do we understand each other yet? My employer runs this neighborhood, and you don't have his permission to open your business here yet. Get me?"

"Clear as crystal," Lyons replied, waiting until the street cop turned the corner. Then he grabbed the enforcer by the neck and slammed him against the brick wall a good foot off the sidewalk.

Wheezing for breath, the crook fumbled for a gun under his jacket and Lyons snatched it away, shoving it into the man's belly.

"I'll say this just once," he growled, shaking the racketeer. "Don't bother us again with any more protection-racket bullshit, punk. Or you die. Plain and simple."

"Yes, sir. Hey, I was only asking," the man croaked, trying to free the grip crushing his throat. "Please, I can't breathe...." he wheezed pitifully.

Lyons released the man and he dropped to the sidewalk. Instantly, the fellow pulled a backup piece from an ankle holster but as the slim pistol came clear,

Schwarz kicked it out of his grip to fly away and clatter into the gutter.

"Now, look," the man started, licking dry lips, "I was only—"

Reaching under his coat, Blancanales drew the Glock and fired. Blood sprayed from the man's shoulder and he cursed, clawing at the wound.

"Scram," Lyons ordered. "Now."

Frantically nodding agreement, the enforcer got to his feet and stumbled down the street.

"He'll be back," Blancanales said, holstering the gun. "With friends to help him even the score. I know the type."

Flexing his hands, Lyons agreed. "With luck, he'll talk to his boss, and they'll try to check up on us."

"Probably have to kill them next time."

"Good," Schwarz said, looking at the blood on the sidewalk. "That way other locals will know we're not cops or FBI." Not even under deep cover was a law-enforcement officer allowed to kill to maintain his or her cover. Only in self-defense.

"Small-time extortion thugs aren't what we're looking for," Blancanales commented dryly, glancing around the intersection. Several people were out and moving, but none of them had paid the slightest attention to the altercation. "But they may be able to lead us to the big fish."

Lyons glanced at his gold Rolex watch, the diamonds sparkling in the sunlight. "Let's go eat. That rib place around the corner smells good."

"For breakfast?" Schwarz demanded, then reconsidered. "What the hell, after all those years in jail, I'm itching for some decent food."

"Fine by me," Blancanales said, putting on his sunglasses again. "The more the locals see us, the better."

As they walked away, a sleeping man in the alley alongside the bustling warehouse watched them depart, then pulled out a very expensive cell phone and placed a call.

"They're here," he said, then closed the phone and moved farther into the alleyway, staying in the dank shadows.

WHEN ABLE TEAM RETURNED a few hours later, the cleaning crew was in the process of packing its equipment.

Going inside, the men couldn't believe the difference. The windows were clean, the broken panes replaced. The lights all worked now, the smells were gone and the floor was freshly scrubbed.

"I'm impressed," Schwarz admitted in admiration. He could see that the rat holes had been stuffed with broken glass and steel wool to prevent new entrance. "These guys are good."

"The best," Blancanales agreed. "Might as well

get started on the Sentries before the furniture arrives.''

"Get hard now," Lyons said softly, pulling out his Glock.

A few moments later a blue SUV Range Rover rolled into the warehouse through the open doorway and four men piled out carrying machine guns. Two more had fire axs.

"Now we talk seriously," the racketeer they'd encountered earlier snarled, his right arm cradled in a medical sling. "Take their guns!"

As the hitmen moved forward, Able Team dived in different directions, their Glocks firing while still in the air. Two of the enemy died on the spot. Two others opened fire with M-16 assault rifles, the 5.56 mm rounds ripping along the concrete floor as they tried to track after the moving warriors.

Hitting the floor hard, Lyons rolled sideways struggling to free the Uzi and rose in a crouch just behind a steel pillar and cut loose a long figure eight of 9mm Parabellum rounds. The driver behind the wheel jerked madly as the slugs took his life, and one of the men with an ax threw it away as he doubled over, collapsing onto the floor.

Lyons hadn't expected the local toughs to come back so soon and with this much firepower. Able Team was in bad shape, and he knew it. They were trapped in a well-lighted room, with the SUV blocking the only door and the rest of the warehouse completely empty. Aside from the support pillars there wasn't so much as a folding chair for cover.

The hit men opened fire again from behind the vehicle, and Schwarz went flat to skip the slugs from his Uzi across the floor and under the chassis, catching two of them in the ankles. As the men dropped, Blancanales finished them off, the tires deflating as the copper-jacketed rounds tore the rubber apart.

"It's only three guys!" the racketeer yelled, pulling a 10 mm Falcon pistol. The gun was blue steel and covered with silver filigree. "Kill them!"

Tossing away his ax, the last hit man pulled out a grenade and started unwrapping the electrical tape holding the arming lever in place.

That was real trouble. Dropping the Uzi, Lyons pulled his Glock and stood to place a shot right into the man's ear, his brains blowing out the other side in a ghastly froth of hair, bone and blood. Then the Able Team leader was pounded four times in the chest from incoming lead. The air was slammed from his lungs and he fell, still triggering the Glock. The bullets punched a line of holes across the SUV, but missed the racketeer.

His teammates stood and raked the vehicle with their weapons in a withering cross-sweep pattern. Windows blew out, paint went flying, the corpse behind the steering wheel shook madly and the racketeer was forced backward, pinned to the freshly scrubbed wall, his chest pumping blood from a dozens hits.

Wordlessly moving his mouth, the man raised his empty hand, trying to pull a trigger no longer there and went still, his head lolling limply onto his crimson splattered chest.

"Welcome to the Big Easy," said a man from the open doorway, the words softened by a pronounced Southern drawl.

Spinning in a gunman's crouch, Lyons almost fired until he saw this was somebody new and unarmed.

"I see you've met the members of the local welcoming committee," the newcomer said, sauntering past the corpses kicking spent brass out of his way. "I came here to talk some business, but perhaps you want me to come back later, after you'd had a chance to clean the place."

"Now is fine," Blancanales stated, the Glock still in his grip as he hit the newly installed control and closed the door to the warehouse, the steel shutters gliding into place on well-greased tracks.

"They work for you?" Lyons demanded, rising stiffly. His chest felt as if it were on fire from the impact of the 10 mm Magnum rounds on his NATO body armor. But this wasn't the time or the place to show how much it hurt.

The newcomer threw back his head to laugh. "These swamp bums? Not in our organization, I can assure you, sir." He strolled over to the dead racketeer.

So Big Red Danvers was aced. No loss there. The

man had only been a punk with ambition. And with his death, another small piece of New Orleans was now back under Family control. Soon they would own the city.

"I always told you it's better to talk first, Red," he said slowly, shaking his head. "The man never could control his temper."

"We can," Schwarz said, dropping his spent clip and quickly reloading. "Now, who the hell are you?"

The dapper newcomer spread his hands wide. "Why, I'm your invited guest, Anthony Giancomo. Fast Tony, to most. Word on the street is that you've been trying to contact my boss since yesterday, and here I am to arrange for a meet. But to see the don, you talk with me first."

"Your boss got a name?" Lyons asked, thumbing the safety on the Glock and tucking it away. This man wasn't part of the arms dealers group that they wanted, but through him they could reach the people, who could reach the Russians.

"Mr. Marasco," Giancomo said. "I'm sure you have heard of him."

Schwarz froze in the act of slinging the Uzi.

"Who was that?" Blancanales asked, the words seeming to echo in the silence of the empty warehouse. No way in hell had he heard that correctly. Flat out impossible.

Anthony "Fast Tony" Giancomo gave a friendly smile, as if he were puzzled by anybody not knowing the infamous name. "Dante Marasco. He's the nephew of old Honey Marasco from Santa Monica. Before Uncle Honey was...retired, he was a very important man in our line of work.

"Sure," Lyons said. "Yeah, I've heard of the man."

CHAPTER SIX

San Francisco, California

An unusually thick fog lay across San Francisco Bay, reducing rush-hour traffic to a crawl along the heavily shrouded Golden Gate Bridge.

Warning horns sounded to steer ships in the harbor away from the rocky shore and the buttress-reinforced Rock Island surrounding the massive support pylons of the majestic bridge. The headlights of nearly a thousand vehicles on the six-lane highway illuminated the expanse of the world-famous bridge with a ghostly nimbus, its orange paint muted into a soft gold by the combination of the fog and the lights. A poet once said San Francisco was at her best when dressed in ephemeral clouds, the same way a beautiful woman became even more provocative when clad in lace and nylons. Nobody who had ever seen the city by the bay wearing nature's finest ever disagreed.

The waters of the bay were slightly choppy from the incoming tide, the tour boats and pleasure craft safe and snug in the slips for the night. But then appearing from nowhere, a Shkval missile streaked across the surface of the ocean faster than the human eye could follow and slammed into the concrete fender surrounding Rock Island like a pyrotechnic thunderbolt. Designed only to break the force of incoming waves, the fender blew apart, and the next Shkval impacted directly into the column of granite blocks that housed the steel columns supporting the southern section of the Golden Gate Bridge. The massive blocks cracked with the first shot but held firm, then shattered with the arrival of another missile. The chilly fog writhed away from the burning waves of heat, only to flow back again to smother the destruction in its impenetrable gray blanket.

Moving with incredible speed, a third Shkval struck the weakened granite blocks, blowing them aside and clearing a path by ripping out massive chunks of the inner concrete sleeve to exposing the bare steel assembly of the primary bridge pylon.

More than 150 feet above, the massive towers of the Golden Gate trembled slightly, the vibrations of the staggering explosions feeding upward to the colossal structure. Slowly, a deep, inhuman groan rose from the weakening steel, and on the highway above, the barely detectable shake became a noticeable sway that started to build in power and tempo. With the fog masking any storm clouds in the sky, the vehicles streaming along the bridge at rush hour were caught totally by surprise and started slipping sideways to slam into one another, horns blaring and alarms keening.

But even as the waters of San Francisco Bay lapped onto the exposed support column, the fifth Shkval detonated directly on the twined steel. Instantly, several of the smaller cables snapped free to whip across the road, smashing windshields, denting roofs and hitting a motorcycle rider directly in the chest. The biker was brutally cut in two, his torso hurled over the side of the bridge to tumble lifelessly down into the gray clouds. Riderless, the bike continued on to slam into the rear of a delivery truck and become jammed underneath, suddenly spraying hot sparks from being scraped along the asphalt. Frantically downshifting, the truck driver slammed on the brakes, but the leaking fuel tank of the Harley ignited from the sparks and the bike roared into flames, soon setting off the double gas tanks of the truck.

Flames washed over a dozen other cars, starting a wave of terror that jammed the highway solid in only seconds. Each terrified driver slammed into others to try to force an escape path. Bumpers locked, more cars crashed into one another and other explosions erupted as the swaying continued to build, more and more of the slim stabilizing cables coming loose to wildly lash across the honking traffic jam. The deck of the bridge was slick with spilled fuel. It was a primed deathtrap waiting for only a single spark to ignite into a hellish inferno. People began leaving their cars to desperately scramble over the other vehicles to try to escape.

Fistfights broke out, guns were fired and the exodus became a melee of insane fighting. More than a dozen fools jumped over the side of the bridge rather than be burned alive. Plummeting through the fog, they lost consciousness on the way down from cranial blood loss and hit the choppy waters.

Flashing red lights and a stridently loud siren announced the arrival of a Coast Guard hovercraft from the inner-harbor rescue station near the old Presido. Working with grim speed, the crew was loading their only weapon, a single 60 mm deck gun normally used for launching lifelines to drowning swimmers. But the sailors had no doubt what was happening in the bay, and were grimly preparing for the very first battle of their long careers.

While the radar swept the sky and sonar probed the cold sea, the crew hunted within the misty depths of the thick fog bank with a powerful laser-beam searchlight to find the source of the torpedoes. Land, sea or air, the hidden terrorists would be found and attacked with lethal force.

Then the sonar went off as a shape passed right by the racing hovercraft. Another Shkval was heading for the crippled bridge support. But even as they banked into a turn, the gun crew struggling to aim the cumbersome weapon, the Russian death dealer sharply angled about as it recognized a viable target.

Unexpectedly leaping from the water on a fiery

contrail, the Shkval brutally smashed into the spinning fans set underneath the thick rubber skirt of the hovercraft before detonating. The debris rose on a boiling fireball, charred bits of the keel slamming into the bottom of the trembling bridge above.

The explosions, the fire sirens, the screams and general chaos combined into a deafening cacophony that almost masked the muted rumble in the sky of fighter jets streaking past the trembling bridge.

"Zebra Dog to Edwards," the lead pilot said into his throat mike, his hands guiding the F-16 with surgical precision. "We have arrived at San Fran. No sign of the enemy activity. But the fog is too thick for a high-fly. We're going in for low-level recon. Over."

"Wave hopping in fog?" the base commander answered from the Air Force base fifty miles away. "I don't recommend that, Zebra Dog. By the time you see something, you would already have crashed into it."

"Only way to find the bastards!"

"No other way, Edwards. If these bastards get off a couple more shots, the Golden Gate will break apart. We have no choice."

"Roger. Proceed with caution. These bastards play for keeps. Over."

"So do we, sir," Zebra Dog growled, arming his missiles and cannon. "Out."

With the Air Force base on red-alert status, the two pilots had launched and gone Mach with the first report of an attack on the bridge. They arrived in under five minutes, but a lot of people could be killed in five minutes.

"Looks peaceful enough," Blue Devil said, flying alongside the other F-16. "Radar is clear, EM clear. Maybe they ran out of Shkvals... Alert! Incoming!"

The second F-16 banked sharply away from the first, and a split second later a missile flashed between the two craft from the cloud banks below and thunderously detonated. The concussion hit both jets hard, shoving Blue Devil free but causing Zebra Dog to go into a tailspin.

Dropping airfoils and fighting the stick, Zebra Dog brought the aircraft back under control and tried to restart the engine. The proximity alarm was beeping dangerously fast, the automatic safety features priming to jettison the pilot clear of the falling plane when the turbos lit and he barrel-rolled away from the water and climbed for height.

"That was a goddamn Stinger!" Zebra Dog gritted through clenched teeth. A heat-seeker. Well, there wasn't much they could do about the volumes of thermal of their engines. Just have to fly faster and trust their reactions would be fast enough to keep them from crashing into anything.

"Here comes another one!" Blue Devil muttered, watching the radar and thumbing a button. "I got 'em, ZD."

Two antimissiles shot from the wingtips of his screaming jet. The rapidly climbing Stinger was destroyed and he slipped past the fireball, the concussion only a gentle nudge this time.

"Nice shooting, Blue," Zebra Dog stated, lowering his speed. In just these few moments, the Golden Gate Bridge was already a good mile plus behind them. Slowly, he began to bank into a turn and head back. "Dammit, we can't see shit from up here, and all the moisture in the fog is blurring the radar. We have to go lower and slower. Time for some wave hopping."

"Roger, Zebra Dog, reducing to stall speed and turning on my windshield wipers."

"I'm going in. Stay on my three, Blue Devil. Concentrate on the port shore. I'll take starboard."

"Roger that, Zebra. Five by five. Time to kick some ass."

Swinging wide out at sea, the USAF F-16 came streaking back across the bay as another Shkval slammed into the steadily weakening support pylon of the trembling bridge. Then just for a second a light flashed on the wraparound controls just above the heads of the grim pilot, and then it was gone.

"Well, I'll be damned," Zebra Dog exhaled as once more the fighters slipped into a banked curve and started back for the bay. "Was that a chemical alert?"

"Smoke!" Zebra Dog shouted in triumph. "The terrorists are using a smoke generator to increase the fog and make themselves invisible in the fog! Damn, that's smart."

"Not smart enough, Devil. Now we got 'em by the

balls. We're going in full speed, hot and hard. Our targeting computer should remember where the bridge is.''

"Damn well hope so. Locking trackers into chemical sources,'' Blue Devil replied, the control board flashing and blinking in a rainbow of technology. ''I have a bogey.''

"Confirmed, I also have a lock on the smoke chemicals. Firing one, firing two.''

"Firing one, firing two!''

The barrage of Sidewinders fell away from their wings, then burst ahead as their rocket motors ignited. The pilots continued on their silent flight through the fog and smoke, Doppler radar showing nothing ahead of them for miles except for the missiles.

Spiraling aimlessly, the Sidewinders almost seemed to be heading straight for the bridge, and Zebra Dog flipped the cover on the master self-destruct to blow the Air Force missiles out of the sky when they suddenly dipped for the water and exploded.

A heartbeat later there followed a series of explosions, the fireballs overlapping into a growing conflagration that violently burned away the smoky clouds to reveal a cargo barge piled high with corrugated-metal shipping containers pumping out volumes of black smoke, the front of the barge open to the water and stacked with what resembled pressurized air tanks. Then the elongated tubes erupted at both ends, revealing their true nature. Shkvals. Dozens of them.

"Got 'em!'' Blue Devil cheered.

Without warning, two winged shapes appeared on the radar going from Mach speed to almost a standstill while in midair. The onboard computer hesitated for only a moment because of the fog, then brought up the ID code for Navy Harrier jump jets.

"Ahoy, Air Force," a new voice said on their general hailing channel. "This is Dragon Rider and Terminator from Sacramento here to help. Sitrep, tango-nine. Repeat, tango-nine."

"Ident confirmed, Dragon," Zebra Dog replied, swinging the F-16 around in a wide curve. "Welcome to Frisco."

"Roger that, Air Force," a woman said, as the huge Harriers slid into motion and took point position alongside the F-16. "This is Terminator. Was that the target?"

"Confirmed," Blue Devil replied, skimming past the flaming wreckage of the cargo barge. "Target has been destroyed."

"But thanks for coming," Zebra Dog added. Then the man cursed as something splashed into the water and started across the bay, building to fantastic speed. "One of the bastards is still alive and just launched a Shkval!"

"We're on it, Air Force," Dragon Rider snapped, the Harrier stopping dead to spin and flash forward. "Terminator, on my six, overlapping fields of fire. Everything we got. Go-go-go!"

Even as the Harriers skimmed along the surface of the bay, their wings crackled with light flashes as the

Navy aviators launched every weapon they had, forming a wall of hellfire across the bay between the Shkval and what remained of Rock Island. The water boiled under the furious assault, and the Shkval exploded only fifty yards from the battered shore.

Incredibly, the aft Harrier then kicked in its belly-jets and descended to land on the steaming rubble of the destroyed fender of the island. A wing snapped off as it brushed a jagged piece of concrete and the crippled jump jet dropped the last few yards to crumple its landing gear into a tangled mess of metal and busted hydraulic hoses.

"If they want the damn bridge," Terminator growled over the radio, "then they come through me first!"

"Way to go, Navy!" Zebra Dog cheered. "Now we'll finish off that last son of a bitch."

"Locking missiles on thermal signature of target," Blue Devil announced. "Ready to launch on your word, sir."

"Negative!" Zebra Dog ordered brusquely. "The CO wants them dead, but intact to trace the source. Blue Devil, Dragon Rider, get onto my six. We're coming in from the shore to keep him away from Terminator. Guns only."

"Roger that, sir!"

"Aye, aye, Air Force!"

"I can see the target from here. Four men, looks like they have another Shkval," Terminator reported succinctly, raising her canopy and drawing a side arm.

"Three, no, six men still moving on the barge. I see more Stingers, but no surviving civilian traffic in the area. The firezone is clear. Repeat, firezone is clear."

"Acknowledged," Zebra Dog said. "Thanks for the ID, Terminator."

"Welcome to hell, creeps," Blue Devil muttered, his words throaty with anger as the man pushed the joystick forward, his hand crushing the trigger.

Swinging around once more, the three military craft spread out in a fan formation and strafed the barge with their machine guns, chewing the men and Shkvals into pieces. Then they swung around once more to finish the job, but the barge already listing as it started to slowly sink into ocean.

Satisfied, the three jet fighters headed out to sea to search for any additional sources of danger while the fourth pilot climbed down from her craft to stand a post in the wall breach and protect the civilians, as so many other soldiers had done before her throughout recorded history.

Minutes later, police and firefighters arrived to handle the riot on the roadway, and ever so slowly, the tremors coursing through the Golden Gate Bridge began to subside, the groaning of the tortured metal going blissfully silent.

Charleston Bay, South Carolina

SITTING AMID the discarded beer cans and weeds alongside a paved highway, the men of Phoenix Force prepared their weapons for the coming assault.

To avoid detection, the Stony Man warriors had been dropped off by Jack Grimaldi in a Huey helicopter a mile away and trekked to that location during the night. The pilot would return to the drop-off point in an hour, or come charging in with guns ablaze in case an emergency evac was needed.

Now the men crouched in a thick growth of elderberry bushes that edged a coastal highway overlooking a cliff that loomed above the Atlantic Ocean. Cut away by aeons of erosion, the limestone descended straight down a hundred feet to the famous rolling hills of South Carolina, the contoured landscape reaching to a white sand beach.

A few sagging boathouses that had seen better days, and some wooden jetties crumbling with age and neglect, extended into the ocean. Terns and gulls nested on the splintery pylons, the weathered wooden posts discolored from the rising tides and the occasional pounding hurricane.

Several miles north of the ancient jetty was the great city of Charleston, its electric halo filling the sky and hiding the thick blanket of stars above in the soft glow of technology.

Set between the crumbling jetty and the city of Charleston was a sleek modern dock, with freshly painted boathouses and a heliport landing field that reached to the front of a large monolithic building stories tall. A helicopter sat on the asphalt field, flotation pods on the landing rails made the aircraft seem to be seaworthy, but the pods merely disguised ATA missile launchers. Video cameras swept the land, sea and sky for possible intruders. Armed guards walked the roof of the building, and encircling the entire property was a tall chain-link fence topped with concertina wire. Savage Doberman pinschers roamed freely along the area between the first and second fences. This was Phoenix Force's target for the night, Lane Importers, a well-known international arms dealer.

Just to the south of the modern dockyard facility, the beach became a jumble of boulders and rock, unsuitable for fishing or swimming, and impossible for any boats to traverse. A winding road led down from the limestone cliff to reach a concrete apron sprawling on the shore. Dozens of motorcycles were parked haphazardly in front of a bedraggled building from prewar days. Green paint was flaking off the cinder-block walls, the roof patched in so many different layers of tar and shingles it rose in a lumpy dome formation. The windows were blocked with sheets of stained plywood, but rods of light streamed from dozens of bullet holes in the sheathing, and from the front door there came the steady mindless thumping of too loud music and countless drunken howls.

The Fat Man Bar and Grill was the shame of South Carolina. The police raided the bar with numbing regularity for drugs, prostitution, disturbing the peace, fistfights and a dozen minor offenses. But somehow the place always stayed in business, and the bikers reveled in their safe haven on the rocky beach, far from the boring, mundane life and just outside the reach of the police past the city limits.

But there was a reason for the continued existence of the Fat Man Grill. Thomas Lane owned the seedy bar, and would have rebuilt the dump if it burned to the ground, because its noise and sleazy customers masked the illegal nighttime business deals that made Lane a multimillionaire: military weapons smuggling. If anything suspicious was discovered, it was always attributed to the bikers, and they often claimed responsibility for the crimes just out of stubbornness and spite to the hated cops. The perfect cover.

The Phoenix Force warriors froze as a car rolled by on the highway, its bright headlights splashing across the bushes for a brief moment, and then it was gone.

While Able Team attempted to burrow from within to find the Russian thieves manufacturing the Shkvals, Phoenix Force was taking a more aggressive tactic. The FBI kept close tabs on several known weapons merchants in America, but did nothing to close them down. Instead, the FBI merely monitored their deals and arrested the customers afterward. This way they had a steady source of reliable data on arms sales, and could stop most hate groups before they could use the weapons they had just purchased. If the arms dealers knew they were being used as stalking goats by the government, they didn't seem to care, grudgingly accepting the immunity from prosecution as the price for losing most of the repeat business.

Located in the underground Annex of Stony Man, Aaron Kurtzman and his team of cyber warriors had hacked into most of the computer files of known weapons dealers, extracting lots of interesting data but failing to discover any connections with the Russian thieves. None of the criminals knew anything about the source of the Shkvals, but each of them desperately wanted a piece of the action.

However, there was one small arms dealer in South Carolina. They couldn't raid it over the Internet, or infiltrate through the telephone lines, the electrical systems or coaxial TV cable. Thomas Lane didn't like computers and instead used an assistant with an eidetic memory capable of recalling everything she had ever heard or read in precise detail. Her name was unknown. Sometimes referred to as ''Kodak,'' an obvious reference to her photographic memory, the mysterious redhead was his walking file cabinet. Lane guarded her at his warehouse-mansion set into the gentle rolling hills of the Carolina coastline. They lived and worked together at the site, rarely leaving the location, and always traveling together with massive security. Rumors claimed the man and woman were lovers, local gossip said she was a prisoner, and hard facts on the relationship were nonexistent.

Then a few months ago, this small-time dealer was suddenly making huge overseas deposits, the source of this new wealth highly suspect because of its timing. Brognola and Price had conferred on the matter and decided it was time for Phoenix Force to pay Thomas Lane a visit.

"He could just be dealing drugs," Gary Manning said, carefully screwing the huge sound suppressor into the barrel of his Barrett Light Fifty. "And not our Russian terrorists."

The mammoth rifle possessed a range of more than 1800 meters, and the magazine held ten rounds that could punch through brick walls and even light tank armor. What the weapon did to human flesh had to be seen to be believed.

"So we shut him down anyway," Encizo replied grimly, stropping the edge of his Tanto combat knife to razor sharpness. The steel sighed as it slipped into the sheath at his hip.

"One less source on the streets," Calvin James agreed, working the bolt on his MP-5 submachine gun to chamber a round.

"Okay, people, here's the layout of this fortress," David McCarter said. The Phoenix Force leader was crouching low in the bushes and holding out his pocket computer for the others to see. The small screen showed a vector graphic of the warehouse and was slowly rotating for a full view. Only half the size of a commercial model, the pocket computer weighed even less yet had greater range and more memory.

"The first floor is a dummy filled with machine tools, injection molds and tractor parts. The second floor is the barracks for his workers, lots of ex-mercs and soldiers-of-fortune there. The third floor is weapons storage, and he lives on the fourth floor. The fifth is home for his personal bodyguards.''

He tapped a button on the computer, and a new picture appeared on the screen. McCarter continued, ''There are AutoSentry machine guns here, here and there, giving damn good cross-fire patterns. The roof and the land around the mansion are heavily mined, the charges controlled from Lane's private office. Every window has bulletproof glass, and every door is solid steel.''

''He lives in a damn vault,'' T. J. Hawkins growled, pulling on a black ski mask and shifting it about to align the holes with his eyes and mouth.

As a disguise it wasn't necessary. The members of the covert team didn't officially exist, their fingerprints and dental records expunged from the government and civilian files when they joined Stony Man. However, the cloth neutralized any possible reflection from their skin or teeth.

''Any chance Lane might use the woman as a shield?'' Manning asked, turning his black cloth cap around so that the bill wouldn't be in the way of the 10-power scope on the Barrett. He was the only member wearing combat cosmetics. The holes of a ski mask often got in the way of the eyepiece for the rifle scope, and that wasted precious seconds to correct. A lot could happen in a few heartbeats; battles were sometimes won or lost in a single instant.

''If she dies, he's out of business. But if she dies,

there are no records to send him to jail,'' McCarter explained, checking his watch. Almost time. "So let's move fast and not give him a chance to make the decision. Lane is a scumbag, and if the FBI doesn't have the balls to blow him away, then we get the job. If you get a clean shot, take him down.''

"No problem," Manning said, wrapping the rifle's shoulder strap around his forearm for a more secure hold.

Opening canvas packs on the ground, the men slipped into a complex harness, strapping bulky canvas packs to their backs. Suddenly, the music swelled from the bar down the beach until the team could almost hear the lyrics. There came a flurry of noise from the biker tavern, a chorus of cheers, a yowl of pain, shattering glass, a single pistol shot, closely followed by the return of the thumping music.

"If we accidentally detonate a couple hundred Shkvals," James said, plainly annoyed, "I don't think anybody in that bar would notice."

"Got that right, brother," Encizo said, tightening the chest strap.

Just then, static crackled in their earphones.

"Firebird, this is Stony Base," Kurtzman said over the miniature com link. "We've cut the circuits to the alarms and land mines. The nest is yours. Good hunting.''

Without another word, the men of Phoenix Force left the bushes and dived straight over the edge of the cliff into the darkness. Only Manning stayed behind, to watch their descent through the crosshair scope of the deadly Barrett sniper rifle.

Show time.

WALKING THE PERIMETER of the rooftop of the mansion, a sentry with a bulky Finnish 20 mm antitank rifle strapped across his back paused to light a joint and drew the pungent smoke deep into his lungs, then held his breath for a moment before exhaling.

The weapon weighed a ton, but scared the hell out of the drunks from the neighborhood bar. Only once had he been forced to use the weapon on some fool grimly determined to cross the fences. A single well-placed shot in the man's chest had blown him completely apart, the head splashing into the ocean, while the boots landed in the bushes. The official police coroner's report cited the incident as a heart attack. Since then, there had never been any real trouble from the bikers, although the guards were extremely careful never to go over there alone. The hillbilly trash was just itching for revenge.

"Boss will ream you a new one if he catches you stoned," the other guard said, his Heckler & Koch G-11 caseless rapid-fire held loose in his grip.

"So don't tell him," the first guard said, taking another drag and passing over the handrolled smoke. "He's so deep in the pockets of the Feds they wouldn't raid us if it was the end of the world."

Accepting the joint, the second man started to reply when feathers appeared on his arm holding the joint.

He stared at them for a full second before slumping to the ground.

"Harry?" the first sentry asked, stepping toward the man when a shadow moved across the moon and he glanced skyward.

Black shapes were blotting out the stars overhead, and even as he recognized the falling objects as parachutes, feathers stabbed him in the chest and left leg. Darts! Even as the guard attempted to reach the monster weapon on his back, a spreading warmth filled his body and the man sagged over, going to sleep.

TUGGING IN THE HARNESS of the para-glider, McCarter swung away from the satellite dish and landed softly on the roof, running for a few yards to regain his balance before hitting the chest release and dropping the chute to the rooftop.

The rest of Phoenix Force arrived seconds later and spread out to secure the rest of the rooftop by more narcotic darts when possible, or their silenced pistols when necessary. Soon six additional men were stretched out.

Going to the front of the building, McCarter loaded his crossbow and fired at a small kiosk near the parked helicopter. The quarrel slammed into the doorjamb with a muffled thump, and a few moments later the door was opened by a man in a T-shirt and denim jeans, holding a magazine and a Tec-9 pistol.

McCarter fired again, the razor-sharp quarrel hitting the pilot in the throat and forcing him back inside and pinning him to the interior wall by the steel shaft. Dropping the gun and magazine, the man clawed at the quarrel, twitched once and went permanently still. Reloading, McCarter put two arrows into the gas tank of the helicopter aviation fuel streaming onto the tarmac.

Suddenly, there was a beep on the rooftop and in the corner an AutoSentry winked into life and swept the rooftop with its single red light, the proximity sensors set above the .38 machine gun looking for any viable targets on its programmed security sweep.

Halfway to the machine, Encizo froze and felt a rush of icy adrenaline in his gut as the deadly weapon pointed directly at him for a very long second, and then moved on, the electronic ID badge taken from a guard recognized by the machine.

Too close. Padding to each corner of the building, he used his knife to slice through the coaxial power cable, rendering the weapons inert.

Prying open a control board, Hawkins yanked out a circuit breaker and pulled in a Tesla ADR power pack. He barely got his hand away when the device visibly pulsed, releasing its stored electricity, and every light bulb in the building blew from the massive power surge. The light streaming from the windows went dark, and cursing started on every level.

Meanwhile, James was using a power tool to remove the screws holding a louvered steel grille in position over a ventilation duct. As it came free, he placed the cover aside and started pulling pins on BZ gas canisters and dropping them down the aluminum duct. The grenades banged and clanged deep into the building, ricocheting off the sides of the duct and disappeared into the bowels of the building long before they started gushing out a stream of thick blue smoke.

The BZ was nonlethal, merely a strong hallucinogenic related to LSD, only without the terrible nightmare side effects. Plus, these were half charges, much too weak to stop the people from escaping, but that was the plan. The defenses of the mansion were much too good, so Phoenix Force would fake a raid and force the groggy arms dealer to leave his impenetrable vault and run straight into their waiting arms.

Soon armed men surged out of the front door, four with KEDR subguns and two holding fat tubular pistols in their hands. McCarter swore at the sight. A Veri pistol! The damn flare guns could illuminate the entire compound brighter than daylight.

Leveling his MP-5 machine gun, Encizo fired a long burst, mowing down the guards, but one still managed to launch a flare while he fell. A sizzling fireball streaked along the ground, bouncing wildly off every obstacle until splashing into the ocean and died.

But just then, a group of people appeared from the boathouse a hundred yards away from the mansion. There was a secret escape tunnel. Dressed in nightclothes and bathrobes, the group started for a sleek hydrofoil moored at the dock. A loud crack rang out from the cliff, and the boat shuddered as its windshield shattered. The group shot wildly into the darkness, the muzzle-flashes resembling burning flowers. Then Manning fired again, and the V-Twin 400 engine cracked apart and whoofed into flames.

"Two men with Uzis," James said, watching through Starlite goggles. "They must be the bodyguards. The fat man resembles our arms dealer and...yes, a slim woman in pajamas, red hair, glasses."

"That's Kodak, the record keeper," McCarter said, swinging up his crossbow and trying for the distant figures.

But the range was too great. The sea wind deflected the quarrel as the group moved around the boathouse to climb aboard a sleek cabin cruiser, the boathouse protecting it from the sniper on the cliff. Then one of the bodyguards appeared from behind the building and cast off the mooring line.

Once again, the massive .50-caliber rifle roared and the guard flew backward into the water with most of his head missing. The woman on the cruiser started to scream as the man gunned the engines into life and started pulling away.

"After them," McCarter said, slinging the crossbow.

But then the team spun at the sound of smashing glass, and saw the incredible sight of a man wearing a helmet and some kind of bulky machine strapped to his back fly away from the warehouse, the top-mounted side bars of the strange device spraying out steady streams of white gas.

"That's a NASA jet pack," James growled, tracking the flight with the barrel of his rifle. Although trained in the operation of the machines, James hadn't seen one in years. The jet packs were difficult to store properly, complex to operate, incredibly expensive and had a maximum flight time of only ninety seconds. Not really enough to reach anyplace, and if the operator ran out of fuel while in midair, down he or she went with a hundred pounds of deadweight pushing all the way.

Without a clear identification on the flying man, McCarter hesitated shooting and merely tracked the figure as it rocketed straight up the cliff and over the top, the white streams from the side bars cutting off just as the escapee cleared the crest and the man dropped a few feet to the rocky ground.

"Hey, what was that?" Manning demanded over the com link. "Goddamn!"

There came the sound of a powerful engine, then headlights splashed over the cliff, and a truck rolled briefly into view as it started down the highway toward Charleston.

Bloody hell, they had been tricked! McCarter knew it had to be somebody very important enough to get the million-dollar jet pack, maybe Lane himself. Or was it reserved for the woman? There had been no way to determine the sex of the flyer. Just because they could see a woman with red hair and glasses on the cruiser, that didn't necessarily mean she was the one they wanted. Lane was a known player and always had a few ladies lounging around in his private quarters.

If this was a simple termination, they could easily kill both parties, but they needed one of these people alive, and with every heartbeat the prey was getting farther away. There was no choice in the matter.

"Gary, block the northbound road, but don't shoot at the truck! That could be Kodak. T.J., cover the road to the south!" McCarter said into his throat mike, heading for the satellite dish. "Rafe and Calvin, with me. Go!"

Grabbing the parachutes, the team tossed them over the edge of the roof and quickly rappeled down the outside of the mansion, bypassing the deadly interior completely. In seconds, they were on the ground, Hawkins sprinting through the minefield toward the barking guard dogs, while McCarter and the others sprinted for the second cruiser tied at the end of the jetty.

CHAPTER SEVEN

Persian Gulf

The *Glory of Paradise* was old and cramped, but its diesel engines were powerful, and the Russian submarine moved through the deep waters of the Persian Gulf with good speed.

However, the air smelled of rank human sweat and tasted like grease. The Iranian captain felt as if he were swimming in dung from the combined odors of sweaty shoes, unwashed bodies, garlic, tobacco and even the hot coppery ozone from the electrical generators. Alone in his cabin, the officer prayed for a single breath of the clean desert wind, dry and clean. On the cramped bridge, he strode the metallic grid of the deck without complaint. Service to his leader demanded that this task be done. For him, that ended any discussion before it began.

"Twelve-mile mark, Captain," the XO called, hunched over the navigation table. "According to the United Nations, we are now in international waters."

The captain snorted in amusement. The gulf belonged to whoever was strong enough to take it. This was where the supertankers passed, and a single working submarine armed with the deadly Shkval torpedo could control the entire area. Even the mighty Americans with their nuclear submarines would stay away from the Shkvals! Sink a few tankers and the rest would start to pay a handsome bounty to Iran for safe passage.

Of course, Iraq, Kuwait and others who also used the Persian Gulf would not approve, and they had Russian submarines of their own. But without the Shkvals, they were powerless.

"Load all tubes," the captain ordered, "Sonar, report on any activity. I want to be ready in case we encounter the Iraqians and their foolish *Sword of the Lion.*"

Enthusiastically, the bridge crew voiced its approval. None of them dared to mention the fact that their own submarine had been named the *Sword of the Lion* before their leader discovered the Iraqis had used it already, and so quickly changed the name of the sub to the *Glory of Paradise.* Which was a much better name anyway.

"Captain, we have contact," the sonar operator said slowly, making sure before he voiced any report. "Depth three hundred feet, twenty knots, diesel engines…confirmed, it is another submarine."

"Range?"

"Nine thousand meters," the sailor said. "North by north-west, sir. Within our territorial boundary."

"Motherless sons of goats," the XO muttered. "Send them a hail to leave this area immediately or we shall open fire."

"Yes, sir," the radio operator acknowledged. He knew the radio only worked in the air, and underwater they had another device. But he really wasn't exactly sure how it operated and so called them both a radio. "Attention, *Sword of the Lion,* attention..."

"God be merciful!" the sonar operator cried, staring at his screen. "Captain, they have launched a torpedo at us! No wait, two torpedoes!"

"What?" the captain demanded, arching an eyebrow in shock. "With no warning or demands? Filthy cowards! Fire our Shkvals and blow them out of the water!"

The XO saluted. "As you command, Captain!"

Moments later two Shkvals exploded from the forward tubes of the Iranian submarine.

"All four Shkvals are running normal," the sonar operator announced with a pride.

"Four?" the captain repeated, swinging around from the periscope. "We only launched two!"

"But there are four in the water," the sailor replied, his voice fading only to come back strong and loud. "Captain! Two incoming Shkvals!"

"God have mercy!" the XO gasped, backing into a corner of the bridge. "We are doomed!"

"Weapons officer, fire all standard torpedoes! Torpedo room, load another Shkval! Engine room, maximum revolutions!" the captain bellowed, sweat pouring down his pale face. "Helmsman, dive seventeen degrees down! Security, release the countermeasures!"

"Too late," the sonar operator said in a whisper, closing his eyes.

With a terrible noise, the great diesel shuddered again as the Iraqi Shkvals tore through the outer armored hull, the inner lining of batteries and then the inner hull to finally detonate inside the vessel. The concussion killed everybody on board instantly, then the sub burst apart, spilling men and machinery into the dark waters.

The Iraqis cheered for only five seconds before starting to scream as the Iranian Shkvals slammed directly into their fuel tanks. The submarine was filled with waves of flame that boiled along the corridors, cooking the crew alive and rapidly building pressure until the sub shattered into an underwater fireball.

Steaming pieces of jagged metal and dead sailors rained down into the murky depths of the Persian Gulf.

New Orleans, Louisiana

HEAVILY LADEN with trays of food, the waiters exited from the left door of the double set, releasing a tremendous clatter of plates from the steamy kitchen of the restaurant. Then the noise was muffled as the thick door swung closed again, only to return as another waiter entered the right door of the set with a tray piled high of dirty dishes.

Giant murals of the Yang River Valley decorated the walls, plastic suits of ancient Oriental armor stood in the corners and the stiff velvet menus were adorned with fancy golden dragons printed on the front.

"I don't like this," Gadgets Schwarz said, taking a sip from his cup of green tea. The checkered grip of a Glock 20 peeked out from within his silk designer suit.

"They're only ten minutes late," Blancanales said, checking the Ingram SMG duct taped to the underside of the table. It was securely held by the sound suppressor and the pistol grip with none of the sticky tape attached to the breech or trigger to hinder operation. They had learned to never trust the Mafia under any circumstances. In fact, the more they smiled, the more likely they were to eat you alive.

"Could be traffic, or a flat tire," he added, looking over the crowd of people in the restaurant. The usual assortment of parents with noisy babies, young lovers more interested in each other than the food, friends laughing at private jokes while they ate. It looked perfectly normal, but looks were usually deceiving.

Pouring more tea into his cup, Schwarz reached down to scratch his leg and check the .32-caliber pistol strapped to his ankle. "How did you choose this place?"

"Neutral territory. Far away from the home turf of both parties," Blancanales said, pouring some tea into his own mug. Aside from the twin Glocks nestled in his jacket, the man also had a .44 derringer hidden inside his hollowed-out wallet. And in the trash can in the alley was a fully loaded M-16/M203 assault rifle combo hidden where nobody could possibly find it.

"We offered six locations and they offered six. This one just happened to be on both lists," Lyons explained, adding sugar to his coffee. Meeting the Mafia Don face-to-face wasn't a good idea now that they knew who he was, but there had been no reason to get out of the meal without blowing their cover story.

"A Chinese restaurant. Well, it's better than Italian. I hate clichés."

"Clichés are only true because they happen so often."

"No, that's a coincidence."

"Or paranoia."

"And who told you to say that?"

"Heads up," Lyons said, glancing at the reflections in the huge mirror behind the lavish bar.

The banter stopped instantly. Pretending to read his menu, Blancanales looked over the red velvet placard and watched as five large men stepped out of a long black Excalibur limousine at the busy curb outside. Anthony Giancomo was with the group. Three of the others had the hard, lean appearance of bodyguards, while the last was a heavily muscled man in a homburg, and holding a cane.

"It's them," Schwarz confirmed.

Blancanales merely grunted at the news.

Beyond the wrought-iron divider separating the private tables from the rest of the restaurant, the other customers started to react to the change as conversations became hushed, and an older couple even rose from the unfinished meal, paid and left quickly. Studying the reversed image in the mirror, Lyons watched as the man with the thick cane said something to Giancomo, who nodded unhappily, then returned to the limousine. Turning clumsily, the Mafia Don and three bodyguards now entered the Golden Pheasant restaurant as if they owned the place.

When the overhead lights hit the men, Schwarz clearly saw the capo's face and felt the years flow away like silver water. Suddenly, he was back with the Death Squad in Santa Monica, California, so many years ago. Flowerchild, Chopper, Deadeye, Bloodbrother... The Mob had caught them in an ambush and everybody died but three members—Mack Bolan, himself and Blancanales. What a slaughter that had been. Bolan returned to finish the job and get his first of many new faces, but Hermann Schwarz would never forget the hit men who had chewed the Death Squad into hamburger. Just a pimply faced teenager at the time, Dante Marasco was an adult now, sleek and heavily muscled with the cold, dead eyes of a professional killer. A major hardcase.

Ignoring the No Smoking sign just behind him, Blancanales lit a cigarette and tried to maintain his disinterested demeanor, even though his heart was pounding. This was the worst-case scenario of every undercover op, running into an old enemy that knew you. If the Mafia capo showed any sign of remembering them, then all hell would break loose, and Able Team would have to take him down right here, surrounded by innocent civilians. The mission would be blown, and they would have to start after the Russian arms dealers from square one again. Valuable time wasted, and countless lives lost over a single misspoken word.

Lyons took a sip of coffee and glowered as the men checked their coats and hats with a pretty Oriental woman. A bodyguard with a goatee stood away from the capo and closely watched the crowd while Marasco flirted with the woman, then another took the point position as the last bodyguard checked his own clothing. The rotation was very well done. These guys weren't street punks with Saturday-night Specials like Red and his gang. These were seasoned professionals.

Frantic waiters tried to clear a path through the other customers as the four men strode across the restaurant, the Mafia Don using the cane and favoring his stiff right leg.

Lyons took the moment to compare the young capo to his deceased cousin. Honey Marasco had been one of the toughest men on the face of the earth. A real monster. Dante was larger and moved with confidence, but that came with the ten-thousand-dollar suits and hired guns.

Long ago, when Lyons was a young cop, he had arrested the teenager for a DWI, and here he was again, a sworn enemy who could blow their cover or deliver the Russians into their waiting hands. Lyons hoped that the former intoxicated youth wouldn't remember him.

Reaching the wrought-iron divider, Dante Marasco stopped for a moment to rest his throbbing leg and scrutinize the three men waiting at the corner table, their backs to the wall. They were hard-looking men, emotionless eyes, with crude prison scars. The Mafia lord had trouble understanding people who killed for blind hatred of others, not for money. That was just stupid. Definitely not the sort of people he would prefer to associate with, but business was business.

As the Don and his bodyguards approached the table, Able Team rose to show respect. While the two groups got the measure of each other, Schwarz took a small Humbug from his pocket and placed it prominently on the table. After a few seconds, the EM scanner blinked green showing no live microphones were within fifty feet of the device. Then one of the Mafia guards laid another Humbug across the table, a larger and less advanced model, then waited until those lights also turned green.

"Clear, Mr. Marasco," the man announced, leaving the device in plain sight. Then he walked behind the Mafia boss to act as a shield between him and the glass windows facing the busy New Orleans street.

"Want to frisk us?" Blancanales offered, the cigarette dangling from his mouth as he opened the tailored jacket to display the two Glock pistols in the double holster.

Staring directly at Lyons, Marasco waved the matter aside. "Not necessary. I would only have insisted if you didn't offer," he muttered, unable to take his eyes off the man across the table. "People who don't carry weapons in our line of work are too stupid to do business with."

"Don't I know you?" Lyons interrupted, getting the jump on the issue.

"No, I don't think so," Marasco said, squinting. "But you do look sort of familiar. Ever done time in Pelican?"

Lyons grinned without a trace of humor. "Made my bones there," the Able Team leader replied, meaning that was where he first killed another man. "Worst food in the world."

The Don grimaced. "Then you ain't never been to Leavenworth."

"Can't be as bad as the chow at Lewisburg ICC," Blancanales said, lowering his sunglasses to peer over the top. "I thought they were feeding us other inmates."

A bodyguard chuckled. "I know that hole. Got a brother in there. I send him soup and buzz whenever I can."

Yeah, Lyons knew about those. Modern jails had a lot of nonsmokers as prisoners. Buying your life with a pack of cigarettes was something out of the past.

Nowadays, it was drugs or packets of soup, small luxury items for the prisoners to enjoy in secret. Buzz was toothpaste with cocaine injected in the middle of the tube. The guards only checked the first squeeze of toothpaste; if that was clean, they passed the rest. Once alone, the prisoner could dump the rest of the untainted cream and rub the diluted cocaine on his gums for a serious high.

"A packet of spicy pepperoni sticks saved my ass once," Schwarz added. "Literally."

"Been there." Marasco smiled, gesturing at his people.

As the men took chairs, the owner of the restaurant came bustling over to take their order, but the Don dismissed him with a glance.

"Food can come later," Marasco said gruffly, resting both hands on top of his cane. "First to business. I only accept cash as payment, no trades, no drugs, no gold, no jewels. Cash."

"How about certified wire bank transfers?" Lyons asked.

As a preparation for the mission, Able Team had over four million in an offshore account in the Cayman Islands. The money was as untraceable as their identities. The previous day, Akira Tokaido had transferred the funds from a numbered Swiss bank account into another numbered Swiss account and then finally into the Cayman Island bank. Each financial institution absolutely guaranteed total privacy.

"Wire transfers are fine," the Don said, leaning

forward, the ornate gold handle of the cane peeking out between his fingers. The walking stick had a 12-gauge shotgun inside that made it heavy as lead, but he liked the feeling of having an extra piece always at hand.

"So what are you looking for?" Marasco asked.

"Military weapons," Lyons replied deep in his throat.

Motioning to one of his bodyguards, the Don nodded as the man poured him a cup of coffee. He liked people who didn't mince around with vague terms. Straight talk from straight shooters.

"Those I have in abundance," he said bluntly. "All you want—Kalashnikovs, Uzis, M-16, G-11, whatever you need."

"Big stuff," Lyons replied. "Armbrust, X-18, Stinger, LAW, Haflas, Dragons, Phalanx miniguns, Hercules cargo planes, hovercraft and better."

Ah, now they were getting to the real purpose of the meeting; the Don could feel it. "Such as?" Marasco prompted, taking a sip of the black brew. Many asked for such big-ticket items; they thought it would impress their enemies. Then they heard the price and asked for something else. Yet for some reason, Marasco had a feeling these men wouldn't balk at the cost. There was an air of determination about them.

Suddenly alert, Lyons saw the shifting of the Don's expression and spoke quickly to stop the train of thought. "We wish to buy Russian rocket torpedoes."

"Huh?" Marasco asked, then looked over a shoulder at his bodyguards. They shrugged in return. "Never heard of them. What are those?"

Knowing that the men were lying, Blancanales explained anyway.

Brushing a hand over his thick hair, the Don exhaled nosily. "That's state-of-the-art. Very difficult to obtain. We have nothing to do with that sort of stuff. There's very little demand for it on the street."

"But you know people," Lyons insisted. "And they know other people, who in turn…" He left the sentence open, waiting for a response.

Placing aside the coffee, Marasco shrugged. "Possibly," he admitted, taking a napkin to pat his mouth dry. "But there would be a fee for my assistance. Say, fifteen percent."

"Ten," Blancanales said, scowling over the smoking cigarette.

"Twelve."

"Done," Lyons stated.

Neither side offered a handshake to seal the deal. There was nothing friendly or genial about the contract. Ethics and morals were a joke to these men. Contracts were signed in oaths of blood, with a lot more coming if either party failed to fulfill its side of the bargain.

"And since we have never dealt with each other before," Marasco commented dryly, "I'll require a down payment in advance. For my time and trouble. You understand."

"Of course," Lyons said, and snapped his fingers.

Reaching inside his jacket, Schwarz pulled out a thick envelope and tossed it to the largest guard, not the Don. That would have been a mortal insult. Marasco should be considered above such things as mundane as money. The man made the catch and carefully opened the envelope to thumb through the wad of green inside.

"Inch and a half," he said, tucking it away. "All hundreds."

"Fifty thousand? That will suffice." Marasco smiled, rising stiffly. "Once we dealt with an undercover FBI team who tried to pay us in five-hundred-dollar bills."

Blancanales frowned. "Banks don't make those anymore. You can't cash them anyway."

"That's correct. Useless money that would have identified us everywhere in the world. Clever, eh?"

"I would have killed them," Lyons growled.

Marasco scowled. "Oh, no. That wouldn't have been wise. I let them meet with other people who tried to kill them. Whichever side won, I still got paid."

"How do we know you're not going to do the same with us?" Lyons asked.

Instantly, the Mafia bodyguards became alert, and the rest of Able Team shifted their positions to reach their weapons fast.

"Why? Because I have a reputation on the street. And you three aren't important enough for me to risk soiling it," Marasco stated bluntly. "I take the matter of honor, and revenge, very seriously."

"As do we," Lyons said.

"Good. Then we understand each other," the Don said with a tolerant smile, the sight as pleasant as an open grave. "Enjoy your meal. It's on the house. You'll hear from me by tomorrow."

Followed by his men, Marasco rose and took his leisure in departing the restaurant to drive away in the waiting limousine.

"We better order something," Blancanales said, crushing out the butt of his cigarette in a butter dish. "Act natural. They may come back or have somebody watching us."

"The deal looks good, though," Schwarz said.

Reclining in the chair, Lyons eased his tense shoulders. "Lots of things can still go wrong. But with any luck we'll soon be introduced to the arms dealers."

"Any prisoners?" Schwarz asked.

"We kill every damn one of the bastards," Lyons stated, waving the waiter over to finally place an order. For some reason he was suddenly very hungry.

As THE LIMOSINE smoothly fed into the downtown traffic, Dante Marasco accepted a painkiller from Giancomo and washed it down with a shot of imported Polish vodka.

"You okay, sir?"

"Fine, fine, old friend," the Don answered, irritated that he was showing any sign of weakness. "Those guys seem to be legit. There can be a tremendous profit from brokering a deal between them and the Russians.''

He patted the leather seats of the Excalibur with an open palm. The limo was a grateful gift from the Russians for bringing them so much business. It was a true pleasure to deal with people who understood such things. Pity he had no idea where they were located, or else the Don could stage a raid, kill them and take over the market. At one hundred thousand dollars apiece, the Shkvals were being snapped up by every piss-pot Third World nation.

''Well, just in case you decided not to deal with them,'' Giancomo said, swaying to the gentle motion of the luxury vehicle as it took a corner, ''I checked with the FBI. The reward for bringing in these escaped killers is almost half a million dollars each.''

''Good,'' Marasco said, clicking on the safety of his cane and laying it aside on the rear seat. ''After the fifth sale, when these men have come to trust us, we'll turn them in and collect from the Feds. A nice bonus. Then we tell the Russians there was a traitor and we need a bigger cut for better security measures.''

''That will work. Unless the Russians think we're lying,'' Giancomo said, glancing out the tinted window.

Just outside, the limo was passing through the French Quarter, and the streets were full of young girls looking for older men to gain them illegal admittance into the better nightclubs. And they were also so grateful afterward. Oh yes, so very grateful.

"Repeat that," the Don demanded suddenly.

The man turned. "Sir?"

"Repeat what you just said," Marasco demanded, frowning as if scrambling to catch a fleeting thought.

"I was saying," Giancomo told him, "that if the Russians think we're lying, there could be a war, and that's bad for business—"

"Son of a bitch," Marasco whispered. Could it be? Was it possible?

"Lying. Goddamn it—Lyons," he said aloud in growing fury. "Son of a bitch. Carl Lyons!"

"The guy who busted you when you were a kid? Are you sure? What in hell would he be doing posing as a racist killer here in New Orleans?"

"It's a sting," the mafioso hissed, his face a mask of repressed fury. "A goddamn FBI sting operation to catch us with our pants down!"

"So we back out of the deal," Giancomo stated. "Tell them there are no more torpedoes."

"Fuck that," Marasco growled, hunching forward, the pain in his leg gone from the rush of adrenaline. "Get the boys moving, call in every favor we have. I want a ring of steel around that restaurant and ain't nobody walking out alive."

"Kill everybody?" Giancomo said in shock. "The women and children, too?"

"Yes! And then burn the damn place down!"

The Mob adviser sighed. "Yes, sir. It will be done."

"No, forget that," the mafioso declared as his face took on a new feral expression. "These undercover cops want to meet the Russians so fucking bad, eh? Then fine. By the time the Feds realize it's a trap, we'll have them in chains.

"And get me the Brazilian," Marasco added, massaging his crippled knee.

Giancomo went pale. "The turkey doctor?"

"Payback's a bitch."

CHAPTER EIGHT

Casax, California

White-hot molten steel sprayed out from the boiling vat as the microwave furnace surged with energy, the relays crackling with the flow of electrical power.

As the molten metal flowed through the red-hot channel to reach the prewarmed molds secure in a bed of compacted sand, Sergeant Jozsef Vadas watched the fiery display through a thick glass wall for a few moments as the noisy automatic machinery gauged temperatures, opened sluice gates and guided the flow of the white-hot steel along aluminum ducts. Just amazing, only the softest metal could contain the strongest. There was such beauty in science, the creation of a weapon pure poetry.

At a control panel on the other side of the wall, a man threw a series of switches, then stepped away from the burning crucible and walked around the thermal barrier and pulled in the cooler air and removed thick asbestos gloves. A digital thermometer on the foot-thick sheet of tempered glass read 120 degrees on the protected side.

"How is production?" Vadas rumbled in his awful voice.

Using a sleeve to wipe the sweat from his furnace-burned face, the curly haired Czech technician smiled.

"Way ahead of schedule," Boris Bezdek replied, his T-shirt drenched with so much sweat the material was transparent enough to see the special-ops snake tattoo on his chest. "But we need more cesium and titanium."

"So soon? How much?"

"A ton."

"I'll have Sergei order two tons. I do not want to be caught short again and slow production."

Removing a canteen from a canvas belt about his waist, the technician opened the container and took a swallow, then liberally poured some over his head.

One of the other foundry workers had tried combating the terrible heat with a cold drink. The temperature inversion gave the man crippling stomach cramps that sent him to the hospital. The trick was to maintain the pain, accept the hellish heat as part of the job and cool down very gradually after going off shift.

"Where are we getting all of the titanium from anyway?" Bezdek asked, returning the warm container to his hip.

"Some bicycle shops, but mostly NASA," Vadas said, watching the liquid steel pour into the mold until the molds back-flowed and the trapped air bubbled out. "When one of their missile hulls is miscast, it costs too much to melt it down and redo, so they dump the hull and order another. Much cheaper that way."

Pulling an overhead lever attached to a complex array of gears and rods, Bezdek cut off the flow perfectly as the air bubbled out of the last mold. "So they make a lot of these?"

"Hundreds. There is a huge junkyard outside of Houston. We have scavengers who buy 'souvenirs' of anything made primarily of titanium and ship it here in boxcars. We pay about a penny on the dollar from the original cost."

"Then sell it for a hundred dollars on the penny." He flashed a grin. "Brilliant."

"Just good business sense," Vadas said, loosening his collar from the waves of heat. "Those final days of the Soviet army everything was in short supply. We had to be creative or else. We became creative."

"And there was nobody better than you, sir!" Bezdek said smartly with a crisp palm-out as if back on the parade ground, then cracked a smile and added, "Except me of course, old man."

Born less than a single day earlier than the private, Vadas accepted the term of affection with as much grace as he could. These were more than his partners, or fellow soldiers; they were his blood brothers. Brothers in blood and fire.

"Indeed. Then get back to work, child," Vadas rumbled, heading for the elevator.

The air grew noticeably cooler the farther he got from the foundry, and he savored the sensation. America was too hot. He couldn't wait until they hit their goal of fifty million dollars a man and they retired to Finland. Lots of snow and lovely pale women, what more could any man want from life?

Passing a computer-operated lathe machining a complex set of cams and lobes for the Shkval torpedoes, Vadas paused as a steam line in the floor vented a huge cloud of white steam to equalize the pressure from the trip-hammers. While he waited for the steam to dissipate, there sounded a muffled boom from the fusing room.

Some metals would only mix under incredibly high pressures and temperatures. Those were achieved with shaped explosive charges through a technique called fusing. That was the secret heart of the Shkvals, the special alloy mixture that formed its armored flat crown. The configuration of the crown made the cavitation occur, which gave the rockets their incredible speed. But only these alloys allowed the flat head to withhold the crushing pressure. Without this special metal, the deadly Shkvals were merely underwater bombs that would detonate at the first pulse of their rocket engines.

The sludge from the volatile mixing was highly toxic and had to be disposed of very carefully. Aside from being extremely toxic, it was also easily traced by chemical sensors. Without proper disposal, the Americans could track them down in a few hours and put the entire operation out of business. Vadas wasn't worried about his own safety or that of his men. The Czech knew that they could fight their way out of any police net. But it would take months to set up shop again someplace else, millions lost in equipment and more millions lost building a new foundry. That wasn't acceptable.

Pausing for a moment in the cool ninety-degree breeze of a ceiling vent, Vadas watched as a forklift rolled by with a small barrel of the sludge, the container marked with the international symbol for a biohazard.

"What is this?" he demanded. "We do not use any biological material in the torpedoes."

Setting the forklift into neutral, Davida Pran leaned forward on the steering wheel and flashed his perfect teeth.

"Something new. Toxic waste kills people, yes? But they do not fear it. On the other hand, biohazards scare most civilians to death. So we pretend a level-four contaminant is actually a level six. Now folks are too terrified to go near the drums to check the contents. Our level-four waste can be run through the city sewage plant, but level six has to be burned."

"Expensive?"

"Very, but excellent camouflage," Pran said, then gestured widely with both gloved hands. "The FBI is clever, but will they look for our chemical signature in the air?''

''It is not the FBI that I fear,'' Vadas replied, ''but the secret police. America says it does not have any, but we both know that to be a lie. Every nation has covert forces, designed to protect and defend at any cost, without regard for the law.''

''We were the shadows for the USSR,'' the man agreed, pulling out a Cuban cigar and biting off the tip before applying a flame. ''Until they fired us. Fired everybody. The greatest military in the history of the world, and they fall because they could not pay their bills.''

''Even soldiers must eat,'' Vadas rumbled in amusement.

Smiling, Pran blew a smoke ring and winked at his comrade before shifting gears and starting forward once more in the chaos of the moving machinery, explosions and bursts of steam. Suddenly there was a gentle vibration on his hip, and Vadas pulled out his cell phone, pushing the volume to maximum.

''Jozsef here,'' he said, knowing the NSA spy satellites wouldn't monitor the short call amid this much ferric metal.

''Sarge, we have a situation,'' Solomon said.

Walking through the factory, Vadas waited for the man to continue. If there had been real trouble, the private would have used the code term ''Admiral.'' But the giant was a worrier, concerned about details.

Which was why he handled most of the deals with the distributors of their weapons. Most.

"The Colombians want a hundred to use against the U.S. Coast Guard so they can make deliveries of cocaine to mainland Texas."

"Can we handle that many?"

"Boris says yes, but just barely."

"Good. Then the problem is what?"

"The PLO wants ten to strike the tourist hotels along the Dead Sea," Solomon paused expectantly.

"Never," Vadas stated, stopping before the elevator. "A distant cousin of mine is married to a Jewish man who works at one of the hotels there. I will never hurt my own bloodline. Offer the PLO a fair price, then have our mercenaries kill them when they arrive."

"Also, interested parties in Australia have offered one million dollars apiece for three Shkvals. I refused."

"You did right," the big sergeant said, pressing the button again to try to make the elevator come faster. He knew the machine didn't work that way, but it was just something that had to be done. "The Aussies would only take them apart and make more for themselves. No major powers get a shipment. That's firm."

Closing the cell phone, Vadas rode the elevator to the third floor of the noisy factory and walked through a set of double doors. The first doors cut the sounds from the machinery by half, while the next finished the job. Now he stood in the quiet cool of a sterile white room filled with computer consoles and scrolling monitors.

Working a laser mouse over a graphic of a lathe, former Colonel Sergei Zofchak sat slouched at a computer console, the raised floor around his boots foggy from the nitrogen cooling system of the massive Cray supercomputers in the refrigerated vault next room.

Vadas said nothing as he noticed that one of the monitors showed a bondage film of extreme violence. Although very handsome, women avoided Zofchak because of his cruel eyes. They were wise. What the Soviet soldiers had done to his mother, the teenager had done in return to hundreds of Russian women in revenge. As an adult Zofchak discovered he had developed a taste for rape and nothing else. Often there was only a corpse afterward. That was a major problem in Europe, but here in America money solved everything.

"How goes the search?" Vadas asked.

"Poorly," the officer said, slumping into a chair. He took a sandwich from a nearby plate, sniffed it and took a bite. Chewing for a moment, he swallowed, then started wolfing it down. "Whoever it was trying to track our messages on the Internet is good, best I have ever seen."

"Interpol good?"

"Better," Zofchak admitted wearily, lowering the sandwich. "And that scares me. It might have been the Orchestra for all I know."

"There is no more KGB," Vadas said, crossing his wide arms and turning his back slightly to the pornographic video. "But you must stay ready, my friend. The American government will try for us again. When they do, find them and our mercenaries will do the rest."

"And if they should fail?"

Vadas shrugged his mammoth shoulders. "Then we shall handle the matter ourselves."

"Good. I enjoyed Reno," Zofchak said, leaning over the keyboard. "Pity there weren't any women in the gang."

A light flashed on the main communications console, and the computer expert flipped a switch to scramble the line signal and give a false location bounced off two satellites. Anybody attempting to trace the call would think they were in Latvia.

"Identify," he said into the desk speaker.

There was a crackle of static. "This Danny Hell," a man said. "And we got trouble."

South Carolina

FIRING WEAPONS, armed guards charged from the shadows, and Phoenix Force gunned them down to reach the docks. The sleek cabin cruiser was already a hundred yards from shore and moving fast for the open sea.

Wetting a finger, McCarter tested the breeze. "About four knots, south by southwest," he stated.

Bracing for the recoil, Rafael Encizo and Calvin James both whipped out M-79 grenade launchers and fired. The fat 40 mm rounds arced high into the starry sky and came down directly before the cruiser in a double explosion on the water.

Still building speed, the craft knifed through the dense clouds of smoke and came out the other side undamaged.

"Thirty seconds," McCarter said, slashing away the mooring line of a small skiff tied to the dock.

Barely more than an aluminum canoe with an outboard motor, the little boat was a tight squeeze for the men, and they had to move carefully to avoid tipping over. Pulling the starter rope, McCarter got the outboard motor coughing into life and pulled away from the dock, the throttle wide-open on the small Yamaha motor.

The swells of the incoming tide were low and gentle, and the skiff soon was past the breakers and into the open sea before finding the cruiser. Running with its lights off, the much larger vessel was almost invisible in the dark Carolina night.

Passing through the last wisps of the BZ gas cloud, the Stony Man warriors blinked hard to clear their blurred vision. Another reason for their ski masks was the military filters sewn into the fabric. Useless against nerve gas, they worked perfectly against such heavy-molecule compounds as hallucinogens, vomit gas and a host of other inhalants.

As Phoenix Force motored closer, the big Detroit

engines of the cruiser cut off and the boat began to slow. Now they could see that the people on board where staggering about as if drunk. Several were simply sitting on the deck swaying to the motion of the ocean. Another blindly walked off the elevated control deck to fall to the main deck in a tangle of his own limbs, while a third bent over the starboard railing and began to noisily retch.

With nobody at the controls, the autopilot had cut off the fuel to the engines to prevent a crash, and now the powerless vessel was slowly starting to turn with the incoming tide washing it back toward Phoenix Force and the rocky breakers.

Then two men appeared wearing bulky gas masks, the old-fashioned kind with goggles over the eyes and spare air tanks. Pulling the arming bolts AK-47 assault rifles, the bodyguards cut loose with a fusillade of rounds that chewed the surface of the ocean as they tracked toward the little skiff.

With lightning speed, Encizo jerked aside as the red dot of a laser spotter touched his chest and a split second later a line of 7.62 mm rounds went across the boat at exactly that spot. A line of holes appeared in the hull and the skiff started taking on water immediately.

Keeping a hand on the tiller, McCarter slapped a sticky wad of C-4 plastique on the largest hole as a makeshift patch while Encizo and James fired back at the cruiser. The heavy 9 mm rounds chewed paths of destruction along the cabin of the cruiser, and the gunmen ducked for cover behind a pair of fishing chairs. Cushioning flew from the seats as the bullets hit.

As the sinking skiff got closer to the listing cruiser, McCarter did his best not to get in the way of the powerless luxury craft and get smashed aside, but time was against them. Maintaining steady cover fire, Encizo and James kept the two men with masks down, until a third man wearing a scuba tank stepped into view from around the main cabin and leveled a LAW rocket launcher at them.

Instantly, the three Stony Man warriors cut loose with their MP-5 subguns in unison, the hellstorm of copper-jacketed lead hitting the man a dozen times exactly as he pressed the launch button on top of the tube.

The rocket streaked past the skiff so close that Phoenix Force felt the hot wash of its fiery exhaust. A few seconds later it hit the sea and detonated in a thundering explosion of water and flame.

"Enough of that shit," James growled through his mask and started shooting up the top deck of the cruiser until the fallout from the blast rained upon the skiff, soaking the men to the skin.

Thumbing another round into his M-79, Encizo fired at the cruiser, the charge impacting on the foredeck and spreading its explosive cloud of gas across the vessel. Driven by the ocean wind, the fumes covered the craft in only seconds before dissipating.

"That wasn't BZ," McCarter stated, angling the

outboard motor to drive them closer to the port side of the ship. "The color was wrong."

"Just smoke," the man replied, moving his boots through the inches of water covering the bottom of the skiff. "But it'll sure rattle the crew after that last dose of BZ."

"Any more?" James asked, peppering the side of the cruiser with a short burst. A face in a porthole disappeared, only to be replaced with a revolver that fired wildly out the opening, hitting nothing but the sea and sky.

"Last one."

"Let's hope it was enough," McCarter said, killing the engine and letting the wallowing skiff creep forward on its momentum to reach the access ladder on the starboard side.

Grabbing on to the ladder, Encizo held the skiff in place while James raked the deck to pave the way and McCarter took the point onto the luxury vessel. As he reached the gunwale, there was a snap from the darkness and a sharp tug hit his arm. Diving aside, he sprayed the MP-5 at the deck trying to wound, not kill his attacker. Masked by the shadows, he had no idea who it was attacking him and they needed that red-haired woman alive!

The dark shape moved again, and the teak deck smacked from an incoming bullet. Grabbing the Gerber combat knife from his boot sheath, McCarter flipped the blade over and threw it handle first with all of his strength. There came a startled cry and a loud clatter as a Colt .380 pistol hit the deck. Rolling forward, the Stony Man warrior came up swinging his MP-5, and bone shattered as he connected with the ribs of a guard. The man staggered backward, both hands holding on to his chest. Firing a short burst into the sky, McCarter could see in the muzzle flash that his assailant was neither Lane nor Kodak. Sweeping the barrel of his SMG gun toward the panting man, he triggered another burst, the 9 mm rounds driving the dying guard over the side and into the Atlantic.

Touching his shoulder, McCarter saw blood on his palm, but only a little. Just a scratch, nothing more. Retrieving his blade, the former SAS officer whistled sharply and stayed alert as the others slipped on board. Below, the skiff started to float away, its bow already swamped from the waves as the craft filled with water and started to drop from sight.

The bodyguard bent over the gunwale loudly retched again as Encizo headed for the bow and James the stern. McCarter went up the short flight of stairs into the raised wheelhouse of the cabin cruiser. A few tense moments later, they met on the port side, assumed positions and kicked open the door to the cabin. Instantly, there came a flurry of gunshots from the dark room.

"He's got a gun!" a woman cried out from inside the cabin.

In spite of the situation, the Stony Man warriors exchanged amused looks.

"Thanks for the news flash, lady," Encizo said in wry amusement, his words muffled by the soaking wet ski mask.

"Windows," McCarter said under his breath, yanking out a spent clip and slapping in a fresh magazine.

The team swung the wirestocks of their weapons onto the portholes, smashing out the glass. Pistol shots replied as they tossed in chemical light sticks. Then the shooting stopped and there came the unmistakable sounds of reloading. The team charged into the cabin and spread out, taking defensive positions behind furniture. The room was an unearthly blue from the weird glow of the military chem sticks.

"Freeze!" James ordered from the left.

"Hold it!" Encizo commanded from the right, trying to confuse the armed man across the cabin.

"Drop the weapon!" McCarter barked, working the bolt of his MP-5. The action ejected a live round onto the floor. It was a useless tactic to try against military opponents, but the sound of a weapon arming often rattled civilians and made some of them surrender out of blind fear.

But not this time. Dropping his empty pistol, a fat bald man hauled a pretty young woman in front of him as a living shield, holding her by a fistful of red hair. She tried to struggle free, accidentally showing that she wasn't wearing anything under her loose bathrobe.

"Is this what you've come for?" the man shouted,

pulling out a 10 mm derringer and pointing the palm gun at the masked invaders. "Now, get off my ship, or she dies!"

"You won't harm her," Rafe said calmly, trying to control the hostage situation. "If she dies, you're out of business."

Lane sneered defiantly. "Yeah? But as cops you can't risk her life, can you? Leave, or I blow her fucking head off!"

In the eerie illumination of the chem sticks, McCarter frowned. The damn man was lucid. The guards on deck had gotten a full dose of the BZ gas fumes, but down here only enough had seeped past the door and air vents to make the people disoriented, but not stupefied. Plus, they were becoming more sober with every breath of clean air blowing in through the busted portholes.

"Please," the redheaded woman pleaded, trying to close the flapping robe. "Mr. Lane, don't kill me! I won't talk to the cops!"

"Shut up," he snarled, sweat appearing on his brow. "They're FBI, bitch! Gotta be."

"No, we're not," James stated, shifting his position.

Squinting hard as if trying to see the men dressed in black, Lane scowled, then an expression of raw fear crossed his pudgy features. As the arms dealer swung his gun hand in toward the woman, McCarter got off a single shot with his machine gun. The man's elbow exploded, the force jerking his hand away from the woman. The hardball round went through her left cheek and out her mouth to smash a mirror on the wall. Cursing loudly, Lane threw the woman forward and dived into an open hatchway. As the redhead fell out of the way, Phoenix Force opened fire, but Lane was already gone.

As James hurried to the redhead, McCarter and Encizo swept down the stairs into the ship. The hold was as luxurious as the top decks, burnished walnut paneling, thick carpeting and an open weapons cabinet alongside a heavy wooden desk. Lane was struggling with something in his hands, and the two men fired in unison, each taking an arm as a target.

Driven against the wall, Lane dropped what he had been holding and writhed in agony from the nonlethal hits.

"Godamn it…you're not…FBI," he panted, blood pumping from both shoulders. "Who…are you…?"

McCarter started to answer when he spied a deadman switch lying on the deck, the green light showing it was armed. Once activated, if the person holding the mechanism released the trigger, it would set off an explosive charge. Kill the person holding a deadman, and you died yourself. But had Lane gotten the chance to set the explosive charge?

As the British SAS officer stared at the wounded man, the arms dealer smiled in triumph.

"Too…late…cop," he whispered hoarsely.

Without a word Encizo turned for the stairs.

James was helping the redhead to her feet, a large

pressure bandage covering half of her face, as the two men charged out of the hold moving fast.

"Move!" McCarter commanded, dropping his MP-5, bodily grabbing the woman to carry her out the door.

Reaching the deck, he threw the redhead overboard and followed just a heartbeat later, with Encizo and James tight on his heels. But it was too late. Even while the team was falling, the cruiser erupted, the fiery light seeming to illuminate the universe.

Thrown dozens of yards away from the blast by the concussion, the three limp men splashed hard into the water and slowly began to sink out of sight.

CHAPTER NINE

Stony Man Farm, Virginia

"...ood evening. This is the news at the top of the hour from National Public Radio," the radio announced. "Only a few hours ago in Sri Lanka, the extreme fundamentalist group the True Path attacked the main naval dockyard of Colombo, the capital city of Sri Lanka, sinking several warships and costing countless lives. The national navy quickly responded with their flagship, but the terrorists escaped unharmed."

A sheet of paper was audibly turned. "Buddhists, Hindus and Catholics across the globe have condemned the cowardly attack on the peaceful nation, and the United Nations has already started airlifting in medical supplies for the hundreds of wounded, while NATO has dispatched a multinational defense force of primarily American, British and Russian ships to protect the city until Sri Lanka's own navy can be adequately rebuilt and to assist in a sea hunt for the terrorists. The government of India denies any involvement in the attack, and has offered what assistance it can to its neighboring nation—''

Barbara Price turned off the radio on her desk, leaned back in her chair and scowled at a map on the wall, a red pin marking every known incident of a Shkval strike. There were so many red pins it was starting to look as if the world were bleeding to death.

''How can they make so many of the things so fast?'' she wondered aloud, lost in thought for a moment.

''Things are getting out of hand fast,'' Brognola said from the sofa in her office.

''Look,'' John ''Cowboy'' Kissinger said from the doorway as he entered the office, ''I found something important.''

Using both hands, the man was holding a plastic box full of computer printouts and top secret documents, and he placed the heavy box on the desk with a thump.

''What have you got for me?'' Price asked, moving her mouse and pad out of the way as she eyed the imposing stack of documents.

''The head of the Shkval appears to be the key,'' he explained, passing over the topmost sheet of the stack, and then giving a copy to Brognola. ''That is what makes the supercavitation effect possible, which is what allows them to move so fast underwater.''

''Some sort of a special alloy?'' Brognola asked, glancing up from the chemical equations on the sheet. ''I can't make head nor tails of this stuff.''

"Bet your ass it's special," Kissinger stated, running a hand across his unshaved jaw. "A titanium ceramic armor that can only be made with high-explosive fusion technology."

"That has a lot of poisonous byproducts," Price commented, placing the sheet aside. Then her face brightened in understanding. "Easily traceable byproducts!"

"Weapons are my line," he said in frank honesty, "and I'm good at my job."

"Damn good," she corrected, lifting the lid of a scanner built into her desk. The monitor of her computer flashed into a view of the document, and the woman hit a button on a small console. The graphic blinked and was instantly on the screen of Kurztman's monitor in the Computer Room.

Pulling out a cell phone, Brognola activated the scrambler circuit. "I'll have DEA start hunting the sewers around every major city. City cops, too."

"No need," Price corrected, rapidly typing in a short note to go with the document. "The EPA already has monitors in the water of all American cities. Aaron and his people can hack in, change the chemical dynamics and start tracking within an hour."

Kissinger pulled up a chair and turned it around so he could rest his arms across the back. "Unless the monitors have been disabled," he said. "Now that's a federal crime with some serious jail time attached, so the big companies would never take the risk.

Which means that the EPA has virtually no defenses on the sensors. They don't need any.''

"But these bastards can and would rig the sensors," Brognola said, leaning forward on the sofa. "But they can't reach them all. There's just too damn many, and if even one goes off, that is all the start we need.''

"It's worth a try," the armorer agreed, "but I'll bet a week's pay, the EPA sensors find nothing amiss.''

"So we also use the DEA," Price said, sending off the e-mail. "Their drug sniffers can also be adjusted to find explosives, so why not poisonous chemicals?''

"If necessary," Brognola said, "The President could declare martial law and we could seal off any city with Army special units and send in the troops to do a hard search for these assholes.''

"God, I hope it doesn't come to that," Price said. "Hal, if the EPA sensors have been rigged, and we have to do a house-by-house search through a major city, that could take weeks.''

"Months," he replied grimly. "But it's still a good angle, and we might get lucky.''

Then the man stood. "Now the two of you get out of here and go grab some chow and a nap. I want another brilliant idea by midnight, and you both look bushed.''

"Actually, that sounds pretty good," Price admitted, rising from the desk. A little spinning flag on the monitor showed that Kurtzman already had read the e-mail and was taking action. "The kitchen staff is gone for the night, but I can fry up some bacon-and-egg sandwiches."

"Sold me," Kissinger said, stepping free from the chair. "I'll make the coffee."

"Deal."

"Better make it strong," Brognola muttered, tapping in commands and codes to get past the White House communications security and reach the President in his private quarters. "It's going to be another long night, and we're nowhere near finding these bastards yet."

"Oh, we'll find them," the gunsmith stated confidently. He glanced at the wall map and added, "Whether we can do it soon enough is what worries me."

New Orleans, Louisiana

"OH CRAP," Gadgets Schwarz said, his spoon paused above the steaming bowl of soup. "They know who we are." Removing the Humbug from his pocket, he placed it on the table hidden from sight behind the dessert menu. Yanking the wire loose that ran to his flesh-colored earphone, the electronics expert thumbed up the volume and voices crackled from the EM scanner, distorted, but still discernible.

"I can see them now," the voice said from the speaker on the bulky transceiver. "They're ordering dessert."

"Well, they'll never finish it." Another voice cackled in amusement. "This is going to be sweet."

"Still say we should hit them outside," another man complained.

"Too many places for them to run. We walk in with guns blazing and blow 'em to hell."

"Except for the big guy, Lyons."

Lyons nearly reacted to the mention of his name, but maintained his composure. Not only was their cover blown, but they also knew him by name. Marasco had to have recalled his face.

"Yeah, the boss wants him alive. Got that?" the gruff voice demanded from the tiny speaker. "There's fifty long in bonus for the guy who brings him in still breathing for the Brazilian to play with."

"I'm calling that!"

"Shuddup. It's an open contract."

"Just be sure to leave your cell phone turned on inside your coat," the man in charge stated. "If there's trouble, we already got people in the back alley."

"I'm well covered," the first man said. "I got Jimmy T-Bone on the roof across the street with a sniper rifle. Ain't nobody coming out of that dive alive, but us and the cop."

"Damn, I thought…" the voice faded away.

Schwarz adjusted the gain on the device to remove a faint squeal of harmonics and another voice answered the first.

"What was that?"

"Why are we rushing this? Let them go home and fall asleep, then we whack 'em."

There was a laugh. "And since when have you ever known Danny Hell to be patient about anything? Just do the job and let's go get a beer."

Able Team nodded at the exchange. Dante Marasco, Danny Hell, the nickname was a natural for the Don.

"Okay, this it. We're going in. See you in five."

"Have fun."

The conversation became the relaying of instructions to the snipers and the men in the back alley. Schwarz lowered the volume, and the three men reclined in their chairs maintaining the illusion they were relaxing after the meal, while they considered every angle. The impromptu trap was good, since they were boxed in tight, but the Mob had done this sort of thing before many times.

Narrowing his eyes, Lyons glanced at the restaurant full of families and seniors. "Okay, we have no choice," he said, taking a deep breath. "We have to meet them outside in the open. Too many civilians in here."

"That was my read on the play," Blancanales said, ripping the Ingram away from the bottom of the table.

"Okay, any chance somebody's got a clever plan aside from charge out there shooting?" Schwarz asked, checking his Glock and snicking off the safety to rack the slide.

"Sure," Blancanales said, pulling out his cell

phone and punching the number for the Farm. Since their cover was blown, it made no difference.

"Price," the mission controller said, answering on the first ring.

"Our cover's blown," Blancanales said quickly, leaning back and smiling as if talking to a friend. "We're in New Orleans and the Mafia is coming in hard and fast. Dante Marasco knows the Russian. We're trapped in a restaurant, civilians everywhere. We going to try to lead the Mob away. This may be our last transmission."

"Understood. Good luck," Price said.

Keeping an eye on the mirror behind the small bar, Lyons saw a civilian Hummer park across the street and men holding shotguns and assault rifles openly step into the street. The hit squad had arrived.

"Anybody want dessert?" the waiter asked, then noticed the profusion of weapons and turned pale.

"Calm down, we're not here to rob the place," Lyons said.

As the waiter stared at the guns, the Able Team leader said, "If you know what a gang war is, then go call the cops, ambulance and the fire department, and I mean right now."

His eyes bulging, the waiter nodded vigorously and walked straight across the restaurant into an office marked Manager.

"Head for the jewelry store on the corner," Lyons ordered above the rising voices of the frightened customers. People had spotted their drawn weapons and were moving away quickly. Good. "Smash open the window and the alarm will bring more cops. With luck we can hide behind the counter and try for the rear door."

"Right," Schwarz said, drawing the word out into a long expression. "We're dead and you damn well know it, Carl."

"Not yet," he said, pulling out a spare magazine from his ammo pouch and placing it into a jacket pocket.

Standing with the Ingram in his left hand hidden alongside his leg, Blancanales straightened his jacket. "Let's do this," he growled.

"Be nice if we had some armor," Schwarz said moving around the table, a Glock in each hand.

At those words, Lyons stopped walking. "Damn it, we do," he cursed, tucking away his piece and grabbing hold of the dining table. The thick cords of hard muscles stood out in sharp relief on the man's hands and neck, his sore ribs feeling as if they were breaking from the strain, but as the Mob hit men reached the sidewalk, the anchoring bolts ripped free from the floor tiles in a crash of splintering wood.

"Holy crap, they know!" the voice cried out from the Humbug on the table. "Hit 'em now!"

"Say what?" a voice demanded, puzzled.

Grabbing on to the center leg, Lyons charged through the crowd of people with the heavy oak table held before him like a medieval war shield. His teammates were close behind him, their weapons drawn and ready.

The customers started to scream, and the Mafia gunners on the sidewalk stared in shock at the sight for a full second. That was when Able Team began to fire at the glass center of the front door. In a hail of bullets, the decorated glass door exploded a rainbow of razor-sharp shards over the hit men, making them flinch protectively, then the Ingram ripped a burst through the open air and they fell away, gushing blood. But even as they died, a few of the men fired back, and Lyons saw clusters of splinters sprout from the underside of the table, impact damage from direct hits on the other side.

Since the piece of furniture was too big for the doorway, the Able Team leader went straight out the picture window in a deafening crash. A man holding a shotgun was sliced apart from the arrival of the glass and dropped his weapon to stagger away, his hands covering the nightmare ruin of his face, blood pouring between his trembling fingers.

Climbing over the windowsill, Able Team reached the sidewalk and started shooting around the tabletop in every direction as more men brought up Jackhammer shotguns. Definitely not tourists. Blowing flame, the automatic shotguns roared louder than thunder, spraying a hellstorm of lead pellets that killed half a dozen people inside the restaurant and blew off chunks of the tabletop.

Tossing the broken piece of wood away, Lyons

grabbed the fallen shotgun from the first man and fired four fast times at the oncoming hit men. Two went down, their legs chewed by the pellets, but the others sprinted for cover. He got another in the back, then the shotgun clicked empty.

With Schwarz giving cover with the two booming Glocks, Blancanales sprayed a burst from the Ingram subgun toward at the roof of the office building across the street, hoping that the target was within effective range. A man cried out a few seconds later, and a body slammed into the street.

"So much for snipers," Schwarz said, reloading one of his pistols.

Tossing away the shotgun, Lyons drew his Glock and fired twice from the hip. A Mafia soldier with an M-16 spun away, losing the rifle, and the front window of the jewelry store on the corner shattered from the impact of a .44 Magnum round. Instantly, an alarm bell began to clang.

Then a car lurched into action and raced toward the Stony Man warriors, crouching before the restaurant. Able Team dived out of the way as the vehicle crashed into the front of the establishment. Both headlights shattered from the impact, fenders crumpling as the remains of the door flew across the nearly deserted restaurant, and the colorful sign of a dragon fell off the side of the building and crashed onto the sedan, denting the roof. Spouting curses, the driver threw the car into reverse, but the vehicle was firmly stuck between the granite columns that served as the jamb for the decorative doorway.

Displaying a wide assortment of weapons, the men in the trapped sedan tried to open their doors only to find the dented roof was holding them closed. Seizing the opportunity, Able Team converged on the hitmen and ruthlessly shot the killers to death through the shattered windows.

Stuffing the Glock into his belt, Lyons snatched an M-16 from a twitching corpse while his teammates did the same. Blancanales hated to lose the Ingram's punch, but he was down to two rounds with no reloads. It had only been an emergency weapon.

Now using the line of parked cars along the granite curbstones as cover, the trio moved down the street in a standard three-man rotation, giving one another cover as they eliminated everybody in sight holding a weapon. Halfway down the block, Schwarz started to ice a man brandishing a revolver, until he saw the fellow was barefoot and wearing a towel around his neck as a napkin. At the very last instant, he jerked the weapon aside and hit the gun instead. The weapon went flying, and the man retreated holding his broken hand.

''Not your fight,'' Schwarz barked, motioning with the assault rifle. ''Leave!''

Nodding vigorously, the fellow turned tail and sprinted down the alleyway, moving a lot faster than was normal for a man of his imposing bulk.

Firing at armed figures on the rooftop, Schwarz

scowled. Great, just what they needed. Local heroes trying to save the nice Italian gentlemen, regular customers, who were being shot at by strangers. What a strange world this was.

Unfortunately, the fat jerk had started his sore shoulder painfully throbbing, and Schwarz realized that he could no longer effectively control the assault rifle. Next time, he might put a round through a civilian's heart, instead of his hand. Dropping the half-loaded clip, the electronics expert tossed the M-16 into the gutter and pulled out the Glock with his strong right hand to rejoin the battle.

More mobsters arrived in a gray BMW sedan, and Blancanales paused for a dangerous second in plain sight to squeeze off a single round and take out the front tire. As it blew, the driver stupidly slammed on the brakes. Out of control, the vehicle veered into the side of a bank at full speed. Windows shattered, and bodies went flying as the armed passengers were thrown from their seats, their weapons discharging, blowing holes through the side doors, the roof and one another. A spreading pool of gasoline began to form underneath the crumpled vehicle. Then a spark from the electrical system ignited the fuel and the wreck woofed into flames.

"Should have worn seat belts," Blancanales advised them, leaving the dying mobsters where they lay.

Bobbing and weaving, Lyons moved past a taxicab. The side window exploded inward and he spun, letting off a long burst for the sky. Another sniper cried out, and a moment later a bloody rifle hit the pavement. Good enough.

Constantly on the move, Blancanales rolled out from behind a mailbox and emptied the M-16 into the backs of two more Mafia gunmen as they hastily reloaded. The 5.56 mm tumblers chewed them apart. Out of ammo, he dropped the spent weapon and took an AK-47 from a man. But before he could check the ammo clip, one of the other men sprawled on the dirty street raised a bloody hand, which held a 10 mm Falcon pistol.

The Able Team commando triggered the assault rifle, and the mobster was stitched with 7.62 mm rounds. The hardman's big pistol boomed as he died, but the round went wild, impacting the side of a parked laundry truck.

Flicking the selector switch to full-auto, Blancanales crouched low as he ran in a zigzag pattern from car to car, constantly firing. Reaching open space, he found two more men loading shotguns. He shot the same instant they did, and he felt a tug on his jacket from a near miss, but the man on the left fell and the other dropped his gun to run away. Saving his limited ammo, the Stony Man warrior let the man escape and moved onward.

A dozen heartbeats later, Able Team joined forces at the corner and swept the area with their weapons, searching for new targets. But there were only dead men and burning cars in sight. Broken glass and spent brass littered the street. People were shouting everywhere, alarms were clanging, car alarms honking and softly in the background could be heard the growing wail of police sirens.

"Let's go," Lyons said.

Moving fast, Able Team slipped into the shadows, climbed a few fences and was gone long before the first police car arrived. All this work, and a chance meeting with an old enemy had ruined the entire operation.

CHAPTER TEN

Stony Man Farm, Virginia

Deep underground, four people sat almost motionless in a hushed room filled with banks of control consoles covered with elaborate keyboards, flickering monitors, winking lights and pulsating gauges. A huge SOTA high-density monitor spanned the main wall.

A fifth man was pacing back and forth in a corner, impatiently watching as the team silently worked the telecommunications systems of the world as they rode the Internet.

This was the electronic arm of the Farm, in the recently built Annex buried underground, away from the main farmhouse. These four people were the invisible soldiers of Stony Man, the vaunted cyber warriors of the covert organization, a cadre of unstoppable computer hackers, part data thieves and part cybernetic assassins, who patrolled the info Net of the world.

Resembling a grizzly bear in a badly rumpled suit, Aaron ''the Bear'' Kurtzman was the head of the cybernetic team for Stony Man. A master in all computer application, Aaron had quit his lucrative job on the Rand Corporation's world-famous think tank to use his skills where they were most needed, bringing a measure of justice to the world, not just making more millions for fat cats already rolling in cash.

"Hunt, any progress on the toxin analysis?" Kurtzman demanded, pushing away from his console and guiding his wheelchair across the room.

"Still processing," Huntington Wethers replied.

Tall and lean with light touches of gray at his temples, the distinguished man had formerly been a full professor at the University of California Berkeley, teaching, among other things, advanced and theoretical cybernetics until the call came to help fight the computer criminals of the world.

"Boston and New York read clear from any fusing byproducts," Wethers added. "I have a hunter program in progress doing the actual checking, but this will take some time."

Pausing his wheelchair to check the data scrolling on the monitors, Kurtzman grunted at the news. "Well, keep at it and let me know when we have some results, negative or positive."

"Certainly."

Now the man in the corner stopped his pacing. "Any other ways to dispose of the stuff aside from pouring it down the drain?" Yakov Katzenelenbogen asked. "Could they burn it?"

"Burn it?" Kurtzman repeated slowly, turning in

his chair. "Yes, they certainly could do that. "But that would require a medical biohazard facility to get temperatures hot enough. Much simpler to just store it in drums, and there's not jack we could do about that. Even though the drums would have to be surgical-class steel, there are millions of those sold each year. Impossible to trace."

"There are 14,750,000," Wethers stated.

"Thanks, teach," Kurtzman grunted.

On the monitor, Philadelphia registered as clean.

"Damn. Then for the moment we concentrate on what can be traced," Katz stated.

"What about a floating crap game?" Carmen Delahunt asked, removing her VR helmet and swiveling to face the men.

"A moving factory," Kurtzman rumbled. "Possible. But the noise of the fusing would attract a lot of attention."

"So they need isolation," Katz said, sipping the coffee. Then he did a double take. "Hey, this is excellent! You finally learn how to make joe, Aaron?"

"Carmen made the coffee," Kurtzman growled irritably. "If you can call it that." The big man looked in disdain at the mug resting in a cup holder attached to his chair. That wasn't coffee; it was just brown water.

On the monitor, Miami ticked off as clean, then Atlanta.

"Took an hour to scrub the pot clean," Delahunt replied. "Isolation, eh? Or maybe just someplace very noisy where the sound of the explosions wouldn't go noticed.''

"Gun range?" Akira Tokaido asked. "Sports arena?"

"Artillery range is more like it," Kurtzman retorted, thoughtfully rubbing a hand on the studded rubber tire of his chair. "We're talking major explosions here, twenty, thirty pounds of C-4 used each time."

Unwrapping a fresh stick of chewing gum and popping it into his mouth, Tokaido nodded as he digested the new data. The handsome Japanese American was the youngest member of the cyberteam. He was a natural born hacker and could instinctively do things with computers that others took years to learn.

"Maybe a rolling mill," Delahunt suggested with a shrug. "Fifteen-ton trip-hammers make more noise pounding steel ingots than you can possibly imagine."

"Maybe," Kurtzman growled, running stiff fingers through his hair. Too many places to check—car crushers at auto salvage yards, stone quarries where explosives were used...the list was endless.

Watching as Columbus, Ohio, registered clean, Wethers removed his pipe and gestured. "Have we considered a mirror?" he suggested.

"Interesting," Kurtzman mused aloud, returning to his console and starting a Boolean search. "Hide the illegal foundry underneath a legal fusing foundry.

Mix the sludge together and who could tell there were two factories?''

"I'll pull up a list," Delahunt said, swinging back to her console. "There can only be so many places that use this level of technology. Certainly no more than a dozen."

But even as she started donning her VR helmet, meters swung into the red zone and warning lights softly flashed on every console.

"Red alert, incoming probes," Wethers said crisply, and the lights in the room momentarily dimmed as the bank of computers on the next level pulled extra juice from the power grid of the Farm.

Katz started to ask a question, then snapped his mouth shut and stayed quiet. He knew better than to bother his team with questions during a cyber attack.

"Somebody backtracked on our downloads from the EPA sensors and has a hot probe running a live trace," Kurtzman stated, flipping switches and palming controls with the speed and grace of a concert pianist. "They're trying to find our location! Give me another landline relay, and get that second firewall erect."

Katz understood the computer babble. They were planning on using a fake ID to lure the invader into a trap and then backtrack on the signal to find their location. Good move.

Moving at blurring speeds, binary commands scrolled by on side monitors. The four threw themselves into the fight, unleashing macros files and switching connections with amazing speed.

"Look at these patterns. They must have another Cray. Maybe two!"

"First firewall has been breached," Tokaido announced, hands flying across the console. "Going to secondary."

"Releasing the ICE files. No good!"

"Jeez, they bypassed the fake phone lines—they're coming right down our throat!"

Katz hunched forward as if braced for a blow. Damn, the enemy didn't fall for the trap. If the firewalls fell and the enemy got their location, an attack force could arrive on their doorstep. Going to the intercom, he relayed the news to Price and Buck Greene. At least the Farm wouldn't be caught by surprise.

"Activating safeguards," Wethers said.

Instantly, automatic scramblers kicked into action, disks were spit from computers so the data on them could not be accessed and several slave computers physically disengaged from the main console, also terminating any possible cybernetic raid. The mighty Crays were no longer attached to the rest of the Farm.

Rubbing his prosthesis, Katz couldn't believe what he was hearing. Who the hell was attacking them? Then he recalled the mysterious enemy behind the hunter-killers. Maybe this was their next strike on America. But so soon?

"I have their identity," Delahunt said. "They're

based in North America. Give me another few seconds...."

"No good! They're still coming!"

"It's not a data raid—they want our location!"

"Blow the cables," Wethers suggested. It was the final resort. With a touch of a switch, a set of explosive charges would blow away a sizable chunk of their cables, physically rendering the Farm inert. They would also be taken off-line for hours, maybe days, until the physical damage could be repaired.

"Don't cut the lines just yet," Kurtzman directed brusquely, throwing compact viruses and tapeworm files at the enemy. Any damage done to the enemy Cray was a point in their favor.

"They're in the United States," Delahunt announced, apparently motionless but doing a hundred things at once in the artificial reality of the Net. A trillion communication lines filled her mind, and the woman raced through the maze following a ghost signal that endlessly changed shape and style. "Just another minute..."

"Akira, use the bomb!"

"That's not going to stop a Cray," the young man retorted, both hands flashing across his keyboard.

"I've made some improvements. Nuke 'em!" Kurtzman ordered.

Obeying orders, Tokaido flipped the arming lever and pressed the button. Instantly, a full broadband pulse of hash washed out from the Farm along the communication lines of the world. Cookies winked out of existence, LANs crashed, ISPs dropped, telephone service crackled with static, cable TV went off the air, buffers cleared and the Internet stopped cold for a full three seconds.

Gradually growing in strength and volume, the Net returned but the electronic presence of their unseen enemy was gone.

"It's over," Delahunt said, removing her helmet as the monitors cleared, the lights ceased flashing, the ceiling lights returned to their usual level of brightness.

"We beat 'em?" Katz asked in concern.

"We survived," Kurtzman corrected, taking the cup of coffee from his chair and draining half of it. "Damn, they were good. These people were waiting for us to arrive, and hit harder and got closer than anybody should have except another major nation. No arms dealer should have this kind of cybernetics, unless they were expecting us to go after them."

"Look at the world map. They found the satellite we're using," Katz stated as the vector graphic of the orbiting satellite high above the base flashed into the wall monitor. "Ten more seconds they would have found us. What the hell were they armed with?"

"Definitely Crays," Tokaido said, massaging his temples. "I recognized the signature. Maybe even Supercomputers, Mark II."

"But we have Cray Fours, so they can't hack us."

"Not unless we monumentally screw up. They can only find us, but that's bad enough."

"We have been given lemons, perhaps we can make some lemonade," Wethers stated, chewing vigorously on his pipe stem. "We can't try to track the EPA sensors again without risking our own exposure. But there is another way."

"The cooling plant," Kurtzman said, a slow smile breaking across his face. "Brilliant. Crays operate with superconductors and have to be kept at arctic temperatures. That means SOTA temperature control systems and a steady supply of liquid nitrogen for the cooling system."

Delahunt shook her head. "That's used in every laboratory and hospital in the world. No way to trace those sales."

"Get the list anyway," Kurtzman directed. "If we find a fusing foundry that gets regular deliveries of LOX, then we may have our arms dealers."

Damn, that was smart. She hadn't thought of the combination. Had the enemy? Hopefully not.

"Lox?" Akira repeated puzzled. "As in the fish?"

"Liquid oxygen, NASA slang," Katz answered.

"Unfortunately, they now know we're out there," Kurtzman said. "Spread the word to Carl and David that we no longer have the element of surprise. The enemy knows we're coming."

"Hell, it's almost as if they were expecting it," Katz added softly, frowning deeply. A grim thought.

Lane Importers, South Carolina

REACHING THE GATE in the fence, T. J. Hawkins fired from the hip and blew off the padlock. As the inner door swung open, waiting guard dogs charged and Hawkins unwillingly gunned down the animals. Moving past their still bodies, he shot off the lock of the outer gate and started running toward the biker bar.

The only access routes to the Lane warehouse were from the sea or air. Having no roads made it that much harder for the police to visit the establishment. However, Hawkins was now trapped with only one way to get off the beach—the winding access road near the Fat Man Bar and Grill.

As Hawkins neared the tavern, the neon lights showing the outline of a naked woman brightened the night. The steady booms of the music filled the air and shook the ground so hard the man thought he was running into an artillery barrage. Parked in oddly neat lines in front of the tavern were rows of motorcycles. A few people stood about on the wooden porch, passing around a bottle of whiskey and smoking loosely rolled joints. Sounds of a fistfight drifted in from the sand dunes, and from the shadows alongside the bar somebody was relieving himself.

"My kind of place," Hawkins muttered, holstering the pistol and checking the ammo clip in the MP-5 subgun.

As he walked toward the crowd on the porch, the bikers reacted in amused shock, checking over the soldier dressed in black military fatigues, ski mask and covered with all sorts of weapons and guns. They started to jeer, then caught his expression. This guy looked as grim as death.

"Who the fuck are you, asshole?" a fat man on the porch snapped, pointing a tattooed finger. Most of the man appeared to be tattooed, and the rest was pierced with steel rings.

In response, Hawkins fired a short burst from the MP-5, the 9 mm rounds drilling into the floor directly in front of the bikers.

"I'm taking that Harley," Hawkins said, indicating the chosen bike with the muzzle of his weapon. "Toss me the keys."

"My bike?" a drunken man snarled, pulling out a snub-nosed revolver. "Fuck you."

Ready for that, Hawkins flipped his hand and a BZ grenade landed on the wooden porch and rolled among the group. It took the drunk people a few seconds to realize what it was, and then to understand it wasn't primed to blow.

"Next one is live," Hawkins said, dramatically pulling the arming pin and also tossing it onto the porch. The pin landed with a musical ting barely audible over the music from inside the bar. "Keys, now!"

The Stony Man warrior knew it would have been safer to simply knock them out with the BZ gas, but then he would have been forced to search for the keys. Time lost he couldn't afford. The escaping truck was getting farther away with every passing second.

"Hey, like sure," a greasy biker said with a grin,

displaying missing teeth, as he rummaged about in his pants. "Like, no problem."

The keys were tossed short, but Hawkins stepped closer and made the catch with one hand, the other filled with the MP-5.

"Like, thanks," he growled, walking backward among the parked bikes and climbing onto the big Harley.

Keeping a careful watch on the bikers, Hawkins kicked the big bike into life, its classic rumble filling the night in mechanized thunder. Suddenly, the music stopped and the door was thrown open wide, showing a mob of leather-clad men and women.

"He's stealing my bike!" the greaser shouted, gesturing with a beer bottle.

A biker wearing a Jesus Saves T-shirt pulled an S&W .38 Police Special. "Kill him!"

Instantly, Hawkins sprayed the doorway with the MP-5 again, taking out the man with the handgun. As the other bikers scattered for cover, the Stony Man warrior aimed a concentrated burst on the cleanest bike in the line. Sure enough, the new Harley-Davidson was carrying a full fuel tank and erupted into flames, covering a dozen other bikes with burning gasoline.

"Our hogs!" a woman wailed, then pulled a brace of German .45 Lugers from under her stained leather vest.

With no choice, Hawkins pumped a single 9 mm round into her leg, then hit the gas and roared away, tossing the primed grenade onto the porch. It rattled to a stop against the side of the tavern and detonated, blowing out the wooden support posts. The roof collapsed, the debris sealing the front door closed.

Gunning the Harley through the soft sand, Hawkins reached the base of the road and twisted the throttle hard once there was pavement under the wheels. As he raced along the curved road, pistol shots sounded from the beach, and he immediately began to zigzag to avoid the gunfire.

Reaching the top of the cliff, Hawkins cut the engine for a moment and listened for the sounds of the truck, but he could only hear more shots being fired from the beach. Pistols at that range? The bikers were determined bastards; he had to give them that much.

But then he caught the sound of running boots from the north. Swinging up the MP-5, Hawkins had the weapon aimed and ready when Gary Manning appeared from the darkness moving at a full run, the huge Barrett cradled in his arms. For a brief instant, Hawkins had a flashback to basic training and all of those early-morning ten-mile runs with full backpacks.

"They went south," Manning said, neither winded nor sweaty from the five-mile dash. "Never came my way."

"Get on," Hawkins said, walking the big bike around to face in the new direction.

Manning climbed on the small saddle behind the man, the dillybar pressing hard against his back in the tight confines, the Barrett crushed sideways across his lap.

Hawkins slung the MP-5 over the handlebars and brought the big motorcycle to life. The big engine rumbled as they swung into the middle of the coastal highway and started building speed.

"Ain't nothing like a Harley," Hawkins commented, grinning behind his ski mask.

"We agree there," Manning said, grinning back, holding on to his black cloth cap. "A BMW is nice and quiet, but what we have tonight is the need for speed."

"Good thing there was a biker bar nearby. Or you'd still be running."

"Hey, all part of my plan."

"You had a plan? Should have told me about it."

The men shifted their weight to lean into the turn as the Harley took a curve in the road.

"Sorry," Manning said, holding on tight. "You're not cleared for that kind of information. But then, neither am I. Can't tell you what I don't know."

"Well, that certainly clears things up," Hawkins said with a grin, forcing the bike to greater speed.

The men rode in silence, watching for any exit roads masked in the night. Since Hawkins was busy driving, Manning pulled on his infrared goggles and watched for any thermal residue alongside the highway that could be the hot engine of a van hidden in the bushes.

After a few minutes, there was a faint explosion

from out at sea, but the dense Carolina forest blocked any possible view.

"Don't like the sound of that," Manning muttered grimly.

"Birdman to Big Mac," Hawkins said over his com link. "Reply, please." But there was only silence. "Birdman to Big Mac or any Stone men, reply, please!"

A faint burst of static from the nearby city of Charleston crackled on the assigned wavelength for the team, but nothing more.

"Shit. Hope they're okay," Manning muttered. "I'll leave my radio open on all channels."

Since there was nothing he could do for the others right now, Hawkins concentrated on the road and the bike. There was a slight drop in the oil pressure that could be trouble if it got any worse. Taking the risk, he pushed the throttle to the maximum, and hoped the legendary motorcycles really were as good as the advertising slogans said.

Following the dark curving road, the Harley climbed on top of the miles, the long minutes becoming an hour. Soon other vehicles appeared on the highway and the men started passing cars, the expressions of the passengers registering shock at the heavily armed, masked bikers. Manning flashed a horrified reverend the old hippie peace sign, and the man displayed a nervous grin in reply, then hit the brakes and quickly dropped behind them.

"Breaker one-nine," a voice said on the CB channel of their com link. "Looking for the local PD or react base. Come on."

Manning hit a radio jammer on his web harness, and the transmission disappeared under a strident squeal of tortured harmonics.

"Hated to do that," Manning said. "If Mac and the others get in trouble, they can't call us for help."

"Yeah, that bought us time, but not much," Hawkins said. "But the reverend will find a phone and call for the cops again to report us."

"So drive faster," Manning suggested.

After a few miles, a truck came into view, driving at precisely the speed limit. There were no markings on the side, no company logo, the light set above the license plate conveniently dark.

Maintaining some distance, Hawkins raised two fingers and Manning switched to com link channel two.

"How do know this is them?" Hawkins asked over his throat mike.

"Only one way to find out." Manning pulled out his side arm and fired a single booming round from the .357 Desert Eagle into the air.

From the side windows of the front cab, men appeared holding MAC-10 machine pistols with illegal sound suppressors. Without pause, they both opened fire, bullets hitting the roadway around the Harley. Revving the engine to the red line, Hawkins popped a wheelie and rode the bike on its rear tire to put some metal between them and the gunners, then charged forward until the bike was only a few feet from the rear door of the truck, where the guns could no longer track.

"Good enough for me," he said as the Harley slammed back on the pavement. Then he drew his Beretta 93-R from a belt holster. "I'll take the left."

"On the count of three," Manning said, leveling his Desert Eagle as the rear door of the truck was raised, exposing a dozen armed men.

In unison, the Stony Man warriors fired their weapons and the rear tires of the truck exploded under the combat rounds. As the truck chassis dropped a fast eight inches onto the rushing asphalt, the men inside went tumbling.

Standing too close to the edge of the door, a man flew out of the vehicle, sailing past the Harley and hitting the pavement to bonelessly tumble end over end for a hundred feet, leaving a gory streak of red in his wake.

Veering wildly, the driver of the truck fought to control the shuddering vehicle as the tattered remains of the destroyed tires were chewed off the bare rims. With sparks flying from the dragging muffler, the out-of-control truck fishtailed onto the gravel berm on the side of the road. Now the rims sliced deep into the soft ground, the muffler snapped off and the vehicle abruptly braked to a rocking halt.

Smoothly coming to a full stop, Hawkins and Manning got off the bike, then flipped it over and ducked behind for cover. Fifty feet away, they could see that the rear of the truck was filled with unmarked boxes and wooden crates, with a NASA jet pack hanging from the wall. This was their target, all right, but without knowing what was in those crates, the men hesitated to shoot. A single round in the wrong place could detonate enough explosives to destroy this whole section of the coastline. And they wanted Lane and Kodak alive. There was no sign of a woman, but she could be in the front seat, or packed in a box.

Gravel flew from the berm as the men in the truck began wildly firing their automatic weapons, tracer rounds stuttering through the night and hitting a lot of nothing. Carefully placing their shots, Hawkins and Manning took out four before the rest got organized and took refuge behind the crates.

"This is the FBI!" Manning shouted, raising his wallet into sight. "Cease firing and come out with your hands raised!"

"FBI my ass!" one of the men snarled, and chattered a long burst at them from his assault rifle,

"Told you that never works," Hawkins muttered, returning fire with his MP-5, the single shots placed with care not to strike the crates.

Then the front doors swung open and two more men stepped into view, each wearing a bulletproof vest and firing a MAC-10 machine pistol, the silenced rounds sounding like stick being dragged along a picket fence.

Choosing his target, Manning swung the crosshairs of the Barrett Fifty onto one man and stroked the trigger. A yard-long stiletto of flame blew from the muzzle and the man's bulletproof vest seemed to explode as he was violently slammed into the truck door snapping off the hinges. Shooting the MAC-10 in a spiral pattern, the other man tried to run, and Hawkins brought him down with a sweep across the legs.

Now the men in the rear of the truck concentrated their gunfire on Manning, so Hawkins gave cover fire as his teammate rolled into the bushes for better cover. A heartbeat later, he reappeared alongside the truck where the defenders couldn't see and started working the bolt action on the monstrous Barrett and blasted a half-dozen rounds into the vehicle.

The big-bore .50-caliber AP rounds punched straight through the steel panel of the vehicle. In a matter of seconds, the interior of the truck had been turned into a slaughterhouse, splattered with bones and organs everywhere.

Dropping the MP-5, Hawkins rose into a kneeling position and attacked the disorganized survivors, placing the 9 mm hardball rounds from his Beretta as fast as possible.

"Clear," he said over the com link, and stood guard while Manning checked the rear of the trunk.

A brief recon showed that none of the dead men were fat and bald like Lane, and certainly none of them were female. Using his knife, Manning pried off the lid of the six crates large enough to hide a human, but they were filled with weapons. The one small crate was packed with negotiable bearer bonds, a fortune in untraceable currency.

"Empty," Manning said over the com link.

"Nobody in the front," Hawkins answered. "So let's go chat with our runaway."

By this time, the wounded man had reached the other side of the highway and was halfway into the bushes when the Stony Man warriors arrived. With a shaking hand he tried to raise a Colt .45, but Hawkins slapped it aside. The gunshot wounds in his legs were bad, but not life threatening, so Manning gathered a fistful of the bulletproof jacket and lifted the guy off the ground to slam him hard against a maple tree. He groaned from the impact and almost passed out from the pain, but Manning shook him awake. This was a mercenary, a hired killer for the arms dealer, and he was getting no more than he deserved.

"Talk or die," Manning growled. "Your choice, pal."

"Please, don't shoot!" the man pleaded. "I'll talk! Please! Whatever you want. I surrender!"

"Where's the woman?" Hawkins demanded from the side.

"Who? Ya mean Kodak? She's with the boss. She's always with the boss."

"Yeah?" Manning said, tightening his grip. "Then who was in the jet pack?"

"I used it," he explained frantically. "I just didn't wanna go to jail. Look, I'm small-fry, I don't know anything."

But he knew how to operate the jet pack? "Then you're useless to us," Hawkins stated, leveling his Beretta.

"Wait!" the man said, licking his lips, clearly about to lie. "Okay, I'm the assistant chief of security, and I know stuff. Plenty!"

"Then what you said before was a lie," Manning said, drawing his .357 Desert Eagle and pumping a round near the man's boot.

Hawkins slapped the man twice. "Then talk," he growled.

"There's a shipment due in Reading, Pennsylvania. We were supposed to meet them at the train station. Pay for it with the bonds. Got a truck hired to carry the missiles back here. Honest!"

It sounded like the truth. "What train?"

"The B&E line from Reno! A Mr. Casax."

Casax. A name at last. "First name," Manning demanded, as the headlights of a car passed by the fight zone. Cops would be here soon. "Description!"

"That's all I got! Casax from Reno. Meet the train at Reading Station!"

"More," Hawkins said, grinding the hot barrel of his weapon into the man's throat.

"Honest to God! That's all I got! I ain't the head guy. I just work security!"

The Stony Man warriors stood for a moment in the cool Carolina forest, listening to the ocean break on the nearby shore and the breeze in the trees. Somewhere an owl hooted and took to the sky.

"Fair enough," Manning said, lowering his rifle as Hawkins tossed the man a medical kit from his web harness. "We made a deal and you kept your end. Now patch the wounds and start walking. But if we ever run into you again, we'll burn you."

The two Stony Man warriors turned their backs on the man for a full second. Then they swung around again with their guns at the ready, catching him in the act of pulling out a snug Belgium Nine derringer from behind his back, the four-barrel palm gun shining in the silvery moonlight from the sky overhead.

"Bad move, punk," Hawkins said as Manning fired the Barrett.

The muzzle flame reached out to touch the man as he slammed backward against the tree, splinters and blood exploding out the other side of trunk.

Checking the corpse for any identification, the Stony Man warriors took his watch, wallet and cell phone. Then they blended into the forest just as three cars screeched to a halt on the highway, the rotating blue-and-red lights slicing through the night to announce that the South Carolina State Police had just arrived in force.

CHAPTER ELEVEN

Zandwoort, Holland

Slowly building in strength and volume, the alarms began to howl in warning for a full minute before the foaming wake of a Shkval cut the surface of the North Sea.

From the reinforced seabed, titanium nets were raised and punched through, mines exploded high and low under the water, but the crushing shock waves and tearing shrapnel were always moments behind the rocketing Shkval. The government of Holland had never thought it was necessary to computerize the national-defense net. Torpedoes were deadly but slow, and a nuclear warhead didn't have to be anywhere near its target, so why bother?

A hundred people were fishing off the parkland along the outer rim of the sloping Zandwoort dike. But at the first howl, they tossed away the poles and frantically started to run away from the incoming wave. They had no idea what it was, but the sirens were taught in kindergarten. If you heard the alarm, then run for your life.

The people driving their cars on the eight-lane highway atop the mammoth dike slammed on their brakes, creating traffic chaos.

"It's going for the gate!" a man shouted, a hand placed to his forehead to block the morning sun.

"Foolishness," a woman stated. "Nothing can punch through those armor plates. There are sixteen, each a foot thick."

"Then we're safe?" another woman asked, glancing behind them toward the polders, the low lands on the other side of the huge dike. Farms and buildings stretched to the horizon, ten thousand homes sitting fifty feet below water level. But the Zandwoort Dike was 150 feet wide, prestressed concrete reinforced with steel beams every four feet. Nothing could punch through that except a nuke.

"God have mercy on us all," an older man whispered, making the sign of the cross.

The crowd watched in horrid astonishment as the Shkval went straight past the concrete slab that housed the sluice gate and slammed into the middle of the dike, at exactly its strongest point.

The explosion seem to shake the world, and debris went flying for hundreds of feet into the sky. The asphalt of the highway buckled and cracked, dozens of streetlights toppled over in both directions for almost a mile, trees were uprooted and the western face of the great dyke shook as if slapped by the hand of God.

Slowly, the concussions eased, and as the smoke cleared, the Zandwoort Dike was badly gouged, a sixty-foot crater blown into its resilient seawall, but the rest stood firm. The damage was minimal.

The crowd broke into wild cheering, when a rumble started under their feet, the vibration building rapidly until it was louder than the explosion of the torpedo strike. Then a rushing roar came from the eastern side of the dike, and the terrified crowd rushed upward onto the highway and past the lines of parked cars to reach the downslope.

There they paused in abject horror as solid rods of blue were shooting out of countless sluice gates as if the armored plating of the defensive locks were wide-open. The saltwater shafts extended for an unbelievable distance, pounding against the downtown buildings in hellish majesty. A modern-style office building was already crumbling, nearly cut in two by the titanic pressure of the rushing ocean. As the stupefied people watched, another building gave way, the windows shattering, the water flushing through the museum and out the other side until the structure began to tilt and break apart, falling to the flooded streets below. People caught on the sidewalks and boating on the canals were deluged by the onslaught, slammed against the sides of homes and cathedrals, their remains mixing with the nightmarish debris of bikes, cars, houseboats and furniture.

"The control room," a policeman gasped in understanding, going pale. "The bastards who did this blew the control room and opened every sluice gate for a hundred miles!"

"My God," the old woman whispered. "What can we…? Is there anything that…?"

His hat in hand, a young soldier hung his head. "Nothing. Everybody below us is dead."

A young girl burst into tears, the sound of her cries overwhelmed by the North Atlantic Sea violently reclaiming what had been so lovingly taken from it the past three hundred years.

Annex, Stony Man Farm, Virginia

"BINGO," Aaron Kurtzman announced from the computer console, fighting back a yawn. "We have a trace on the cell phone Gary reclaimed in South Carolina. The last call was placed to California."

"That's as close as you could get?" Price demanded.

The world situation wasn't good. The central wall monitor was displaying nothing at the moment, but a side monitor was showing a detailed graphic of the world, the number of red dots marking a Shkval strike increasing with alarming regularity. Soon, wars would start as the chaos grew like a cancer across the globe.

"Did our best," Kurtzman rumbled, rubbing his eyes. "None of the memory buttons had been set, a wise precaution on their part. But we contacted his wireless service and complained about unauthorized calls on the bill. They sent us a complete listing, and the only number not accountable is in California.''

Raising his mug, the man seemed surprised to find it empty. Hadn't he just filled it a minute ago, or had that been an hour?

"California," Price prompted.

"That's where the trail ends," Kurtzman said, rolling over to the kitchenette. A new pot of coffee was brewing, and it smelled like his formula. Good. "Any further details are scrambled, lost, or the records deleted. Not conclusive evidence of the arms dealers, but highly suspicious.''

"So this Casax tracks their phone calls with their Cray and burns the records the same way we do.''

"That would be my opinion. If there was one thing telephone companies do not lose, it is the location of a paying customer.''

California, eh? Price checked her status sheet. Yes, the dead chief of security had his watch set for Pacific standard time, not the East Coast, where he had been found. Another tenuous link to the West Coast. It wasn't much, barely a gossamer thread, but it was their first step in the right direction to find the arms dealers.

"How's Phoenix Force?" Katz asked from a console. The screens before the man showed the war status of the Farm above, and of America at large.

"Battered, but alive," Price replied, a jumpy black-and-white monitor giving her a view inside a helicopter. "The cold water woke them up, and they made it to shore after the explosion."

"Pity about Kodak," Katz said, looking at a list of the known dead. Accidents happened in battle. The Stony Man warriors had lost her in the explosion, and her lifeless body washed ashore the next day in North Carolina. Good thing Hawkins and Manning had caught that truck; the data about the train was the Farm's first solid lead on this matter to date.

"The woman worked for a known arms dealer, so she knew the risks. I'm only sorry David didn't have a chance to debrief her. Bear, anything yet on the name Casax?"

"It's simply not enough to work with," the computer expert stated. "Could mean something, or nothing. Maybe they threw some Scrabble tiles on the floor and chose a name for their group that way. British Intelligence uses that all the time. The word is impossible to figure out since it means nothing. Called a Qwerty code." He saw her lack of understanding. "Take a look at your keyboard."

Price glanced down and smiled. A Qwerty code. How simple. "Or maybe it's somebody's name," she suggested.

"Nothing so far, either as a family name, or first," Akira Tokaido stated. "I'm trying anagrams, reversal, replacement transfers and simple combinations—C. Asax, Charles Axe and so on."

"Any results?"

He sighed glancing a scrolling list. "Too many."

"Take an hour," Price advised, hearing the exhaustion in his voice. "Get some sleep."

"I'm fine," Tokaido said, forcing himself to sit straighter at the console.

"That wasn't a request," Price said, firmly. "Take a shower, change your clothes, get some sleep. Tired minds are blunt swords."

Removing his headphones, the young hacker gave a weak grin. "Well, if you're going to quote Sophocles, what choice do I have?" he said, and stumbled from the room, looking more dead than alive.

Price didn't correct the mistake. The phrase was her own, and if Akira thought it was from the ancient Greek playwright Sophocles, then he was even more exhausted than he appeared.

"Nothing on the byproducts yet," Carmen Delahunt reported. The woman looked tired, but she was still going strong. Unlike Tokaido, she was taking fifteen minutes every hour to nap. "I'm checking the last status report of the EPA rather than access a current report. Also checking the air-pollution records, just to be thorough."

Pushing back her chair, Price walked over to see the results. "Good idea. Anything else?"

"The liquid nitrogen was easy. It's heavily regulated. But again, too many locations."

The mission controller pointed at a submonitor. "Concentrate in California."

"Way ahead of you," Delahunt replied, returning to her task.

A staffer brought in a tray of sandwiches and departed. Grabbing food, the three cyber warriors dived into the electronic maelstrom of the Internet, and the silent battle raged once more, minds and iron will against the technology of the unknown enemy. Slowly, time passed in tense silence.

"Finished," Hunt Wethers announced, not moving from his previous position hunched over the keyboard. "I have the name of the shipping carrier, Consolidated Cargo. They own a thousand railroad cars, two of which are leased to Casax, Incorporated."

Rolling up the sleeves of her red flannel shirt, Price arched a questioning eyebrow.

"It doesn't exist. Just a name on paper."

Damn. Maybe it was a Qwerty code. "Find us the location of those two cars," she directed. "Even if they're empty, there could be clues to the whereabouts of the American factory. Soil samples we can trace, something."

"Already accessed," Wethers replied, and tapped a key. The main wall monitor flashed into a picture of a document. "The B&E Railroad, the *Delta Sue* diesel locomotive, Consolidated Cargo mass shipment, cargo container lot 178, bound for Reading from Reno, Casax Inc."

Reno again. Interesting. Hadn't there been a recent gang war there? "Katz, have the FBI check the EPA sensors in Reno. We'll handle the train," Price stated, palming a control to bring up a map of Central America. Reno to Reading was about two thousand miles, and the actual Shkvals could have been brought on board at any point along the route. If any were actually there.

Flipping a gang bar on her console, a red triangle appeared on the map indicating the exact location of the freight train, Indiana heading into Ohio. Estimated eight hours to Reading Station. Damn. When the people on the train aren't met by Lane's men, they would know something was wrong, blow the cargo and disappear. The only direct link to the Russian thieves gone forever.

"Aaron, send full data files on B&E Railroad to Able Team. They're closer than anybody else," Price ordered. "That train is to be boarded before reaching Reading Station and the cargo examined at any cost."

"On it," the big man said, swiveling his wheelchair into the console. His hands began moving with lightning speed across the controls.

Biting a lip, Price then added, "And send Phoenix Force to New Orleans and get Marasco. Offer full immunity if he talks."

Removing the pipe from his mouth, Wethers asked, "I beg your pardon, Barb, but why not the other way around?"

"The Don knows what Able Team looks like," Price explained, linking her console to the Crays below to watch the progress of the EPA sensor reports. "Lyons couldn't get close enough to try and cut a deal with him now. But Phoenix Force can."

"Federal immunity to a Mafia Don," Katz muttered. The man's thoughts on the matter were clearly readable.

Price shrugged. "This is more important than petty revenge. Too many civilians have died already. I don't care what it costs to get the job done, but that damn weapons factory must be shut down!"

"Agreed," he said, shaking his head. "But cutting a deal with the Mob leaves a bad taste in my mouth."

"Me, too. And if he refuses to cooperate, they're to terminate with extreme prejudice," the woman said calmly, watching the data scroll. "Although, I think it much more likely that he'll try to lie his way out."

"They usually do," Katz muttered, placing the call.

Casax, California

HANDS FOLDED behind his back at parade rest, Jozsef Vadas looked out the window of his apartment located above the foundry.

Although it was night outside with dawn hours away, the great city was still alive, cars speeding by, night clubs and restaurants open, searchlights sweeping the sky announcing the grand opening of something or other. The very air seemed to pulse with the rhythm of life. It was exciting, but he longed for the peace of the Carpathian Mountains. The constant killing was beginning to affect his dreams. The bloodshed would continue until his men were rich—he had made them a solemn promise—but his heart was no longer in the job, and he wished to go home.

Across the apartment, the other Czechs were at the dining table, sorting the stacks of cash and preparing another deposit into their offshore bank accounts. It occurred to him that if anybody really wanted to stop terrorism, all they had to do was to bomb Switzerland and the Cayman Islands out of existence. No secret bank accounts, no more terrorists. But of course, that would never happen because the people in charge of any government always had their bribes stashed away in a similar account. America had missiles, Australia had distance, but Switzerland was the best defended nation in the world because it held the purse strings.

"Our present situation is not acceptable," Vadas stated, turning from the picturesque view and his dark thoughts of retirement. "An unknown group blocked our trace, and now a Mafia contact claims a dead policemen was disguised as a terrorist and wanted to buy our product."

"Is he dead?" Davida asked, pausing in the counting.

"The Don says yes, but I think he lies."

Moving a stack of hundreds in a bank deposit bag, Boris Bezdek frowned. "Any other of our wholesalers no longer available?"

"Lane in Carolina does not answer his e-mail. I fear the worst," Sergei Zofchak said pointedly.

The sergeant took a chair, the stout wood creaking

from his weight. "Sergei, hack into his computer and burn all records of our transactions."

"I cannot. He uses a secretary with a photographic memory."

"How clever. Then send some mercs to kill her," Vadas ordered, then added, "And Lane also. Tell them to expect resistance, possibly Delta Force troops."

"Sarge, this matter is getting out of control," Solomon said hesitantly. "These Americans are much better than we ever imagined."

"That is a fact," Vadas conceded, picking up a stack of cash six inches thick and casually tossing it back onto the table. "And only fools fight in a house on fire. My friends, it is time for us to leave. Sergei, finish the deposit. Boris, close down production and start dismantling the equipment. Davida, have our people in Mendoza City start preliminary operations on establishing a new factory. Solomon will carry the templates."

"Too bad," Pran said, looking at the empty white cardboard box sitting on another chair. "I love American pizza."

"Once we reach full production, we'll have it shipped down to us, my friend," Bezdek said, slapping the man on the back. "By topless Hollywood models!"

The soldier made a noise. "Too skinny. I want a woman with some meat on her bones. A good Russian girl."

"You and your foreign women." Zofchak chuckled. "Something wrong with Czech girls?"

"No accent." He smiled. "I like an accent, English, Spanish, Russian, very sexy stuff."

"French?"

Pran frowned deeply. "Woman must shave. I do not want a man with tits."

"I do," Solomon said with a crooked grin. "But until I find such a person, regular men will do."

The group shared a laugh with their huge comrade. For most of his life, the giant soldier had been forced to pretend he liked women while in the Soviet army. The Communists took a very dim view of homosexuals. A bullet in the back of the head was their usual response. But in the independent Czech Republic, nobody cared, though nobody would hire him, either. Vadas was delighted to take him on as a business partner. The man was a splendid soldier, and what he did on R&R was of no concern to anybody else.

"We'll destroy the factory as we leave," Vadas said, pushing himself off the chair. "The computers can fire off our last batch of Shkvals at the city above once we are clear. It will take the government years to sift through the rubble."

"Not enough," Zofchak growled, tapping a pencil against the legal pad covered with columns of figures. "This is costing us millions, so they must pay billions. We'll leave them something to truly remember us."

Bezdek furrowed his brow. "Such as what?"

"San Offrey," he answered, and the others nodded in agreement. An easy, almost foolish target. Sometimes the Americans were so stupid it was baffling.

"During the national riots, we shall slip south and mix with the Panama Canal traffic. Davida, call our people in Argentina. Mendoza City will be our new base of operations. Delivery will be more expensive, but down there we shall own the police and be completely safe. The Americans never find us again."

Akron, Ohio

MORNING WAS JUST lightening the sky, adding warm pinks to the purple of night. A large grassy field spread along the side of a gentle hill ending in an embankment. The seclusion and beautiful view of the majestic lake and pastoral city below combined to make the isolated area a favorite romantic spot for local couples. Just a Lovers' Lane, similar to a hundred thousand others in countless small towns across the nation.

"More wine, my sweet?" the young man asked, offering a frosty bottle dripping condensation.

Smiling shyly, the woman started to reply when there was a strong gust of wind that violently shook the tress. Dust clouds rose, and the blankets billowed up as she fought to keep her dress from going over her head. Instantly wary, the young man stood blinking at the sky above as he flipped the wine bottle over by the neck to brandish it as a weapon, displaying important information about his past. It was a classic bar-fight technique.

"Jesus Christ!" he cried, suddenly dropping the bottle. Grabbing his companion by the hand, he pulled her up and shoved hard. "Run, babe! Run!"

A single glance in the same direction told her more than enough, and the teenager effortlessly kicked off her pumps to start racing barefoot over the lush summer grass, soon leaving the boy behind. Across the park, other couples were running for their lives in various stages of undress, heading for their cars parked under the canopy of trees.

Seconds later, the Apache Longbow gunship landed on top of the fluttering sleeping bags, and three men in full combat gear piled out of the military helicopter.

Revving in power, the massive gunship rose into the brightening sky and started angling away to the north, keeping as far away as possible from the train tracks running through the Allegheny Mountains. A single sighting from a passenger on board the train could ruin the entire deployment, especially since there was no way to hide the Hellfire missiles and 35 mm rocket pods of the sleek gunship. The black-suit pilot would stay within radio contact of the team, but would take no action until they requested his assistance.

"The bridge is south by southeast of here," Gadgets Schwarz directed, checking a compass on his wrist.

Combat boots pounding the ground, Able Team took off at a full run in spite of their body armor and backpacks. The men were outfitted in regular combat gear, Blancanales and Schwarz with M-16/M-203 combination assault rifles, and Lyons toting an Atchisson shotgun.

"Stay frosty, guys!" Lyons said gruffly, jumping over a low fence designed to keep people off the grass. "I'll be damned if we're going to fubar this mission like New Orleans. If we blow it, there's nobody else to catch the slack."

Minutes later, the men of Able Team crested a low hill to find themselves standing before an old, abandoned bridge from the Public Works Era of the Great Depression. The granite blocks were tinged with green moss, the trestle furry with rust, and the cobblestones on top were worn smooth with age. Even the crossway itself ended on both sides in fields of grass, the ancient road once served no longer even existing. However, a very modern-looking railroad track ran directly underneath the ancient bridge, and as the men stopped there came the telltale sound of track switches engaging, connecting the northbound rails to the eastbound.

Going to the stone cap, Lyons dropped a surveyor's plumb line over the side and read the distance. "Twenty-five feet," he reported, releasing the line. "That gives us a four- to six-foot drop. Should be no problem."

"Six feet onto a moving train," Blancanales added,

tightening a belt across his chest. "And we have to land on the last carriage so nobody sees. If we miss or slide off, we'll bust so many bones we'll be riding a chair like Bear."

"Oh, don't be melodramatic," Schwarz chided, looking over the edge. "We'll probably be sucked under the wheels and killed instantly."

"Really? That's so encouraging."

"Always glad to help."

Softly in the distance, there came the sound of a blaring horn, its strident tones audibly growing in strength every second. A moment later, a dot appeared on the western horizon and began to swell. The train was moving with express speed through the rolling plains of Ohio, heading straight into the Allegheny Mountains of Pennsylvania.

"Too fast," Blancanales said grimly. "Damn engineer must be trying to impress the boss and reach Reading early."

"Can we still make the jump?" Lyons asked with a frown. "There's graveyard of difference between thirty miles per hour and fifty."

"Damned if I know, but we got a choice?"

"Not really."

"Get your pneumatics ready," Schwarz told them, checking the compressed-air cartridge in the grip of the odd pistol in his belt.

Deafeningly loud, the triple diesels at the front of the freight train sounded the warning horn again, the single great headlight in front shining for a good half mile ahead of the express. The train was heavily loaded with over a hundred cars. Lyons knew that was about average, but somewhere in that mix were the two from Casax, maybe all together or separated by a dozen innocent cars. There was no way of knowing. The enemy was here, but still hidden. The arms dealers were very good. Able Team just had to be better.

"It's occurred to me," Schwarz stated, watching the express train hurtle toward them, "that we're very close to the Ohio National Guard armory. Think it's a target?"

"No water."

"These things are rocket powered," Schwarz retorted. "Who says a Shkval can't fly for a short distances?"

Frowning, Lyons had no reply to that chilling thought.

"Here she comes!" Blancanales announced.

The bridge trembled as the freight train thundered underneath. The cars rumbled below the men with the familiar click-clack, click-clack of iron wheels, and many seconds passed before they caught the roof light of the caboose.

Words were useless, so Lyons simply pointed at the train and jumped. He fell the few yards and hit hard, sprawled on his belly to spread the force of the impact, which elicited a sharp pain along his bruised ribs. Instantly, he started to slide backward off the caboose, pushed by the strong wind of the speeding train. In lightning speed, he drew a knife and buried the blade in the wood roof to brake his slide. As he came to a halt, the Able Team leader drew a mountain-climbing pistol and fired a piton into the roof, then started looping a rope through the steel anchor for a secure grip.

Lyons wasn't worried about alerting anybody inside the caboose with the noise. The car should be deserted with the entire crew working the triple diesels at the front of the massive locomotive. The caboose was there purely because of union regulations, to give the crew a place to go for a hot lunch and to sleep on the twenty-four-hour trips. But since the only way to reach the caboose on a freight train was from the ground, and it took time and a full mile of distance to stop the huge locomotive, the crew almost always ate cold lunches in the front control room to save time and trouble. However, their grandfathers had gone on strike to get the rights to a caboose over a hundred years ago and nothing short of hell would make them give up the unnecessary luxury.

Firing another piton into the wood, he tightened the rope and checked behind. Schwarz was nearby cinching his rope through another piton, but there was no sign of Blancanales.

"Pol, report!" Lyons whispered into his throat mike.

"Yeah, yeah, I'm fine," the man answered as a gloved hand rose into view from behind the caboose. Climbing onto the roof of the carriage, Blancanales shot in a piton and roped himself to safety.

The men clung tightly as the train tilted slightly, taking a long curve in the track. Slowly the cars straightened and the team started crawling forward onto the curved roof of the cargo containers. Unfortunately, this wasn't a passenger train with interconnecting doorways at each end, safety railings and windows. This was a freight train, each car sealed tight to prevent pilfering. A hundred cars, each with only two possible entrances—the side door, which was impossible to open at these speeds, or the roof hatch, which was locked from the inside.

Along with their other weapons and sensors, each man also was carrying a DEA ammonia sniffer. Human sweat carried traces of ammonia, and urine a lot. If there were arms dealers riding with the Shkvals, they would need a chemical toilet to use for the long journey, and that would require ventilation holes. The team was counting on guards being along for the ride. If the Shkvals were alone, there was no way to find them.

A slow hour passed as Able Team inched its way along the different roofs of forty cars, going from a wooden boxcar to modern-day modular steel, and then along the slick railing of a pressurized liquid tanker. The hull was bitterly cold, and the team was shivering before reaching the next car.

"Liquid helium," Schwarz read from the warning label painted on the frosty side. "Christ, if that got breached, anything hit by the stuff would shatter like glass from the intense cold."

"Think it might be a double container?" Blancanales asked. "With the Shkvals inside another hull in the middle?"

"Too cold," Lyons stated. "The machinery would rust and the electronics would start to malfunction."

"Maybe. But still a damn good place to hide the torpedoes. It's the last place we would ever look."

"And the last we will," Lyons added. "But only if necessary."

The conversation stopped as the men ducked and another low bridge flashed by above. If anybody raised a head at the wrong moment, he'd be decapitated.

"Enemies underneath, death on either side, stones bridges coming at our heads…hey, Carl, can I transfer back into the Army?" Blancanales asked, crawling onto the next car.

Using his knife blade and rope, the former cop stayed alongside his teammate. "Sure. Just take me with you," he said in a rare moment of humor.

"Just a second," Schwarz said, adjusting the ammonia sniffer strapped to his forearm. "I have a reading."

Holding a small plastic mirror in his gloved hand, the Able Team leader read the sign on the side. "Wrong ID number. This carriage is full of fertilizer. Good cover for the ammonia."

Blancanales looked over the edge of the container and turned back to the others with a smile.

"No external lock on the door," he reported.

"Fertilizer isn't a hot commodity to steal," Schwarz said over the com link as he ran a trace with the EM scanner. There were no live proximity sensors or pressure plates in the roof to reveal their position.

"But ever since the Kansas City bombing, it is a controlled substance," Lyons corrected grimly. "If the company lost a single bag, they'd have to pay heavy fines. It should be locked."

"Probably is, then," Blancanales replied, "from the inside."

Bracing his boots against the edge of the cargo container, Schwarz starting pulling out shaped charges of C-4 plastique. If there had been a vent hole, even a small crack, he would have used the U.S. Army laptop in his shoulder bag to send in a fiber-optic probe and see what was inside the steel box. But they were going to have to open this can the hard way.

"Should we check the rest first?" Schwarz asked, laying the plastique in a rough circular pattern near the sliding side door. The door would be the only section of the car they could be sure was free of any Shkvals as the arms dealers would need to keep the exit clear so they could load and unload the weapons.

"This will alert anybody else on the whole damn train," Blancanales added.

It was a good point, Lyons conceded. But the train was already past the Ohio Arsenal and heading for the Pennsylvania border. Pittsburgh wasn't far away, and the terrorists could have bribed the drivers for an unauthorized stop.

"Do it," he ordered, going with his gut instinct.

Attaching the electric firing squibs, Schwarz started humming under his breath, the throat mike catching the occasional piece of the song.

"Is that the theme to *Mission Impossible?*" Lyons demanded, crawling away from the explosives.

In response, Schwarz smiled and pressed the detonator. The plastique gave a loud whomp and a section of the roof blew inward, leaving a jagged hole. Taking the point, Lyons swung his head and the Atchisson into the container looking for targets. Smoke from the explosion clouded the air, and the concussion of the blast still reverberated inside the steel box, masking any movements. Flipping over, the Able Team leader dropped into the car and landed on the crumpled section of the metal roof.

As the breeze from the roof sucked out the smoke, Lyons saw that most of the container was filled with plastic bags of fertilizer, but a small group of men was scrambling into the far corner, cringing in terror. A big fellow in mostly rags was brandishing a homemade knife made of a shard of glass wrapped in what looked liked duct tape.

"You keep back there, buddy!" the hobo said in a not very threatening voice, quaking in fear.

But Lyons didn't buy the setup for a moment. Then he heard a cough from behind the stack of fertilizer bags. He glanced at the floor and saw scratch marks from a false wall. Got them! But his face had to have betrayed his emotions because the hobos dropped the glass knife and started to draw Beretta 93-R pistols. They were fast, and had the element of surprise, but Lyons beat them to the draw. The Atchisson ripped a short burst of 12-gauge rounds. That whole section of the container exploded in blood and rags.

"Feds!" a man shouted from behind the wall of bags, and the fertilizer exploded as a rifle boomed.

The heavy slug hit Lyons in the chest, slamming him backward, his NATO body armor deflecting the round but knocking the breath out of him. Spraying the bags with a full clip of shells, he then dived behind a corpse on the floor as his teammates appeared from the roof, spraying the gaping hole in the false wall with their M-16/M-203 assault rifle combos. Men screamed as the tumblers hit the steel wall and ricocheted out of sight.

"Shift," Lyons subvocalized into his throat mike, and as the other members of Able Team separated, he tossed a primed concussion grenade into the hole.

The Stony Man warriors opened their mouths and covered their ears, and the blast still buffeted them hard. Then the stack of fertilizer bags toppled over, exposing the wooden expanse of a false wall. But even as they started forward, small hatches dropped open in the wood and AK-74 assault rifles sprayed steel-jacketed lead in random patterns.

As he thumbed fresh rounds into the tubular magazine of the Atchisson, Lyons knew the men behind the wall had to be badly dazed from the grenade, if not permanently deaf, so he ignored them for a moment and concentrated his weapon on the hinges. The steel fléchettes chewed the galvanized iron apart, and with the sound of splintering wood, the door dropped away, exposing the startled gunner. Blancanales and Schwarz hosed the men in controlled bursts, then reloaded and moved past the corpses.

They stayed low, moving fast along a narrow passage that followed the exterior wall of the container for several yards before ending with a steel grille. The cargo container was a fortress!

As the trio appeared at the grille, the ceiling lights blinked out. Flipping down their infrared goggles, Able Team saw two men carrying Kalashnikovs step into view. The covert-ops veterans fired in unison and the guards fell back, the grille decorated with red.

Blancanales shoved the small barrel of his M-16 through the grille and fired off short bursts while Schwarz used a key-wire gun on the lock. In seconds the mechanism yielded to the locksmith tool, and Lyons took the point again, the booming Atchisson clearing the way as they penetrated deeper into the shipping container.

Keeping a mental record of their progress, the Able Team leader knew the box was running out of space and wasn't surprised when they found a hatchway built into the wall. A secret doorway connecting the next container to this one full of troops? Made sense.

Using brute strength, Lyons and Blancanales forced the sliding hatch aside as Schwarz laid on more plastique, the ground rushing at deadly speed below the narrow space between the two containers.

"Fire in the hole!" he warned over the com link, and took cover as the gray wads of plastique blew a split second later.

The sliding hatch was punched off its track and went flying into the next container. A man caught directly in its path shouted in pain for a brief moment before he was slammed aside.

Heavy slugs from enemy gunners slammed against the outside of the steel cargo container.

When the gunshots paused, Lyons and Schwarz flipped the spoons on gas canisters and tossed the grenades into the next carriage. Able Team quickly donned gas masks. Billowing tear gas poured from the rolling can and started to fill the air. Soon men were cursing and gagging, one screamed wildly and machine guns raked the doorway, doing little damage. A small man with an M-16 tried to charge across the space between the two containers, and Lyons triggered a point-blank blast from the Atchisson. His arms gone from the elbows, the mutilated man staggered, then tumbled down between the railroad cars where the clacking wheels tore him apart.

Clearing a path with individual shotgun blasts from the Atchisson, Lyons crossed over and quickly stepped aside to get out of the way of his teammates.

There were no false walls or trick grilles dividing this container, only a pair of massive lattice supports holding a dozen Shkvals each, their weird flat crowns and rocket vectors alternating in different directions.

"Pol on the left, Gadgets take the right," Lyons ordered, moving along the central passage. "I've got the slot."

A shadow moved and Lyons fired. A burst of M-16 fire drilled in from the left, and the same twice from the right. Then the Stony Man warriors were past the stacks of rocket torpedoes and facing a single Shkval resting in a chain hoist.

Standing behind some wooden crates, two men had the hull of a Shkval open and were doing something to its internal works. The rear rocket flared for a second, throwing out a volcano of heat along the enclosed carriage. But then the rocket cut off, only to flare once more for a slightly longer moment.

Lyons couldn't believe the sheer audacity of the plan. The crazy bastards were trying to launch a Shkval and fry Able Team alive with its rocket exhaust!

"Charge!" Lyons shouted, surging forward.

Cutting loose with everything they had, Able Team ran straight for the rocket chewing apart the wooden crates, and they made it past the belled cone of the rear vector just as the rocket roared again for several seconds. The Shkval started to move forward in its sling, then the motors cut off again and Able Team scrambled over the crates, blowing the technicians apart.

There was nobody else in the shipping container,

and the team removed its gas masks, then quickly reloaded.

"Any chance that this thing is going to start again?" Lyons demanded, gesturing at the Shkval as he rammed fresh shells into the Atchisson.

"No way. It's not designed to launch this way," Schwarz said, slinging the M-16/M-203 over his shoulder and checking the complex maze of electronic circuitry and smoothly machined cams filling the guts of the deadly machine. Yanking a wire loose, he then removed a circuit board and tossed it away.

"It's dead now," he announced, then scowled and plunged his hands back into the microchip innards of the Russian weapon.

"And so are all of the arms dealers," Blancanales complained, checking the pulse of a man sprawled on the floor. "Damn it, we need prisoners."

"At least we got the shipment intact," Lyons commented, tugging on the chain of the harnessed Shkval. Why was this one in a special sling? It certainly looked like the others. Maybe it was the self-destruct torpedo positioned to stop the weapons from falling into the hands of the government.

"This could have been a lot worse," he stated, relaxing his stance slightly.

"It is worse," Schwarz stated, retracting himself from inside the torpedo and going to the nose. Drawing his knife, he carefully scrapped the blade along the neck of the hull, peeling off long strips of the satiny paint and exposing four brightly colored rings.

"Is that the damn Russian bar code for a nuke?" Lyons asked, pointing with the Atchisson.

"Unfortunately, yes." Schwarz sheathed his blade. "We're in big trouble."

Lyons turned toward the electronics expert "You mean it's armed?" he demanded, swinging the autoshotgun toward the open service panel. The best and fastest way to deactivate a nuclear weapon was to shoot it to pieces. The internal arming mechanisms were very delicate. The C-4 might still explode, but there wouldn't be a nuclear chain reaction.

"No, this only has a conventional warhead," Schwarz said, pushing away the barrel of the weapon. "But it was originally armed with a tactical nuke."

Just then the train shook slightly as it jounced over a switchback junction, starting to move toward the north and away from Pittsburgh.

"Which means that our Russian thieves now have a nuke," Lyons growled, clicking on the safety of the alley-sweeper.

"I'm afraid so."

"Damn!"

Resting the stock of his assault rifle on a hip, Blancanales scowled deeply. "Possibly several. Who knows how many of these that they stole from Murmansk were equipped with atomic charges?"

"And if the arms dealers don't have them anymore, then somebody else has bought the nukes," Lyons said, glancing over the gory litter of the battle inside the steel container. The dozens of Shkvals stacked neatly in their cushioned lattice no longer seemed quiescent, stored weapons inert and harmless.

Goddamn it, they were almost on top of this mess and it suddenly got a thousand times worse. A Shkval with a nuclear warhead. Just one of those could reduce a major city into rubble with a death toll in the millions. Choose the right city and it could start a war that would engulf the world in flames.

"I only hope there is something here that gives us a clue to the whereabouts of Casax," Schwarz added. "The numbers are falling and we're still standing on square one."

"We better call Barb," Lyons stated, adjusting the controls on the radio to the scrambled channel reserved for priority broadcasts. "This is now a national emergency."

CHAPTER TWELVE

Bella Donna Estates, Outside New Orleans

His boots wedged in the fork of a banyan tree, Spanish moss hanging from the branches like lacy fog, David McCarter balanced the Steyr SSG-69 sniper rifle in his hands. Studying the palatial mansion below through the telescopic sight, the man didn't like what he saw.

The lush grounds were surrounded by a six-foot-tall brick fence, on top of which was another six-foot-tall iron fence. An imposing barrier, if not for the fact that the main gate was wide-open. A dozen Mafia hardcases stood around the front lawn of the four-story mansion, the holsters of their shoulder rigs clearly empty. Two stocky pit bulls were securely chained to their doghouse, every light turned on and the open garage door showed the parked limousine and crew wagon, a muddy blue Hummer.

The side-by-side front doors of the antebellum-style house were flung ajar, and sitting in an easy chair in the middle of the greenhouse was Dante Marasco chain-smoking cigarettes. A small table along-side the man held a thermos and a telephone. His cane was leaning against a far wall, yards away.

"Could be a trap to lure us in, expose our position," McCarter said, placing another pound of pressure on the trigger of the Steyr. A featherweight more and the Mafia Don would leave this Earth in an explosion of brains and glass.

"No way," Rafael Encizo said over the com link. "This guy has done everything but run a white rag up the flagpole. What more do you want?"

"Yeah, guess so," the Briton reluctantly agreed, releasing his grip on the Steyr rifle. His natural inclination was to never deal with criminals, but Price wanted information more than bodies, so he would give the Don a chance for his life. But one wrong move, and Phoenix Force would level that blood-money mansion.

Placing the sniper rifle nearby, McCarter pulled a cell phone from a leg pouch in his fatigues, turned on the device and dialed the number printed on the telephone in the greenhouse. The Mafia Don jumped as the phone rang, and he picked up the receiver on the second ring.

"We can kill you at any time," McCarter said, knowing that Encizo had turned on the voice scrambler and the words were distorted beyond recognition.

Taking a long drag off the cigarette, the Don held the smoke for quite a while before exhaling. "Yeah, I sort of figured that," he said, twin plumes of smoke trickling from his nose. "When my temper cooled last night I realized what a shitstorm this had become, and figured the only way out was to cut a deal."

McCarter didn't reply, but looked at James on the ground below. Encizo glanced up from the U.S. Army laptop hardwired into the field radio and shook his head. The call wasn't being traced or recorded.

"The welcome mat was a good idea," McCarter stated calmly. "We came fully ready to simply level the place. You took a big chance that we wanted something more than you under the ground."

"Which is why I sent my wife and kids away," Marasco stated.

"Good. Now here is what we want—"

"Hold it," Marasco snapped, gesturing with the cigarette arm. "I ain't talking with no voice on the phone. Prove to me who you are."

Covering the cell phone, McCarter touched his throat mike. "T.J., show the man," he directed. "But just T.J. Gary and Cal, stand ready and watch for enemy flanking. This still could be a trick."

"Roger," Hawkins replied, and there came the muffled sounds of metallic clacks and thumps.

A few moments later a keening whistle cut the air, the noise growing steadily louder until the front gate of the estate detonated into a fireball of smoke and shrapnel. The bodyguards on the front lawn were thrown to the ground by the concussion, and a dozen panes cracked along the front of the greenhouse.

"Enough!" Marasco cried, standing. "Cease fire,

you crazy mothers! Okay, I believe you! You're the goddamn Army, Delta Force, whatever.''

The former British SAS commando growled, ''Just a concerned citizen.''

''Right, and I'm Joe Pesci'' the Don muttered, removing the cigarette to tap off the ash. ''Now if you assholes know anything about me, then you know how fucking much I do not want to do this. Okay, I'm caught and today is my turn in the barrel. What's the deal?''

''You retire as of this moment,'' McCarter stated, allowing some of his hatred to show through. ''You get so much as a parking ticket and we come back. In force.''

''Yeah, I expected something like that,'' the man said sitting back down again and lighting another cigarette. ''What the hell, I got enough stashed away. That it? I go legit and you're happy?''

''Not quite,'' McCarter growled, shifting his position in the tree to lift a pair of field glasses to his face. The computerized range finder adjusted the focus automatically and the Mafia Don came into wire-sharp clarity. ''We want everything you have on the Russian arms dealers selling the Shkvals.''

''Russian? Geez, you guys aren't anywhere near as good as I thought. Maybe I should reconsider the deal,'' the Don said with a bitter laugh. ''These soldier boys are Czechoslovakians, or just Czechs, if there's a difference. Who knows with these piss-pot

Third World nations. I heard them mention going home to Prague once and looked it up.''

Czech soldiers? That would certainly explain their hatred of the Russians, and how they knew where the Shkvals were stored. So they were from the days of the Soviet Union, maybe security troops. When the USSR broke apart, Czechoslovakia became free, the army was disbanded, thousands of soldiers out of work and a few started their own business. The only business they knew was killing. Everything fell into line.

''More,'' McCarter stated gruffly, looking over the grounds with the field glasses. For a moment, he could have sworn there was some movement in the trees beyond the mansion, but with so many squirrels and birds, it was difficult to tell.

Touching his throat mike, McCarter said, ''T.J. and Cal, do a recon, southwest sector. Possible enemy activity.''

''Well, I got a California telephone number,'' Marasco started to say.

''Useless to us,'' McCarter said brusquely. ''I want names and an address.''

''Yeah? Then tough shit. Ace me,'' the Mafia Don stated, annoyed, crossing his legs at the ankles. ''I was merely their wholesaler for the south, not in bed with the guys. One of them really likes pizza, and another is gay. That help any?''

''Hardly,'' McCarter drawled. ''You're giving me

shit here. Unless you have something real, I've no use for you.''

"South side clear," Hawkins said. "But I found a radio-controlled toy stuck in a tree to shake the leaves as a diversion.''

Damn! The enemy was already here. Had to be the Czechs, or their Spanish mercs. "Get hard, people!" McCarter commanded. "Red alert!''

"Okay, okay, Los Angeles," the Don growled, grinding out the cigarette on the table. "I heard one of them complain about the pizza at a Lakers game. It was a home game that night. Now that is all I got. Honest to God!''

That was enough. Concentrating all of their efforts on one city, the warriors could pry these bastards out of hiding in twenty-four hours.

"Phoenix One to Stony Base," McCarter said into his radio, switching frequencies. "They're in L.A. Repeat, they are in Los Angeles." Then the man cut off the reply from the Farm as there was a familiar flash of light from the hillside overlooking the bayou mansion.

"Incoming!" Manning shouted in warning over the com link.

Streaking across the swamp came a fiery slash that went straight through the open doorway and impacted in the foyer. A thunderclap shook the entire building, the windows blowing out in a shower of glass, tall columns supporting the colonnade tumbling away as the whole front of the mansion began to sag and break apart.

"Sweet Jesus!" Marasco cursed, rushing to the greenhouse wall and pressing his face against the glass to see. "What the fuck are you people doing? I thought we had a deal!"

"That wasn't us. Hold," McCarter snapped, covering the cell phone and touching his throat mike. "Cal, Gary, try for a pincers strike and bring down the shooters. Alive if possible, but watch your arses."

"On it," Manning replied, sounding as if he were already running.

Just then, another LAW rocket came from the hillside and struck the garage. The vehicles lifted off the ground as their gas tanks exploded, flame stretching out to the front lawn. A bodyguard caught by the fire burst into flames and fell to his knees, shrieking while the others ran about in blind panic.

"Hold, my ass," Marasco barked, rushing to a flowerpot and plunging his hand into the peat moss to come out with a snub-nosed handgun wrapped in a plastic lunch bag. "What sort of a double cross are you guys trying to pull here? We got a deal!"

Sweeping the forest and hills with the field glasses, McCarter bit back a curse, but knew there was no choice. As long as the mafioso kept his side, they had to do the same.

"Meet me at the gatehouse!" the Don commanded, heading for the door. "I have another car down the road in a fishing shed."

A back door, eh? Clever. "Stay exactly where you are!" McCarter ordered into the cell phone, grabbing his MP-5 subgun from a branch. "Do nothing!"

There was another flash and a third LAW streaked in to hit the mansion again. The building was writhing in flames, red-hot embers swarming into the smoky sky. On the lawn, the remaining bodyguards were taking refuge along the brick wall. Without guns, the men had no clear idea of what they could do under attack.

"What, are you insane?" the Don shouted, thumbing back the hammer on his plastic-wrapped gun. "They're dropping bombs on me!"

"The rockets are hitting exactly where you are not," McCarter corrected sternly. "They can see you in that glass house. This is a ploy to lure us out of hiding. Not terminate you!"

"So I'm bait for both sides," the mafioso growled, crushing the receiver in his hand. "Damn you all. Now stop wasting time talking and go kill the sons of bitches."

Turning off the cell phone, McCarter had to admit the Don was cool under fire. He had to have inherited a modicum of brains along with the famous Marasco balls.

"Cal, open fire in a spiral around the last seen launch," McCarter snapped into his throat mike, working the bolt on his MP-5. "T.J., pound the top of the hillside with your mortar. Force them down into the swamp where they can't use the LAW. Rafe and I will take them out. And watch for sleepers in the trees and the water. These aren't amateurs.''

''Roger!'' Hawkins replied, and seconds later there came the telltale whistling once more and the crest of the hillside began erupting in explosions, pieces of uprooted trees and fireballs dotting the crest of the ridge.

Descending from the banyan tree, McCarter and Encizo took off at a full run into the swampland. Staying on dry land as much as possible, they soon had to start wading through the dark waters, mud sucking at their boots. A profusion of Spanish moss and vines hung from the banyan trees, seriously reducing visibility. Swarms of fish filled the water, while snakes slithered in the mud and toads festooned nearly every tree trunk and rock. Somewhere close, an alligator bawled in anger, then went silent as another barrage of 60 mm mortar rounds detonated on the hill, coming ever closer.

''I have visual contact,'' Manning said, then came the telltale boom of his Barrett Light Fifty. ''Missed! The target is four men in ghillie suits. Repeat, four men. Heading your way.''

The ghillie suit was a full-body camouflage suit covering a soldier from head to toe. There was even a hood for the face. In swamps and dense jungles it made the person wearing it almost invisible.

''Night vision,'' McCarter said, flipping down the goggles of his helmet. He caught a brief movement to the west and stopped firing just in time when he recognized James.

The pounding fury of the 60 mm mortar rounds was shaking the swamp by now, leaves and soldiers falling off the trees. Screaming birds were racing through the treetops away from the explosions, and then two of the trees detonated, clearing away the moss and leaves for twenty yards, dozens of dead birds falling into the watery swamp.

"Claymores in the trees!" Encizo warned, firing his MP-5 in short bursts. A nearby tree shuddered as a shower of antipersonnel fléchettes hit the muddy water.

"Rafe, hold your position!" McCarter ordered, kneeling in the filthy muck and triggering a long burst into the curtains of Spanish moss. Dead birds fell into the water, disturbing clouds of buzzing mosquitoes.

Steadily, the hammering of the mortar grew in volume and power, the knee-deep swamp shaking with every blast.

"Three o'clock clear," James reported.

"Nine o'clock clear," Manning added. "Looks like they're coming straight for you, David."

"Good!" McCarter growled, spraying the woods directly ahead with a figure eight of 9 mm rounds.

"David, I have to ease off the attack. The rounds are falling too close to your position," Hawkins warned over the com link. "Any closer and I'll be mailing your family a folded flag!"

"Keep that mortar going!" McCarter demanded,

stitching an alligator that rose from the reeking mud. The deadly animal rolled over as it died, exposing its pale belly to the sky. "Drive those bastards to us and that's an order!"

Suddenly, there was a fiery flash of light and a LAW rocket streaked toward the soldiers. McCarter and Encizo dived into the swamp and the rocket zoomed by to hit a sunken log. The bayou rocked from the force of the blast, black water and mud spraying out in every direction.

There was a blur of green and Encizo fired. Not at the movement, but at the nearest tree. The trunk splintered from the 9 mm rounds and a man cried out, stumbling into view holding a bloody neck, a dagger of green wood sticking out of his spurting throat. Knowing the merc was already a dead man from the cut artery, McCarter mercifully put a burst in the man's head and the corpse fell with a splash.

The strident concussions of the 60 mm rounds were starting to slap the faces of the Stony Man warriors when three more camouflaged figures finally burst from the dense foliage, firing AK-74 assault rifles with 30 mm grenade launchers attached underneath the main barrel.

Stepping behind a tree, McCarter took the lead man and tried to simply wound him in the legs. But just as he fired, the man tried to dive out of the way and his chest got riddled with bullets. He flopped into the water and stayed there facedown.

"Alive, we want them alive, damn it!" McCarter

barked. "Rafe, Cal, put them in a box! Gary, close the lid!"

The two commandos bracketed the last two mercenaries in a withering cross fire, the water jumping all around them from the incoming lead. Trapped, the mercs launched their 30 mm grenades into the woods, adding to the pyrotechnic chaos but nothing more.

Then the Barrett spoke, slamming the AK-74 out of the grip of the bigger merc just as he was thumbing in another 30 mm shell. The weapon shattered from the impact and flew away in pieces as the gunner clumsily clawed at his web harness trying to draw a side arm, but his flopping hands were useless, every bone in them broken from the sledgehammer hit of the .50 hardball round.

Manning stroked the Barrett's trigger again, blowing a chunk out of a banyan tree alongside the mercs and they desperately went back-to-back, one struggling to reload his pistol while the other simply stood there, flicking his eyes from left to right seeking any avenue of escape.

"Cease firing, T.J.," McCarter said in his throat mike, and a ringing silence washed over the swamp.

The two groups looked hard at each other for a long minute, then the first merc threw his pistol into the dirty water and raised his bloody hands.

"Take them," McCarter said, ready for betrayal.

Encizo worked the bolt on his MP-5 as James stepped into view from a curtain of Spanish moss. Then Manning arrived brandishing the Barrett rifle, and seconds later Hawkins joined the scene, sporting a brace of the MP-5s. The appearance of so many seemed to take the fight out of the prisoners and they submitted to a search without incident. Everything taken off them was placed in a plastic bag and sealed tight.

"Start walking," McCarter ordered, gesturing with his MP-5.

Sloshing through the swamp, Phoenix Force and its prisoners began heading toward the roadway to the north and a waiting helicopter.

Letting the others get slightly ahead, Encizo pulled out his cell phone and tapped in a number.

"Yeah?" a voice asked suspiciously.

"It's over," he said into the cell phone. "You're safe for the moment, but I would seriously consider moving to another country for the sake of your family." The Stony Man warrior then turned off the phone, slipped it back into the cushioned pocket on his leg and rejoined the others, herding the mercs to some place private for a thorough debriefing.

CHAPTER THIRTEEN

Oval Office, Washington, D.C.

The room was quiet and cool, the drapes closed on the windows, the ventilators only giving a hushed murmur. Sitting behind his desk, the President of the United States was shuffling reports, reading most of them at a single glance.

"So you got a latent print off one of the Shkvals and it matches the statement of the captured mercenaries," the President said, laying a document aside. Where his fingers touched, the security paper was turning a brilliant crimson. His were the only prints on the Russian report.

"Yes, sir, the enemy now has a name. A Soviet special-forces counterinsurgence team known as Red Dagger," Brognola said. "Officially disbanded in 1997, but apparently they're still together. The man in charge is former Sergeant Jozsef Vadas. His XO is a former lieutenant-colonel, and the rest are lower ranks, but real hardcases—trained as Spetsnaz, Kremlin special ops, counterterrorism, political assassination, you name it. Back in the old days, these were the people trained to hunt and kill rogue KGB agents. They have eliminated entire civilian villages during missions and are utterly ruthless.''

''A Czech sergeant planned all of this?'' the President asked, shaking his head. ''Incredible.''

Brognola leaned forward in his chair. ''Mr. President, sergeants run the army of every nation, and always have. They know how to do everything, including bust the rules to get the job done.''

''The possibility of this Red Dagger having a tactical nuclear device is a major concern. Are you sure it wouldn't be best to declare martial law and send troops into Los Angeles?''

''Sir, that's the absolute surest way I know to make these men use the nuke,'' Brognola said resolutely. ''Our teams will find them quietly, with a minimum of lives lost.''

The politician leaned back in his chair. ''Estimated time frame?''

''Unknown, sir. This could be done by tomorrow, or next month, or never. We're not gods, and do lose a battle sometimes.''

''Unacceptable,'' the President told him.

Brognola frowned.

''Don't misunderstand me, Hal,'' the Man corrected, sitting upright once more. ''I know that sometimes we lose, even lose big. That's just a reality of life. Nobody wins forever. What I meant is that the unknown factor is unacceptable. I'm receiving more and more reports of Shkvals striking civilian targets around the world, and now I'm waiting for one of these to be a nuclear strike. A single tactical nuke detonated offshore could destroy Los Angeles, New York, London, any major coastal city.''

Brognola understood. If a tac nuke was detonated in downtown Los Angeles, it would destroy ten square blocks. Maybe half a million people dead. But if the nuke was detonated in deep water along the coast, the boiling wave of radioactive steam and mud would form a tidal wave that could smash the city flat. Same size bomb, ten times the number of people killed.

''Hopefully, they don't know how to use a nuke,'' Brognola said. ''But looking at their background, it's rather unlikely. I assume the Navy is on full alert, sir?''

The President laid his hands upon the desk and leaned forward. ''Hal, we're on war status. Def Con Four. In fact, only an hour before this report arrived, the White House press secretary announced that I would be spearheading a conference on terrorism to discuss these worldwide attacks. We're going for maximum coverage—newspapers, television, cable and every superpower will be sending a representative. Mostly just ambassadors. Only the prime minister of England has the guts to join me in person on the dais for this media conference.''

''Very tempting, sir. But I don't think Vadas and

his people would be stupid enough to try for such a target. The security will be too good.''

''That wasn't the idea, Hal. This is to be a public show of strength, to prove we aren't afraid of the terrorist groups the Czechs are supplying. Any sign of weakness will only encourage them to do more. If this lures Vadas out of hiding, then I trust you to catch him. But for a hundred other political reasons, this conference must be held, and soon.''

Setting his jaw, Brognola considered that statement. For political reasons, America never openly declared war on Colombia and napalmed the coca fields into ash. For political reasons, Congress had been allowed to play with Vietnam like a game while brave men lost their lives in foreign paddies for a decade. For political reasons, the Korean War hadn't been settled in an hour with one ICBM on Chinese soil.

''Understood, sir. Camp David as usual, sir? No, that's too close to the sea,'' Brognola added immediately. ''How about the UN Building in New York? No, that's even closer. Damn it, sir, every major city has a source of water. There is no conference center completely distant from a waterway. Even Salt Lake City has a river and a dam. How about Cheyenne Mountain?''

The President waved that aside. ''Not enough exposure. Besides, it has already been publicly announced that the conference is going to be held at

San Clemente. Several former presidents will be in attendance with me, along with the foreign dignitaries.''

"No," Brognola stated flatly. "Absolutely not. That's only eighty miles from L.A. If anything happens, all of you could be killed!"

Patiently waiting, the President said nothing as he watched the Justice man shift mental gears.

"Damn, you do have to hold the conference," Brognola stated, backpedaling. "The world media must be running with the story by now. If you were to cancel, the Czechs would guess why and leave Los Angeles immediately, and we might never get this close to them again."

"Exactly," the President said simply. "Bad timing, but there is nothing we can do but proceed and make it appear that we're in the dark. Thankfully this isn't ancient Rome. Even if something does happen to me, America will go on."

"Accepted," Brognola said with a wooden face, masking his true emotions on the matter. "But to be realistic, security will be tight. I'll have the ARS go over the retreat and conference hall with a microscope long before the first Marine honor guard arrives."

"I certainly hope so," the politician said, glancing at a picture of his wife and children on the littered desk. "Do your best to keep me alive, Hal, but get these people at any cost. That's more important."

Brognola stood and held out his hand. The President stood and they shook, two soldiers committed to the battle.

"Don't worry, sir," Brognola said. "Stony Man won't let you down."

Los Angeles, California

WAVES OF HEAT shimmered off the black tarmac of the private airfield as the Hercules C-130 transport rolled to a stop. With a hiss of hydraulics, the rear hatch eased to the ground and three men strode from the plane carrying black gym bags. The rest of the field and airport were empty. But that was why Able Team had chosen the location.

The captured mercs hadn't been able to give a location for the Czech soldiers. Their dead commander had handled all communications with the Czechs over the Internet for security reasons, and their pay had been transferred from a Swiss bank to their Cayman Island account by encrypted transmissions.

However, Kurtzman discovered the money in the wallet of the dead merc was mostly crisp new hundred-dollar bills—but slightly stained with a lubricant. Cash withdrawn from an ATM. Using a Department of the Treasury hunter program, the computer wizard backtracked the serial numbers on the money to a large transfer of overseas funds handled discreetly by a bank in the Fox Hills area of Los Angeles and withdrawn as cash. That wasn't such an unusual occurrence in major cities, where legitimate businessmen and criminals both needed untraceable funds for bribes and payoffs. But other bills listed in the same withdrawal also appeared in deposits made by local stores.

Bull's-eye. Money from the withdrawal that paid a mercenary soldier also bought groceries and assorted sundries in one L.A. neighborhood. That could be where the Czechs were hiding. The arms dealers had expertly laundered their dirty profits from the sale of the Shkvals into legal millions, and only paid for items using cash, but cash taken from an ATM where every serial number on every bill was digitally recorded.

Unfortunately, the dispersal pattern of the purchases was too random for analysis, but that was where Able Team would start its hunt, the Fox Hills Mall. This slim lead was still their best chance to find the Czech merchants of disaster and bring them down hard.

Watching the big men from behind a chain-link safety fence, a slim brunette in a neat pantsuit waved at the trio and started for the gate when somebody bumped her from behind. Instantly, she shot out a hand and caught the man by the throat, crushing his windpipe. Helpless in the woman's grip, the fellow could only wheeze and start to turn red.

"Give it back," she ordered in a stern tone, holding out her empty hand.

Fumbling frantically, the thief returned the wallet he had lifted from her purse.

After checking to make sure the money and credit cards were still in place, the woman released her grip, giving a little shove at the end to knock the pick-pocket to the ground.

"Next time you do a fine-wire, I'll blow your god-damn head off," she said sweetly, brushing back her short jacket to expose the automatic pistol in a hip holster.

Massaging his throat, the thief whispered an apology and hurried away, mixing with the ground crew and the few students for the parachute school.

Nodding to the security guard at the open gate, Able Team walked around the metal detectors and walked toward the brunette heading their way.

"Trouble?" Blancanales asked, tilting his head forward to look over his sunglasses.

"Nothing important," Toni Blancanales said with a smile, and hugged her brother. "Damn, it's good to see you."

The conversation paused as the students walked out onto the tarmac while the skydiving instructor constantly fed them last-minute encouragement. A few of the older students looked pale, but resolute to get their first taste of air.

Shifting the weapons bag in his grip, Rosario Blancanales kissed her cheek. "You look good, kid. Lose some weight?"

"Nice try, 'Politician,' but you say that every time we meet," Toni replied, releasing the man. "It doesn't get you off the hook for not writing more often."

"Hey, I've been busy."

"Iran, New York, Paris, yes, I keep track."

Gadgets Schwarz draped an arm around her waist and gave the woman a friendly hug. "Did you get us transport?"

"No problem. Able Group Security aims to please," she stated, returning the gesture. "A van is over in the main parking lot. I set it up just the way you like it."

"Thanks," Lyons rumbled, moving past the cinder-block airport terminal, a fat seagull watching from the roof of the tower. "By the way, any local news that might tie in with our perps?"

"Such as?" she asked, bumping a hip into the ex-cop as a way of saying welcome home.

He gave a rare smile. Toni was the sister of his brother-in-arms, and Carl Lyons felt like an uncle to the young woman. Aside from his son, Tommy, she was the closet thing to family he had still kicking in the world.

"Well, any buildings burn down only to explode when the basement caught fire?" he suggested, heading toward the parking lot. "Flocks of birds falling dead from the sky, ships sinking without a known cause?"

"The fire and ships I understand, but dead birds?" Toni bit a lip for a moment. "Oh, from the burned-off poisonous byproducts. Nothing like that. L.A. is just L.A., as always. Nothing suspicious."

Grunting in reply, Lyons strode along the black asphalt and looked over the peaceful airport, allowing himself to feel the heat of the West Coast seep into his bones. He preferred the quiet greenery of Virginia, but L.A. charged his soul, made him feel more alive. It was a hard, unforgiving city, with mean streets like nowhere else in the world, but L.A. was home to him, and that's all there was to the matter.

As the four people climbed inside the vehicle, Toni ran a quick check on the internal security systems. The rear of the spacious cargo van was packed with electric equipment and an assortment of weapons. The rear windows were also tinted to prevent casual observation of the military hardware. It was nothing like the legendary War Wagon, but more than heavily armed enough for this mission.

"We're clear," she stated, placing the EM scanner into a pocket. "No bugs, no bombs. Now what the hell is so damn important that you couldn't discuss it over a scrambled phone circuit?"

While Gadgets checked over the radio equipment and jacked his laptop into the coded modem, her brother and Lyons brought her up-to-date on events. When the equipment was ready, Schwarz hit a button on the burst transmitter and the announcement of their safe arrival squealed straight up into space, the report compressed into a half-second tone that was impossible to trace by triangulation or intercept. The Farm couldn't directly communicate with Able Team without compromising the mission, but at least the electronics wizard could keep Price and the others apprised of their whereabouts and status on a regular basis.

"Damn, so the Czechs are here in L.A.," Toni said, starting the engine and pulling out of the parking lot. "I was afraid of that."

"They're here at the moment," Lyons told her, opening the equipment bag between his feet and using a speedloader to fill the cylinder of his Colt .357 Python revolver. "But when Vadas and his people find out the railroad shipment has been seized, they'll either try to silently slip away or blast an escape to freedom."

"Both are bad news," she agreed, slipping effortlessly into the highway traffic. "What's Phoenix Force doing while you're checking the stores in the Fox Hills area for a lead?"

Removing his jacket, her brother slipped on a shoulder holster. "Now that we have a target zone," he said adjusting the strap, "Carmen was able to focus a NASA satellite on Los Angeles and find elemental traces of fusing byproducts in the atmosphere over the city. With the shifting winds there's no way to determine a focal point, but nobody legal would waste money incinerating the toxins. It's illegal to burn, and cheaper to bury."

"Unfortunately, there were sixteen legal foundries registered in the greater Los Angeles basin, and maybe that many again illegal ones," Schwarz explained, shutting down the communications gear.

"Fusing is a very profitable business. Even more so if you don't obey the government EPA regulations."

Adjusting her sun visor, Toni whistled. Well, well, a new crime was born every day here. Welcome to L.A. "Say roughly double that many illegal sites... Damn, Phoenix Force has its work cut out trying that angle."

"We all do," Lyons said, looking over the new construction as they entered the outskirts of the sprawling metropolis. New buildings, new billboards, the city was never the same even after a short time away.

"How are you going to play it?" she asked, angling through the traffic. Talking on a cell phone while applying lipstick, a platinum blonde in a pink Lamborghini tried to cut off the van, and Toni fought down the urge to block the way and allowed the woman to take the lead. This was business—stay low, be cool was the key.

"We're going in as loan sharks collecting on overdue vig," Lyons said, tucking away his weapon, then pulling it again to check the draw. Satisfied, he holstered the piece and leaned back in the seat. "I was thinking you might handle a few of the better stores in the mall itself as the FBI investigating credit-card fraud. That way we don't have to keep changing clothes to stay in character."

"No problem."

"Got a cheap blue suit?" Schwarz asked, racking the slide on his SPAS-12 shotgun custom-mounted under the main barrel of his M-16 assault rifle. The shotgun was loaded with stun bags in the hope of taking at least one of the Czech soldiers alive.

"Sure do. Standard FBI uniform and the bad flats to go with it," Toni replied, shifting gears and taking an exit onto southbound Route 405. "Along with a fake commission book that's so good it scares the hell out of Brognola. That'll get me into their files. Anything special you want?"

"Sure," Rosario said, thumbing a 40 mm round into the breech of the grenade launcher attached to his assault rifle. "Find out what Casax means. That'd help a lot."

As the van began to enter the city proper, the woman furrowed her brow at the word and started to speak, then paused. Casax. Why did that name sound so familiar?

Computer Room, Stony Man Farm

"ANY LUCK on tracking the sale of the Cray computers?" Barbara Price asked as she entered the Computer Room and approached Kurtzman's station.

"Nothing so far," Kurtzman replied, rubbing his face. There was a half-filled mug of coffee on the top of his console, and snack-food wrappers littered the floor.

"Cray makes a lot of them," the computer expert said, turning to face the mission controller. "And six have been stolen across the world in the last ten years.

Who's to say we're not facing a Japanese Cray stolen over there and shipped here?''

"Wouldn't the liquid-nitrogen cooling system make it a four-star bitch to move?" Price asked.

"Only needs that when it's working," Kurtzman replied. "In shipment it would just be mere electronic equipment."

Too bad, Price thought, taking a chair then hitting a button to delete the e-mail. She had been counting on finding the Cray since the liquid-nitrogen angle had failed to pan out completely. There were simply too many legal uses for the volatile fluid. There had to be four hundred liquid-gas companies that sold thousands of gallons every day. Even NASA sold off the excess from its plants in Houston and Florida. Liquid nitrogen had no street value, and as a weapon it was worse than useless. Blow a tanker of fifty thousand gallons and people who were standing a hundred feet away wouldn't be killed. It vaporized incredibly fast in the open.

"Any reported thefts of liquid nitrogen?" she asked hopefully, opening an encrypted message from Brognola. The ARS had cleared San Clemente and the President was on his way. Every military base in the area was on full alert, ready to strike. All they needed were the coordinates of a dedicated target to blow it off the map.

"Lots of small thefts, mostly from college science labs," Kurtzman said, running stiff fingers through his hair. "Every year some idiot frat boy loses a hand trying to use the stuff to chill a keg of beer. But those are only liter bottles, nothing in the quantities we're talking about.''

"Damn," she muttered.

"Okay, heads up, people!" Katz said, rapping his prothesis on the console for their attention. "We've hit a brick wall, so let's take a different approach. I want police reports of any unusual smells at night, or gunfire with no body discovered. Also, anybody admitted to a hospital with heat exhaustion, severe stomach cramps or frostbite.''

"Frostbite?" Delahunt repeated. "Ah, from the liquid nitrogen for the Crays. Understood.''

"Now, if they run, what's the best route out of the city?" Katz continued. "I want the plans for the local sewers, phone-line access tunnels, geological-probe data along the fault lines. Cargo manifests for every plane in LAX going anywhere. And not just planes large enough to carry the five men and a single Shkval, but for every plane. They might be traveling individually to confuse the trail. Remember, these people are trained to hunt and kill terrorists. They know how to disappear in crowds and start riots to avoid capture.''

"It's almost as if we're facing the Soviet version of Stony Man," Akira Tokaido muttered.

Glancing at the young man, Price admitted, "That's a lot closer than you want to know.''

"Hunt, check the 911 records of the phone company. Look for reports of any unusual explosions or sick children with fast and abnormal heartbeats,'' Kurtzman directed.

''I see, children finding any C-4 would play with it like modeling clay and get C-4 poisoning,'' the professor muttered around his pipe. ''I'll hit the street clinics first, then the EMTs and then the major hospitals.''

''Good man. Akira, keep after the enemy Crays. Katz will spearhead this for the moment. I'm going to ride command with Barbara and Hal on the conference in San Clemente,'' Kurtzman stated, both hands busy on his control board. ''Carmen, hack into the local banks, link to the security cameras and run a face-identification program. We only have a picture of the Czech officer, Zofchak, but that's one out of five and we might get lucky.''

''Banks are too limited. I'll try the streetlights,'' Delahunt said, her hands playing across a keyboard with a concert pianist. Monitors were flashing with command sequences and coded files. That should work, Los Angeles was one of the very first major cities to install cameras at intersections to get the license plate numbers of speeding cars. Damn, the local PD had some good encryption on those!

''Need a hand?'' Kurtzman asked, flipping a switch to slave a section of his master console with hers. But as his side screens blinked into life, he saw she was already past the police firewall and into the city-wide system.

''Akira, if Carmen finds anything, follow her lead,

but take no direct action without my direct authorization. We may only get one shot at these people.''

''Way ahead of you, chief,'' Tokaido said, sliding a new CD into his built-in stereo. His earphones began to move from the loud music, but his face took on a serene expression as he rode the matrix of the world searching for any trace of the enemy Cray. One by one, he shielded off the known Crays in the nation, Pentagon, IRS, CIA, Microsoft, until he was alone in an electronic spiderweb of trip wires, poised and ready, eagerly waiting for the prey to show itself and be destroyed.

''There's still another matter,'' Katz said gruffly, the laser printer at his console already sighing as it started feeding out police reports and newspaper clippings. ''Vadas will either leave the Shkvals behind because they're too heavy, or take some along to help blow their way to freedom. I need to know the theoretical range of a Shkval traveling through the air.''

The destructive power of a Russian VLR-36 tactical nuke he already knew in full detail. And if forced into a corner, Stony Man would allow the arms dealers to escape alive rather than let Los Angeles be destroyed by a radioactive steam cloud. But the teams would rather die themselves than allow even one of the Czechs to escape alive and start this nightmare all over again somewhere else in the world.

''Full stats on the Shkvals. On it,'' Price said, and hit the intercom button. ''Attention, Cowboy, please report to the Computer Room at once.''

"On the way," his voice crackled from a speaker.

Katz grunted. "I also want silhouette files of the rocket exhaust of the torpedoes, thermal patterns and shock-diamond configuration. Send those to CINC-PACFLT at Coronado Base in case we need an air strike."

"You're planning for the high command of the Pacific Fleet to launch a naval air strike on downtown L.A.?" Price demanded, swiveling in her chair. Coronado Base was the Navy's equivalent of Cheyenne Mountain in Wyoming. The island hardsite was designed to protect, by itself, the entire western coast of America. A fortress supreme of ICBM missile batteries, aircraft-carrier attack groups, entire submarine fleets and the legendary headquarters of the Navy SEALs.

"Hoping? No. Planning, yes. We must prepare for what an enemy can do," the veteran explained succinctly, "not for only what they might do."

Grudgingly, the woman accepted that. "Fair enough. But L.A. is a big city," Price said. "Five million people. That's an ocean of humanity for the Czechs to hide within."

"No, it's a cage," Kurtzman countered as the door to the room began to cycle open and Kissinger walked in with an armful of papers. "And we're going to lock the door and drown these bastards in their own damn blood."

CHAPTER FOURTEEN

Casax, California

With a metallic bang, the power switch was jerked open and the great hum of the microwave blast furnace slowly died away until there was only silence. The metal walls of the furnace still radiated a terrible heat, but the sting was already gone as the hundreds of pounds of molten steel started to cool.

Turning, Boris Bezdek and Davida Pran looked up from their work sheets and saw Jozsef Vadas standing near the control board with his hand still on the switch.

"The Americans have captured the Pennsylvania shipment," the big man said bluntly, "and terminated our mercenaries in New Orleans."

Bezdek muttered a vulgar word in Czech, and Pran spit on the floor.

"Did any of them talk?" Bezdek demanded.

Vadas shrugged. "Unknown. But it is a chance we cannot take."

"How soon could they attack?" Pran asked, shrugging his wide shoulders. A KEDR subgun was suddenly in his slim hands, and he worked the bolt to chamber a round.

"If they knew our true location," Vadas said bluntly, "they would already be here."

Nervously, the men listened for a moment, but there was only the steady ticking of the cooling furnace and the soft hiss of a steam-line safety valve sputtering away the last of its pressure.

Shaking off the apprehension, Bezdek placed the clipboard into a trash can and pulled on a pair of canvas gloves. "I'll start packing the C-4," he said, flexing his hands. One of the first lessons learned in handling raw plastic explosives was to wear gloves, or else your body absorbed some of the nitroglycerin from the claylike blocks and soon you were as sick as a dog with the heart rate of a humming bird.

"Take no supplies," Vadas ordered, then patted his shirt pocket. "Sergei and I each have a copy of the blueprints for the Shkvals burned onto a CD. That is all we need to start anew in Mendoza City. Speed is important now. Load the boat and the Eighties with all of our cash and weapons. Leave everything else. Solomon has already started activating the C-4 charges to destroy the factory."

"What about the Shkvals?" Pran asked in concern, glancing across the factory. Filling a nearby lattice were a dozen of the deadly rocket torpedoes, everything installed except the fuel for their compact engines.

Furrowing his brow, Vadas scowled. "How many are completely finished as of right now?"

"Fourteen."

Surprising news, and much better than he had hoped for. "Arm the boat, and put two in each Eighty. Just in case."

"No good," Bezdek countered. "The boat is full already. We packed a shipment to deliver to the Colombians."

"Then leave the torpedoes," Vadas stated. "We shall set them to launch into the city after the roof blows off of this location."

Just then the elevator opened and Solomon walked out with a large munitions bag draped over a powerful shoulder.

"When?" Pran asked, slowly tucking the KEDR away under his arm.

Vadas started for the elevator, his steps audible in the warm stillness. "We depart at noon."

Extracting a Russian satchel charge of C-4 from his bag, Solomon placed the explosives at the base of a steel pole that supported the concrete ceiling, wired in a radio detonator, set a secondary fuse and moved on, his hands already preparing another charge for the next pole.

"Are we still going to blow up San Offrey as we leave?" Pran growled.

"Why not? San Clemente is only forty miles away from the nuclear reactor," Bezdek said, jerking a thumb at an expensive stereo near the refrigerator. "I heard on the radio that the American President will be giving a speech on terrorism there tomorrow. The radioactive steam cloud from the Shkval strike will cover half the state.''

Vadas hit the call button and the doors opened. ''Even better,'' he pronounced in his horrible voice. ''All the more chaos to aid our departure.''

''And revenge,'' Pran growled.

His craggy hands full of squibs and timing pencils, Solomon looked up from the delicate work. ''Do we have time to blow up the beachfront reactor at San Offrey?''

Stepping into the elevator, Vadas turned to face his brother soldiers. ''Of course, comrades,'' he said as the elevator doors began to close. ''There is always time for revenge.''

Fox Hills Mall, Los Angeles

TONI BLANCANALES WALKED along the sidewalk of Rodeo Drive, heading for the next store on her ever shortening list. The clerks at the Curtis Mathais stereo store had been polite but useless. The same with the tailors at the Armani suit store. Her next stop was one that Able Team should have handled except that it was located between two of her other stops, and this saved time. A pizza shop. Talk about a long shot.

As Toni pushed open the door, a bell suspended overhead on a coiled spring sounded.

''Good morning, miss, how may I help you?'' the

clerk behind the counter started, then his voice faltered at the sight of the grim woman in the dark blue suit.

"Hank!" the clerk shouted over a shoulder.

A large fat man in a red-and-white-striped apron rushed out of the back room, his pudgy face and hands coated with flour. "What?" he snapped, then scowled.

"FBI, Special Agent Gable," Toni said, showing a commission booklet. "I need immediate access to your delivery records."

"Sure, sure, no problem," the man said nervously, wiping his hands clean on the apron. "What is it, some sort of drug-ring problem or something?"

"Sorry, but I'm really not at liberty to discuss the details, sir," Toni said in a hard, clipped voice. "Now if you will just show me the records, please."

The clerk nudged his boss with an elbow. "Hey, doesn't she need a warrant or a writ or something for this?" he asked.

"Do you want me to come back with a writ?" Toni said, deceptively friendly, leaning on the counter to make the men step back. "I can and I will. But it'll waste two hours of my time, and that will make me very unhappy."

"Yeah, well, if that's the law," the boss started hesitantly, clearly unsure of how to handle the matter.

"By the way, is this building up to the codes?" Toni asked, glancing around the store and running a fingertip along the top of the cash register. She made a disapproving face. "Tsk, tsk, how filthy. Is the fire inspection up to date, tax records in order for you and every employee you got? Then again, the Board of Health should really see this place. What a mess. I would be doing the city a favor closing this dump down for a month or two."

"A month?" the boss squeaked. "I'll be out of business closed for a month!"

Toni nodded in sympathy. "That would be a shame. Although, of course, if I had those records, the Bureau would be much too busy handling real criminals to waste a single second on some minor code violations. Now you were saying about the records?"

The clerk opened his mouth to speak, then shut it with a snap and went to answer the ringing phone.

"Yeah, yeah, I get the idea. Jeez, you Feds are pushy," the boss grumbled. "The delivery sheets are back in my office."

Following the fat man through the busy kitchen of the take-out joint, Toni let him open the door to the office, then sent the fat man away so she could be alone. The room was small, painted a utilitarian green, with painfully bright fluorescent lights, a pressboard desk, a cheap folding chair, a battered metal filing cabinet and a row of lockers lining one wall for the employees to hang their street clothes. A combination changing room and executive office. Very classy.

The top drawer of the file cabinet held employee records, job applications, medical leave and the like.

The next was filled with hanging manila folders covering a wide assortment of topics, including the delivery records. Checking the dates given by Gadgets, the woman soon found the address, five large pizzas with everything. Wasn't it five soldiers who attacked Murmansk, and were believed to be working with Vadas. Circumstantial evidence at best, but another link in the chain.

As a private investigator for Able Group, Toni was more familiar with Santa Monica and Malibu, but she recognized the neighborhood the address was in from the news reports on television. A run-down suburban area to the west of Fox Hills. Lots of gang wars, car junkyards and machine shops. A real bad neighborhood, and a prime location for Czech soldiers to hide their weapons factory.

Toni started to return the paper to its folder when a penciled notation on the margin caught her attention. The delivery person had been met outside of the house and paid on the curb. Damn! The house was just a blind drop chosen at random for the pickup. Checking to see how often the arms dealers got a delivery, the PI found a dozen more deliveries of five pizzas, also with blind drops on the sidewalk. But always at a different location.

Feeling a rush of adrenaline, the woman pulled out her pocket computer to check the location of the houses on a city map and immediately saw a pattern. Why hadn't they thought of this earlier! Where else in L.A. could the men have been hidden? It was so simple, it was brilliant.

Whipping out her cell phone, Toni started to call Lyons, then paused. If the arms dealers were this close, they might have their Cray monitoring the local wavelengths for keywords. Taking a moment, she tapped in the number and waited for a ring.

"Yeah?" Lyons answered. In the background came traffic noises; the men must be riding in the van.

"Uncle Able? This is Sister Phoebe," Toni said, deliberately mispronouncing the word just enough to let it sound like FBI.

"Did ya find what I asked for?" Lyons growled.

"Yes, I did, Uncle," Toni answered calmly. "They're in the river, down in the storm drain."

A MILE AWAY across town, Rosario Blancanales slammed on the brakes and brought the van to a rocking halt on top of an overpass. The men craned their necks to see over the berm of the road and down at the yawning chasm of a storm drain. Designed for the runoff water when the summer storms hit, the deep culverts stretched for miles across the entire city like open concrete veins.

"The storm drains," Schwarz said, scrunching his face. "Dry riverbeds that connect to the sea. Christ, those are perfect for smuggling the Shkvals into the city, especially during a rainstorm."

"There's something like eight hundred miles of the tunnels forming a maze under the city," Lyons added, remembering an old police lecture when he was just a rookie. "The DPW is adding new tunnels all the time. Not even the city has an accurate map anymore."

As cars behind them began to honk their horns, Blancanales put the van into gear and started moving again. "Knock a hole in any basement foundation and the Czechs would have direct access to the ocean!"

"Eight hundred miles of subterranean tunnels," Schwarz said, looking away from the window. "How the hell are we going to recon that by ourselves? It would take years to cover every side tunnel and passageway, even with a pack of ATF dogs trained to sniff for C-4."

Turning the steering wheel, Blancanales slipped the van into a parking space near the guardrail where they could still see into the storm drain. Over two hundred feet wide, maybe fifty deep with steeply sloping sides, the artificial river was only a dirty stream of water about a yard wide at present, the trickle meandering down the middle of the huge culvert. Tufts of weeds grew here and there, garbage was strewed about and a rusted shopping cart stuck out of a mound of mud.

"Eight hundred miles," he repeated. "We'd need an army."

"We have an army," Lyons said, pointing out the other side of the van into the distance. "And they've already done the advance recon for us."

The other men changed directions and saw a group of cardboard boxes arranged underneath a tall bridge.

Dressed in rags, some homeless people were cooking food over a smoky fire of burning car tires.

"They go everywhere," Lyons stated. "If anybody knows what's happening underneath the city, it's them."

"Good thing we're loan sharks," Schwarz said, fluffing the collar of his new silk shirt, partially unbuttoned to display the gold medallion hung around his neck. "Because the homeless really don't like cops."

"Well, it's certainly worth a try," Blancanales said, slipping the van into gear and starting for the nearest access ramp.

Reaching a cutoff a few blocks later, Schwarz got out to jimmy the padlock holding the wire gate shut, but found it was already disabled. Maybe by the homeless trying to keep some privacy, and maybe not. Taking it slow, Blancanales rolled down the steep embankment, then across the stream to openly approach the homeless people.

As the van approached the group, several women herded small children into the makeshift shelters of the cardboard boxes, and men armed with homemade knives and lengths of iron pipe formed a protective line.

Parking some distance away to appear less threatening, the men of Able Team got out of the vehicle and walked toward the frightened group. Most of the people in sight were dangerously thin, badly malnourished.

When Able Team was about ten yards away, a man ordered them to stop.

"What do you want, Officer?" he demanded suspiciously, tapping the iron pipe in his palm.

"We're not cops," Blancanales said, stuffing his hands into his pockets to appear less threatening.

Another man with long greasy hair snorted in contempt. "Bull," he croaked in a hoarse voice. "Ain't nobody comes here but cops and sob sisters, and I don't see any religious pamphlets, which means you're cops."

"Whoever we are, we're looking for some information," Lyons said, "and we'll pay well for it."

A boy looked eagerly at his father, but the man shook his head. "Go away," he muttered, thrusting the homemade shiv forward. "We don't know anything about anything. Wherever you're looking for, it isn't here."

"How can you say that," Blancanales said patiently, "when you don't know what it is yet?"

"Ain't nothing here but us," the old woman snapped from behind the men, her gums empty of teeth. Her age could have been forty or ninety; there was no way of telling.

"Look," Lyons started, but stopped as their faces took on an expression of terror when there came the sound of a revving car engine.

"They're back!" a man cried.

"Run for your lives!" another shouted at Able

Team as the rest of the homeless dived for cover inside their packing crates and boxes.

The sound of the finely tuned car engine got rapidly louder. Streaking down the access ramp was a small, bright yellow MG coupe. The Able Team commandos stood their ground, waiting to see what was going on, and watched as the little sports car streaked along the culvert passing the ramshackle tents of the homeless. Lyons saw a glitter of something shiny in the air then a glass bottle shattered on the side of a packing box and erupted into flame.

Lyons was shocked. A Molotov cocktail? The laughing driver of the MG spun the tiny coupe around and raced past the homeless again, tossing another bottle out the window. But this time, the three Stony Man warriors cut loose with their handguns and the container shattered in the air, raining fire on the muddy creek and nothing else.

Whooping and blaring the horn, the two men inside the MG hit the gas and started to race away, but Able Team dropped into a firing stance and cut loose. Sparks flew off the trunk and rear bumper of the imported sports car from the barrage of ricochets, then a tire blew off the rim and the racing vehicle sharply lurched up the embankment and went into a slide as it hit a slick patch of mud. Out of control, the coupe banked too hard and flipped over, tumbling back down to the dirty concrete floor of the culvert and landing right side up.

As Able Team sprinted toward the battered roadster, both of the doors flung open and two well-dressed young men staggered into view, one of them holding a hand to the side of his bloody face. Seconds later the inside of the MG whoofed into flames with a shattering of glass, showing that there had been a lot more of the Molotov cocktails inside the coupe.

"My car! You bastards ruined my car!" the bloody man yelled.

The other drew a nickel-plated Colt .32 pistol and worked the slide. "I'll kill you bums for that!"

Able Team shot in unison and the armed man flew backward with a dozen rounds in his chest.

"No. You shot him," the driver gasped in shock, lowering his bloody hand. "Why did you do it? We weren't hurting anybody!"

"You firebombed families!" Schwarz snarled. "Women and children!"

The young man seemed confused. "B-but they're just bums," he said in explanation. "Not real people like us. They're nobodies. Who cares? We do it all the time."

They'd done it before? No wonder the homeless were so wary of strangers. Breathing deeply, Lyons felt a burning anger, and he dropped his Colt Python to advance upon the man with only his bare hands. The wounded driver had to have seen the murder in Lyons's face because he went deathly pale.

"If you touch me, I'll sue!" he warned in a quaking voice. "I'm rich! My lawyers will eat you alive in court, and you'll live for the rest of your life paying my lawyer.''

Lyons remained silent, flexing his big hands menacingly.

Finally understanding the situation, the driver clawed under his shirt to pull out a Beretta .22 Marksman. Instantly, Lyons rolled out of the way and Blancanales took the down the gunner.

Going to the bleeding forms, Able Team checked to make sure the men were dead, then tossed the bodies into the burning MG to make it look like an accident until the bullet holes were found. Reloading their weapons, the men returned to try to help with the fire, but it was already out, the cardboard shed burned to the ground in only minutes.

Most of the homeless were already on the move, slinking down the culvert between the piles of old tires and storm-tossed wreckage. The covert specialists knew that the police would eventually arrive, and it would be better if nobody was here to answer any questions.

A limping man worked his way to the team and just looked at them for a while before speaking. ''They've been doing that for months,'' he finally said. ''Killed three of us so far.''

There was no hint of gratitude in the sentence. It was just a statement of fact.

''Well, they'll never do it again,'' Blancanales said. Thrill killers, the worst scum in the world. At least the Czech arms dealers did it for money, not just to get their jollies off inflicting pain on others. Somehow that made them less evil than joy-riding yuppies armed with the flaming bottles of gasoline. The Able Team commando shook his head. It was a mad world.

"No cop would have done that," the man said, rubbing his stubbly chin.

"Told you we weren't cops," Lyons said, then turned and started for the van. But he only got a few yards before a voice called out for him to halt.

"Yes?" Lyons asked patiently.

"I guess you ain't cops," the man said sullenly, scratching under his rags. "Big men, foreign accents, been moving machinery at night. That what ya looking for?"

Lyons nodded.

The man jerked a thumb over his shoulder. "Two miles to the north, tunnel 34. Nobody goes there anymore. Haven't for a year. Anybody goes into 34, never comes out again."

Schwarz was already pulling a map of the drains on his handheld computer.

"Ever?" Blancanales asked.

The man shook his head. "They just vanish. We often camp in front of it, so we know at least one direction the cleaners won't come for us."

Pay dirt. That must be the entrance to the maze. From there they could find the factory.

"Cleaners," Lyons repeated. "That your name for the freaks trying to clean the streets of you."

The homeless man shrugged. "You helped us, now we helped you. We're even. Go away."

"We can help more," Blancanales started, reaching for his wallet.

Furious, the homeless man snarled, "Yeah? You got jobs for us in that pocket? That's what we need, jobs. Not a goddamn handout, not fucking charity. Jobs. Any job." His angry eased as quickly as it came, and he shrugged in resignation again. "Oh, just go away."

"No," Lyons said gruffly, removing his jacket. "Because I don't take charity either, buddy. You warned us before they attacked, and you damn well didn't have to do that. So we're not even yet." Unbuckling his shoulder rig, Lyons passed over the holster, the .357 Colt Python and a handful of speed loaders.

"Protect your family," the former cop said. It wasn't a request.

His hands full of the weapon, the man looked Lyons straight in the eyes for the very first time, nodded in thanks and started limping away after the others.

"Sometimes I think we're fighting the wrong war," Schwarz said, the smoke from the smoldering cardboard shed wafting over them.

Lyons disagreed. "Same war," he muttered, "just different battles."

"Let's check that tunnel," Blancanales said, heading for the van.

CHAPTER FIFTEEN

Culvert City, West Los Angeles

Attaché case in hand, Calvin James walked from the building of All-Steel Foundries and climbed into the van, trying not to wrinkle his expensive clothes.

"Move on," he reported, loosening the Hugo Boss tie. "This place is clean."

"Too bad," Hawkins said, starting the engine and moving into the stream of traffic. "This was our most likely candidate."

Phoenix Force had started to check the legal fusing factories for a secret second manufacturing plant. It was a long shot, but every possibility had to be investigated. But so far, nothing.

If there had been time, McCarter would have preferred to pretend they were mercs and try to get hired by the Czechs on the Internet, but that subterfuge would have taken days, maybe weeks, to pull off correctly, and right now this was a race against the clock. Which meant more direct and more dangerous tactics. There was no other way to find the Czech soldiers but to walk into each factory and do a hardsite recon for the target.

"I'll take the next," McCarter said, straightening his collar.

Driving along Rodeo Drive, but not the nice section of the world-famous road, the team angled onto West Jefferson and passed by several machine shops until reaching a newly refurbished brick building that read California Steel and Experimental Alloys.

"Well, what do we have here?" Encizo asked, working the arming bolt of his MP-5.

"Casax," Manning whispered, sweeping the front of the factory with the scope of his Barrett.

"Could be," McCarter agreed, checking the 9 mm Browning Hi-Power tucked into his belt. The building stood by itself with empty lots on both sides and a junkyard directly behind. It couldn't have been more isolated while still inside the city limits of Los Angeles.

"If I'm not back in twenty minutes, assume the worst and come get me," the warrior advised, checking his hair in the rearview mirror.

"We'll come running," Hawkins stated.

Taking the briefcase from James, McCarter exited the van and started across the street toward somber brick monolith of California Alloys.

Opening the front door, McCarter found himself in a small alcove. Closing the street door, he pressed a button on the second door to announce his presence. The secretary behind the receptionist desk buzzed him in, but as he entered the lobby he suddenly knew that something was wrong. The secretary glanced at a hooded monitor, then snapped her head toward him in horror.

Instantly, McCarter drew his weapon, and there was a sharp sting in his neck, a feathery tuft visible just above his collar. A tranquilizer dart! A wave of drunken warmth blurred the world around him, and McCarter tried his Browning at the tinted front window to alert the rest of his team. But his hands were already numb, and as he struggled to regain control of his body, a big man stepped into view from a corridor and loaded a dart into an air pistol. It had to be Jozsef Vadas. This was the weapons factory! McCarter got off a single round from his weapon, the 9 mm hardball slug cracking a tile. Then Vadas fired another dart and hit the Stony Man warrior in the thigh. McCarter threw himself forward but stumbled over his own feet and fell down a tunnel of darkness.

DRUMMING HIS FINGERS on the steering wheel, Hawkins impatiently checked the dashboard clock. ''He's late. David must have found them.''

''Or he's digging for more info. Should we go in and risk blowing his cover?'' Encizo asked, pulling on NATO body armor. The multiple layers of Teflon, titanium and Kevlar stopped most small-caliber rounds, along with knives and hammers. The only drawback was that it couldn't be worn secretly under street clothes. The angular contours that maximized deflection were unlike anything human.

"Contact the Farm," Manning suggested, doing the same. Every combat instinct the soldier had told him the balloon had gone up and McCarter's life could now be measured by the ticks of a clock.

James went to the burst radio and prepared a message, but as he tried to broadcast there came a wailing keen that filled the van.

"Damn airwaves are being jammed," he cursed, turning off the communications set. "I'd say that he found Vadas."

"Let's find out," Hawkins growled, stepping onto the street. But even as he walked around the parked van, the building across the street went dark and steel shutters rolled down to cover the doors and windows.

"The target has gone hard!" Manning pulled the Barrett from the vehicle and worked the bolt. "Hit them now!"

Grabbing weapons and munitions bags, Phoenix Force raced across the street, preparing their weapons and spreading out into an assault formation, even as gunfire opened up from the rooftop of the building, strafing their vehicle.

Computer Room, Stony Man Farm

"WE HAVE A PROBLEM," Carmen Delahunt said calmly as the monitor on her console went white with hash. "Half of L.A. just went off the air. Full-spectrum jamming, TV, CB, cell phones, everything is dead.''

"So find me somebody in the other half," Kurtzman snapped, his hands throwing levers and flipping switches. On the status board, satellites in space began to change their orientation and now point their transmitters at western Los Angeles.

"Contact Carl!" Price snapped. "Find Jack Grimaldi! Organize a rescue team stat!"

"No response from either," Akira Tokaido reported. "Trying secondary venues."

A tense silence filled the room as the electron riders of Stony Man waged their special kind of invisible combat, possibly a million lives riding on the outcome.

Casax, Basement Level

HOLDING OPEN the door for his men, Jozsef Vadas watched as Bezdek and Solomon dragged the stranger to a chair and tied him forcibly into place with strong nylon rope. Both of the men did so without their usual professional demeanor, and the former sergeant noticed each had cut lips and Solomon was favoring his right eye, the skin already darkening into a black eye.

"Son of a bitch has the constitution of an elephant. He woke in the elevator," Bezdek growled, giving the big man a brutal blow across the face.

McCarter turned his head to soften the blow, but blood still flowed from the side of his mouth.

"Get his cell phone," Zofchak ordered, shining a lamp on the prisoner. Pran passed it over, and the Czech electronics expert pressed the autodial buttons and only got a dial tone. Then he tried a few different combinations with a similar lack of results.

"Wiped clean after each call," Zofchak announced, tossing the phone to the floor. It landed with a clatter and broke apart, then he ground the components under the heel of his combat boot to make sure a location signal couldn't be broadcast. Their Russian radio jammers should have the entire city off the air, but it never hurt to be sure.

Solomon drew a knife and pressed the stud, a six-inch blade snapping straight from the handle. "He's a cop and I say we slit his throat then run," he growled.

"He fights too well for a policeman or FBI agent," Bezdek said, licking a busted knuckle on his left hand. His shirt was badly ripped, and the head of his snake tattoo peeked out of the gaping rip in the cloth.

"FBI? What are you boys, nuts or something?" McCarter shot back, trying to put a quaver in his voice and sound frightened. "Look, I don't know what you're doing here, drugs, whatever. It ain't my business. Hell, I blow a little snow every now and then myself. It's good for a man. Keep the old pipes clean."

Grabbing a fistful of McCarter's hair, Vadas yanked his head back and forcibly looked inside the man's nose.

"No scars. He lies. He has never used cocaine."

"Kill him," Solomon said. "If the Americans are here, we must depart at once."

"With such a prize in our laps?" Vadas said in his distorted voice. "Do not be foolish, my friend. We have laid our plans and are in no immediate danger. If this is their spy, he will know much we can use to escape the waiting net."

"What in hell makes you think I'm a cop?" McCarter stormed, putting everything he had into sounding innocent and buying more time for his teammates to bust in and stage a rescue.

While being tied, the Briton had expanded his chest as much as possible, and when he relaxed there was a definite looseness in the ropes. Already he was working on the knots trying to get loose. And while the Czechs had taken his gun and backup piece in the ankle holster, in his shirt pocket was one of Cowboy's trick pens that fired a single .22 cartridge. Not much power and no damn range, but jammed into a man's ear it killed as surely as a grenade.

Sliding a knife from his pocket, Vadas snicked the blade into existence and cut open McCarter's jacket, exposing his arm.

"We have very sophisticated X-ray scanners in the foyer," Vadas explained. "You carried a gun, but many do that in L.A. It is a dangerous city. But you also had this." Shown to the rest of the Red Dagger team was the tattoo of the British SAS.

Trapped, David McCarter couldn't believe the bad

luck. The arms dealers had state-of-the-art counter-terrorist Doppler X ray installed at the front door. Goddamn, he had been caught before pressing the buzzer. Even as a hand came free from the ropes, hopelessness brushed the soldier's heart for a moment, then the Stony Man warrior grew resolute.

"There's nothing I can tell you," he stated firmly. "Do your worst."

"Gladly," Solomon whispered, grabbing one of the Briton's ears, and pressing the knife blade to the soft flesh.

Just then, faint machine gun fire sounded from the PA speaker in the corner of the ceiling, and a massive explosion boomed from across the foundry.

"What is happening?" Zofchak demanded, grabbing a KEDR subgun from the wall and working the bolt.

"Alert," a computerized voice spoke calmly over their earphones. "Perimeter breach, sections one and nine. We have intruders. Repeat, we have intruders."

Moving with lightning speed, McCarter dropped the last rope, then stood and rammed the trick pen into Solomon's ear. With a muffled bang the Czech's brains blew out the other side and the former SAS commando held the corpse as a shield as the rest of the furious Czechs sprayed him with 9 mm rounds.

STRIDING THROUGH the billowing smoke of the crumbled storm drain wall, Able Team spread out, firing their weapons at anything that moved. Thermal sensors had found the warm foundry easily. But when they tried to report the location to the Farm, the jamming field told the team the gig was up. The disguised door refused to yield to Schwarz's EM scanners. However, the wall blew apart nicely to a U.S. Army satchel charge. Two mercs died on the spot, still trying to arm their weapons, and Blancanales and Schwarz tore apart four more with deadly fusillades of 5.56 mm tumblers.

Ruthlessly, Lyons cleared a catwalk with a stuttering burst from his Atchisson, then ducked to reload as his teammates used 40 mm antipersonnel rounds in their M-203 grenade launchers. The massive shotgun rounds blew hellfire amid the machinery, the lead pellets zigzagging everywhere madly. Another merc cried out as he fell into view from behind a forklift, and Lyons finished him off with a thundering round from his backup .357 Colt Python.

"Double Charlie!" a familiar voice shouted and there came the sound of machine gun fire.

Holstering the pistol, Lyons cursed. Double Charlie, that was code for a friendly trapped by the enemy. Shit.

"Shoot to wound," he snapped and headed in the direction, ramming fresh shells into the Atchisson. Blancanales and Schwarz were close behind, reloading the 40 mm grenade launchers.

As the team rushed past an elevator, a group of big men poured from a doorway firing machine pistols in every direction. The group split apart and raced deeper into the foundry, leaving a trail of blossoming smoke grenades in their wake. Blancanales fired his M-203, the 40 mm grenade missing the men and streaking away to explode in a deafening metallic crash. The rest of Able Team sent a few bursts that way as a bloody David McCarter stumbled into view from the doorway firing a KEDR subgun at the fleeing group. The man was bleeding from a dozens place, but otherwise the man seemed uninjured.

"One Czech's down," he snapped, firing again until the KEDR clicked empty, then he tossed it away. "Those were the rest of the bastards."

"Where's the rest of Phoenix Force?" Schwarz demanded, tossing the man a 9 mm Beretta pistol.

An explosion sounded from somewhere above as McCarter made the catch and dropped the clip to check the load before slamming the magazine back into place.

"I'd say that was them. But we can't wait. Every second lets Vadas and his dogs get farther away. Did you see where they went?"

"They split up, two that way, two that way," Lyons said, gesturing.

"Bloody hell!"

"Better stay with us," Blancanales suggested. "There are mercs everywhere!"

Sparks flew off the concrete floor and bullets musically ricocheted away, but there was no sound of gunfire.

"Sniper!" Lyons warned, and the men went back-to-back to make sure they didn't shoot one another in the thickening smoke.

In a practiced move, each man took a different direction and laid down suppression fire. With a cry, a merc fell from above and landed with a sickening crunch alongside a silenced KEDR subgun.

Tucking the Beretta into his belt, McCarter raided the body for spare clips and took the silenced weapon.

"Back in business," he said. "Let's get the buggers."

"Oh, shit," Schwarz said softly, still in the same position from before. Reaching into the shadows under a steam pipe, the man pulled out a Russian satchel charge, the timer blinking with a red armed light. Quickly, he disarmed the bomb and threw the secondary radio detonator away.

"Here's another!" Blancanales called, gesturing at a canvas bag lying on top of a pressure line feeding to the microwave blast furnace.

"This whole place is mined to blow." Lyons touched his throat mike, but the strident howl of the jamming still filled the com link. Communication with the others was impossible.

"It's a lot worse than that," Schwarz said, going to an empty lattice that stored Shkvals. The rocket torpedoes were now standing upright and hardwired together with electronic circuit boards. It was clear the weapons were set to launch skyward once the roof was blown off by the satchel charges, or maybe they could punch through. Torpedoes usually needed a good thousand yards to arm their warheads so they wouldn't harm the submarine launching them.

"Damn it, we don't have time to wait for my team to handle this!" McCarter growled as another distant explosion shook the foundry. "The bleeding Czechs are getting away!"

"Can you stop them from launching?" Lyons demanded.

Slinging his M-16/M-203, Schwarz got busy with both hands with the complex array of wiring. "Damned if I know," he muttered. "These boys really did a job on the controls. But I'll do my best."

"I'll help," Blancanales offered, opening a tool kit and pulling out an electronic probe.

"No, I can do this faster alone. Get out," Schwarz said, yanking open the hatch on a torpedo and pulling out a circuit board, then cutting a wire. "Don't worry, I'll stop these from going off. You just get Vadas."

Lyons nodded and McCarter squeezed the man's shoulder, then the three warriors charged into the billowing smoke after the escaping arms dealers.

Standing alone amid the ticking satchel charges, Schwarz feverishly started to defuse another rocket, trying desperately not to think about additional snipers, reserve mercs or his own imminent demise.

CHAPTER SIXTEEN

Rappelling through the gaping hole in the roof, the men of Phoenix Force fired their weapons at the scurrying mercs below and landed amid their strewed corpses in the office cubicles.

There was no sign of McCarter or the Czechs among the dead, so Hawkins and Manning did a recon through the offices while Encizo took out the video cameras and James plugged an EMP bomb into a wall outlet. The accumulators hummed in building volume as they charged and then the entire building went dark from the electromagnetic pulse sent through the electrical wiring, the enemy Crays off-line and harmless. Unfortunately, the jamming still continued.

Once Hawkins and Manning were finished checking the second floor, Phoenix Force took the stairs to ground level and kicked open the stairwell door before exiting. A hail of bullets hammered the jamb, and Manning kicked open the door again as Encizo dived through, firing his MP-5.

Dropping her KEDR subgun, the secretary behind the reception desk staggered under the 9 mm hardball rounds and slumped into her chair. The Stony Man warriors were quickly realizing there were no civilians in the entire building; this was a military hardsite plain and simple. But they still had to go slow and careful. McCarter was somewhere among the enemy, and there was a chance that he was alive.

While James pushed the corpse from the chair, Hawkins pulled the pin on a grenade, then rolled the chair through the double doors leading to the ground-floor foundry. Cries of surprise rose from the other side, then the concussion grenade blew, slamming the mercs off their feet. Phoenix Force charged the doors firing their weapons with precision, watching for civilians and McCarter, but there were only armed men and soon another section of the stronghold was cleared of personnel.

The foundry was in full operation, automated lathes slicing curling strips off spinning bars of metal. A laser behind a safety wall of green-colored glass flashed as it stabbed holes through finished sheets of armored alloy, wide conveyor belts moved along through the steam pipes and a huge crane with a catwalk overhead dangled a forest of steel chains. There were a million places for people to hide amid the machinery, and a thousand things that would explode at the touch of a bullet. But this was exactly the sort of situation the men of Phoenix Force had been trained for, and they reached the far side of the plant alive and with only minor scrapes and cuts.

Suddenly, strident alarms began to howl and red lights started flashing above every doorway.

"Alert. Alert," a calm artificial voice said. "Intruders in section three. Repeat, intruders in section three. Kill on sight. Repeat, kill on sight."

"Have to catch us first," Manning snarled, firing the Barrett. The wall speaker exploded into electronic trash and the howling alarm went silent.

"I thought we aced the Cray," Hawkins said, scowling, dropping a clip and reloading from the bulging pouch on his designer belt. There had been no time for the team to change into fatigues, so the NATO body armor, weapons and web harness were strapped over the designer suits.

"Must have been a backup not wired to the power system," James answered, firing his MP-5 from the hip.

On a catwalk overhead, a merc loading an AK-74 assault rifle staggered and lurched forward to tumble down into the open vat of white-hot steel. His body flashed from the awful heat, instantly reduced to smoke.

The team waited for any response to the noise, but the automatic machinery continued to thump, making more and more armor plating, but not the easily recognizable crowns for the Shkvals.

"There's another foundry," Hawkins stated. "Find a secret elevator!"

"On it!" James said, whipping out an EM scanner

and starting to probe the walls with fluxing magnetic fields.

Weapons at the ready, Phoenix Force kept guard while the tech did a probe and abruptly faced a black section of wall covered with a corkboard full of work sheets and safety notices.

"There!" he said, studying the handheld device, then cursed. "Shit, we've got company coming!"

"How long?" Hawkins demanded.

Thumbing a control slide, James saw an indicator on the scanner flash with a building rhythm. That was a lot of mass coming from below, range twenty yards, eighteen, fifteen...

"Ten seconds, maybe less," he snapped, tucking away the scanner and swinging up his machine gun.

"Okay. Just the way we did in Beirut," Hawkins directed, steel sighing as he pulled a knife from a sheath behind his back.

While the others drew their own blades, Manning yanked the pin on a flash grenade and placed it on the floor before the corkboard. Then the rest of the team faced away from the grenade and braced for the concussion.

Seconds later the wall split as the hidden elevator arrived and the grenade went off in a blinding flare of light. Caught point-blank, men yelled inside the elevator and Phoenix Force rushed forward. As each man was identified as not being McCarter, his life was ended with a swift slash until the new arrivals were dead.

"Found the jamming unit," Manning announced, checking through the twitching corpses. He lifted the gory device, almost losing his grip from the slippery blood across the Russian broadcast unit. He tried pressing the button on the miniature control panel but nothing happened.

"Shit, the code isn't punched in," Manning cursed. Wasting no more time, he tossed the jammer into the air and Encizo blew it apart with a single round from his MP-5.

"Stony One, this is Stony Two," Hawkins said into his throat mike, the high-pitched squeal finally gone.

"Thank God, you're back on the air. Get out of the building!" McCarter ordered in their earphones, the words crackling with static and interference. "The foundry is mined to blow!"

"Understood. What is your location?" Hawkins requested, adjusting the gain and volume.

"Never mind us!" Lyons answered. "We're in pursuit of Vadas through the storm drains under the city. But two of his people remained behind."

"Find and terminate!" McCarter grunted, and there came the background noise of machine-gun fire and screeching tires.

Able Team had to be in hot pursuit of the former Czech sergeant. "Confirm, immediate evac," Hawkins replied as there came a steady thumping that the men could feel through their combat boots.

In an explosion of masonry, something huge

crashed through a side wall, slamming aside a thousand-pound forklift as if it were a toy. The Stony Man warriors scattered for cover as the roaring machine plowed through the foundry, smashing machinery and steam pipes until ramming straight through the exterior wall to reach the parking lot. Its eight massive tires bumping high over some motorcycles, smashing them flat, the Russian BTR-80 Heavy Armor APC jounced over an Excalibur limousine in the parking lot to slam through a chain-link fence and reach the city street.

"Hit it!" Hawkins ordered, spraying a figure-eight pattern with his MP-5. The brass shells arched from the ejector port and fell tinkling to the terrazzo floor.

Phoenix Force opened fire with their MP-5s, raining copper-jacketed lead onto the Russian "Eighty" with no effect as it careened off the side of a building, removing a huge section of granite and bricks, then rammed past the Stony Man van full of their equipment, busting it apart to finally straighten its course and charge down Jefferson Road.

Pedestrians ran for their lives, and compact cars tried to dodge out of the way only to be crushed flat under the armored transport, windshields shattering as the trapped civilians briefly screamed and went horribly silent.

Dropping clips and reloading, Phoenix Force kept firing until the speeding APC took another corner and was gone from sight, leaving death and destruction in its wake.

"Son of a bitch," Manning cursed, levering another round into the Barrett. Even the monster .50-caliber weapon lacked the firepower to dent the Russian APC.

Hawkins glanced around, fully aware of the ticking bombs that could detonate any second. Their van was totaled, the limo gone and any civilian vehicle they could steal wouldn't have a chance in hell against the armored Eighty.

"Stony Two to Uncle Jack," Hawkins snapped into his throat mike. "We have a problem."

"Yeah, I see the bastard!" Jack Grimaldi replied, the steady throb of helicopter blades in the background. "The crazy bastard is going straight along Rodeo Drive."

"Can you get in a shot?"

"No way! The street is too crowded. My missiles would only kill innocent bystanders. There's a school nearby and kids are everywhere!"

"Well, stay on his ass! Don't let them get away."

"Roger! Out."

Just then a sharp whistle cut the air, strangely echoing over their earphones.

"Here's another APC!" Encizo announced, waving from the hole in the wall.

Rushing through the crumbling breakage, the men of Phoenix Force found two more BTR-80 A/80S armored personnel carriers sitting in a section of a warehouse converted into a military garage. The first had its louvered hood removed, the guts of the engine laid out on clean gray cloth obviously undergoing repairs. But the second APC appeared to be intact, eight tires inflated, both of the eight-foot-tall radio antennae and the sixteen-foot-long whip antenna in place, the body draped with sand bags and fuel cans.

Eight feet high, ten feet wide and twenty-five feet long, the APC was sheathed in 12 mm of reactive armor plating and proof to most air-launched missiles. The windows were covered with armored traps, gun ports dotted every side and there was a front-mounted 7.62 mm chain gun and a roof-top 14.5 mm antiaircraft cannon. Smoke generators were mounted front and aft, along with 30 mm grenade launchers. There were no doors, only ferruled roof hatches that could be dogged from the inside sealing it completely airtight.

The amphibious craft was state-of-the-art, the best the Russian army had in the field, and only an American M-1 Abrams tank could challenge the sleek war machine with total impunity.

Oddly, sandbags lay in a rough outline of the first APC, the attaching ropes cut. Hawkins didn't like that. Why would the Czechs remove the sandbags? Those were excellent protection from incoming missiles. Maybe to save weight. But these brutes could haul tons of men and supplies. Oh, hell.

"The other APC has Shkvals on board," Manning stated. "If that amphibious vehicle reaches the ocean, nothing in the water could stand in its way."

"Then we stop it on dry land. Okay, clean house!"

Hawkins ordered into the com link, and the team swarmed over the second APC, wasting precious seconds checking for booby traps.

Feeling the pressure of the clock, the men finally gave the all-clear and Encizo climbed into the driver's seat, gunning the massive tandem set of 260 horsepower diesel engines and throwing the APC into gear. Shuddering and banging, the BTR-80 crashed backward through the loading doors of the warehouse and into the bright noon sunlight. Going right off the loading dock, the APC dropped four feet to the pavement without harm, its superslung undercarriage and eight tires easily absorbing the impact.

Gunning the engines, Encizo shifted gears and started through the vacant lot after the first APC, rolling over mounds of trash and rubble with equal ease until they were on the street.

Even as the Eighty started along Jefferson, a huge explosion shook the Casax foundry and flames rose from the basement level to tongue the sky above.

BURSTING OUT of the storm drain into the bright noon sun, Able Team and McCarter instantly saw Vadas and the others again, the men leaning low in their Yamaha motorcycles, blue smoke streaming from the tortured air-cooled engines.

Keeping a hand on the dashboard, McCarter was leaning out the window and firing his stolen KEDR subgun, while Blancanales did the same out the side door of the van, his M-16/M-203 chattering nonstop at the riders, but the arms dealers were weaving back and forth, making themselves difficult targets. Inside the storm drains, they had first driven with the headlights off through the inky blackness, ghosts masked by shadows.

When Blancanales tried using Starlite goggles to keep track, the former Czech sergeant and his men started tossing out road flares and damn near blinded the man before the automatic cutoff saved his sight. After that he and McCarter switched to infrared, but that was useless when the enemy started dropping grenades in their wake. The two Stony Man commandos maintained a steady barrage at the bikers, but with Lyons weaving frantically to avoid the military charges, only one merc was killed after a hundred rounds fired, Vadas and the rest reaching the outside world completely untouched.

The bikes really increased speed upon reaching the sunlit culvert, and Lyons started angling for the access ramp to cut them off. Only a hundred feet of culvert remained before the start of Ballona Creek. The Czechs were trapped.

Incredibly, the men didn't even try to leave the concrete canyon but went straight off the end of the breakwater. As they fell the twenty feet to the sluggish waters of Ballona Creek, Vadas and a curly haired man expertly dived away from the tumbling machines and knifed into the waters like expert swimmers. The rest of the riders hit the creek with less grace, but also vanished beneath its murky surface.

Braking to a halt at the edge of the culvert, Lyons and the others piled from the van and rained lead into the creek, dropped their spent clips, reloaded and did it again. However, there was no sign of blood in the water, and no bodies rose to the surface.

"This is a trick," McCarter said, slapping his last clip into the KEDR machine pistol. "Vadas is a trained scuba diver."

Thumbing fresh cartridges into the Atchisson, Lyons cursed in understanding. The arms dealers had to have placed air tanks under the water for just such an escape as this.

Working the bolt on the M-16 to free a jam, Blancanales glanced at the oily creek lapping the sloping concrete embankment of the culvert. "The water ends here," he said as the brass came loose and bounced off the ledge to splash into the creek below. "So there's nowhere else to go but out to sea."

"They might take a side feed," McCarter suggested, squinting to see into the distance. There were no air bubbles rising to mark the use of scuba tanks, so Vadas had to have rebreathers.

"Can't. There are no tributaries," Lyons said gruffly, returning to the van and gunning the engine. "This used to be a real creek, before L.A. paved the thing. It's a single straight feed to the Marina del Mar and open ocean."

"Can we cut them off?" McCarter demanded, climbing into the passenger seat and slamming the van door closed.

"Gonna try," Lyons said, heading for the access ramp.

The gate at the top was missing, so the Able Team leader charged straight to Alsace and went the wrong direction on a one-way street to reach West Jefferson. Or rather, a piece of the road since it actually was about a dozen different streets all given the same name and stretched halfway across Los Angeles like a crazy snake meandering through the hills and valley.

Siren wailing, a police car suddenly appeared and tried to block the speeding van. McCarter used the KEDR to blow out a tire and the driver braked to a halt in the middle of an intersection, the second cop already talking on the radio.

"Drive faster," McCarter suggested, tossing away the dead subgun and taking an M-16/M-203 from a gun rack on the wall.

Tires squealing as the van took a corner on two wheels, Lyons grunted, "That was the plan."

As the van skirted along the edge of Ballona Creek, Blancanales scanned the waters with binoculars.

"There they are!" He pointed into the sluggish river. "Eleven o'clock!"

"Got them!" McCarter confirmed, peering through the low-magnification scope built into the handle of the assault rifle. "Due west near the far bank!"

Watching the traffic, Lyons hadn't seen what they found, but he accepted their call and, wildly shifting gears, he twisted the steering wheel with all of his strength. The van nearly flipped as it banked into the turn, then the headlights loudly shattered as it crashed through the safety fence along Jefferson, tearing down a whole section.

At full speed, Lyons sent the vehicle straight over the edge of the embankment and was airborne for only seconds before violently slamming into the river.

Braced for the impact, the men didn't lose their seats. As water began to pour in, the team checked its weapons and waited until the water covered the windows before swimming from the sinking vehicle.

Fighting the undertow of the van, the Stony Man warriors tried to find the scuba divers, but visibility was poor in the polluted river, and the Czechs were almost upon them before they had a chance to react.

The odds were bad, five to three, but the Stony Man commandos chose a man and attacked, diving below the swimmers to slash knives upward at their kicking legs. The divers tried to evade, but two were wounded across the thighs, red blood fogging the water. Lyons and Blancanales converged on the closest merc and gutted him like a fish, then stole the scuba tank. McCarter held off the others with a sizzling flare, until he thought his lungs were going to burst, then Lyons slipped the mouthpiece of the rebreather between the Briton's lips and the Phoenix Force leader sucked in a lungful of oxygen.

At that point, Vadas and the curly haired man broke away and started swimming hard, the last two Czechs staying to block any possible pursuit.

By now the mercs had gotten out their own knives, ignoring the pistols in their belts as useless in the creek. More often than not, a pistol fired while submerged would back-blast and take the shooter's hand off at the wrist. Equipped with the finest handguns in the world, the two groups of soldiers were reduced to simple blades and raw muscle. Hand to hand fighting while underwater, the direst kind of combat.

Their own lungs starting to feel the strain, Lyons and Blancanales pressed the attack and grappled with the enemy divers. Seizing the deadly opportunity, the Czechs attacked, the blades of their knives thrusting hard at the bellies of the Stony Man warriors. But the high-tensile steel only clanked against the NATO body armor.

Dressed only in a business suit, McCarter was busy strapping on the rebreather as Lyons and Blancanales now rammed the handles of their knives into the face masks of the divers, blinding them with a rush of water, and used the distraction to slice open their vulnerable throats along the carotid artery. The Czechs thrashed from the stinging pain, but slowed their motions after only a few seconds and then went terribly still.

Wearing the rebreather, McCarter fed Lyons and Blancanales oxygen as they took the weight belts and rebreathers from the dying men, along with their pistols. The Stony Man commandos were larger than the Czechs and thus the weight belts were too light to keep them submerged. But the weapons helped balance that shortcoming, not precisely, but close enough.

Swimming onward, the trio continued on a straight course, with no idea of what they were searching for next.

Past the concrete lining of the reinforced creek, the bottom became sandy, dotted with rusted machinery, shopping carts and assorted detritus of the city. But the debris of humanity soon was left behind and the sea bottom became smooth sand dotted with small outcroppings called pinnacles.

Motorboats cut the surface above the commandos, and visibility was much worse in the sea, roughly ten feet, the salt badly stinging their cuts and scrapes. Suddenly, there was a wide shadow and a heavy rumble as a yacht from the Marina del Mar passed by overhead. This close to the shore, the currents were mild but steadily moving to the left, and the team had to constantly fight to stay on course.

Checking his illuminated sports watch, McCarter saw the depth was close to fifty feet, the dark green of the limitless ocean lying before them as immutable as interstellar space.

Glancing over a shoulder, Lyons raised a single finger for their attention, then jabbed it downward and slowly extended his hand. Although the com links were totally waterproof, radio waves didn't work well underwater and gestures were the only reliable form of communications.

Blancanales nodded in comprehension, and only

yards away there was a surge of powerful currents as the trio crossed over an edge of an aquatic cliff, the sandy bottom dropping far out of sight.

Well trained in the SAS, McCarter knew about such things. It was a canyon, possibly hundreds of feet deep, maybe even more. They should have expected this. A surface ship would be regularly checked by the Coast Guard and harbor patrol, but some sort of a submersible sneaking along the ocean trench could stay down here for weeks, maybe months without being detected, depending on its equipment. And these Czechs were very well equipped. But what was it, a diving bell? Or maybe another relay point with fresh scuba tanks, cash and weapons for the men to use by going back to the shore and mixing with the civilian boaters. Maybe even a DSRV, or minisub. Anything was possible.

Waving a hand, Blancanales pointed ahead and shook his head. McCarter nodded and pointed downward. Lyons silently agreed and led the way by kicking for the depths of the Pacific, heading into the unknown.

CHAPTER SEVENTEEN

As the Russian APC crested a low hill on Jefferson, the city spread before them. Smoke and destruction were everywhere, bodies dead in the road and others crawling away leaving behind a bloody trail from crushed limbs.

"Target location!" Hawkins demanded, tightening a fist until his knuckles turned white. The murdering scum would pay for this senseless slaughter with their lives.

Unfortunately, there had been a reason why the Czech soldiers hadn't taken both of their working APCs. This one had some kind of engine trouble. There was a steady banging that didn't seem to affect the engine in any way, but it was only a matter of time. He only hoped the damn thing held together long enough for them to catch the arms dealers and settle this today before any more people died.

"Radar is clean," James reported, operating the scope.

At the steering wheel, Encizo added, "Infrared also clear. The other BRT-80 is too low to spot this way."

"There!" Manning said, pointing skyward at the U.S. Army Comanche gunship hovering in the air.

"They're a mile due west," Grimaldi said over the com link. "Heading like a bat out of hell along Rodeo."

"Roger that," Encizo answered, and threw the huge machine into gear.

The banging got louder as he hit the turbocharger and the tandem engines roared as the APC rapidly built speed. Using the turbo would drain their fuel reserves, but speed was the top priority.

Taking the corner, the BTR-80 brushed past a dry cleaning truck, ripped most of its side off, then rolled over a mailbox, smashing it flat as Encizo did his best to avoid the terrified people frozen on the crosswalk.

Once on Rodeo, the rest of Phoenix Force prepared the weapons of the vehicle while Encizo put the pedal to the floor and started following through the trail of disaster from the second APC.

"There!" Hawkins shouted as the enemy BTR-80 came into view.

Traffic was going wild as the armored transport smashed aside the larger civilian cars and simply rolled over the smaller ones. Desperately, Encizo fought to avoid hitting any of the crumpled wrecks as James switched frequencies on the radio and called for ambulances. He couldn't read any of the Russian on the controls, but the numbers were the same and the rest he did by guesswork. But he barely got the message out when the radio began to squeal loudly from more jamming.

"Sons of bitches!" Hawkins cursed, firing his MP-5 at the enemy APC, but the 9 mm rounds did nothing to the Russian giant.

"My turn," Manning growled. Standing in the top hatch, he worked the bolt on his Barrett Light Fifty and fired. The sound of the big-bore rifle was deafening within the metal confines of the Russian APC, but the rear of the second vehicle exploded in flame as a reserve gas tank detonated from the arrival of the .50-caliber round.

Dripping flame, the machine didn't even slow, and stubby KEDR subguns poked out of the aft ports and started throwing lead at Phoenix Force, sparks flying off the armored prow from the incoming rounds.

"Damn, the Russians make good machines," Manning snarled, working the bolt to jack out the spent shell. "We need better than this Barrett to stop them."

Glancing around the inside of the transport, the Stony Man warrior saw several attaché cases and weapons crates, but inside were only AK-74 rifles, KEDR subguns, assorted ammo and some grenades. Nothing that could stop the juggernaut of the Eighty.

"Any weak points?" Encizo demanded, ducking as a chance round impacted on the Plexiglas shield covering the driver's view slot.

"None that I know about," Hawkins told him, firing a long burst from his MP-5 under the vehicle to no result.

Suddenly, the radar started to beep loudly as two police helicopters arched into view around a hotel. Moving fast, the two took an advance position before the speeding enemy APC and began to descend.

"They'll be slaughtered," Hawkins growled, then flipped up the commander's hatch. His business suit fluttering in the wind, the commando fired his MP-5 at the other APC as a diversion.

Joining the effort, Manning stood in the rear hatch and fired the Barrett as fast as he could work the bolt. The big rounds slammed into the rear tires, but nothing happened. The military tires were designed to withstand the explosive efforts of land mines.

"This is the LAPD!" a magnified voice commanded from above, sounding louder than thunder. "Stop those vehicles now! You are all under arrest!"

The swivel hatch on top of the Russian APC rotated a half turn, and the 14.5 mm cannon stuttered flame. A police helicopter shuddered from the arrival of the explosive shells stitching along its aluminum hull. The windshield shattered, the engines exploded into flame, the passenger fell from his seat only seconds before the aircraft vanished in a fireball.

The blast echoed along the city streets, shrapnel raining down for blocks. The other police chopper immediately angled away, closely followed by a small news helicopter.

As the Czech gunner tried for the escaping helicopters with the blazing chain gun, a squat, angular gunship streaked from the sky on an interception course and moved between the two, taking the hits itself. The U.S. Army Comanche shook from the pounding rounds, but its belly armor held, and the forward Gatling cannon opened up, the armor-piercing DU rounds tearing up the pavement as if it were wet paper.

Then a flash came from the top hatch of the APC, and a missile streaked skyward. The gunship dodged, but the Stinger slammed into its tail, completely removing the rotor assembly.

Spewing oil and black smoke, the Comanche began to spin and dropped out of sight behind a row of stores.

Finished loading in a belt of ammunition, Hawkins opened fire with the 7.62 mm coaxial gun, the individual reports merging into a single smooth roar. Then the soldier abruptly stopped as he saw the hardball ammo ricocheted off the armored ass of the BTR-80 and impacted civilian cars everywhere. Windows shattered, people dropped screaming, and a streetlight exploded into bits.

Then the Czech APC fired at them with the 14.5 mm KPTV minigun, and more ricochets filled the area.

''We need some combat room!'' Hawkins growled, his hands white from fighting the urge to press the triggers.

''This is what the bastards are counting on!'' James

replied, slowly and carefully shooting his 9 mm Beretta out a gunport. Another gas can exploded, and the Czech arms dealers stopped shooting until the flames were gone and they could open the rear ports again.

James dropped the clip and reloaded. "Bastards know that we can't fight back because we would have to kill our own people to get them. As long as they stay on crowded streets, we can't do anything."

Just then, the reactive armor dented from the hammering arrival of a heavy 14.5 mm round.

"But they sure can chew the shit out of us," Hawkins snarled, lowering the useless MP-5 and pulling out a red-striped canister. "I have a thermite grenade that'll stop that thing, but we gotta get some clear space!"

"And if you can hit a moving target that's shooting back."

"I'll hit them," the big man growled.

Watching the fuel steadily drop, Encizo asked, "I wonder where the hell they're going? Must have some sort of an escape plan in case of trouble. These guys are much too good not to have something arranged."

"Maybe they plan to use the nuke," James said simply, rapping the side of the BTR-80. "This baby is NBC rated."

Hawkins scowled. Christ almighty, what a horrible idea. Ten city blocks would instantly vanish in a monoatomic fireball. The shock waves would topple skyscrapers across the city, possibly even trigger a quake from the faults under the city. He knew the

Army Corps of Engineers routinely injected tons of high-pressure graphite into the faults below the city to ease the possibility of a major quake. But a nuke could easily circumvent that procedure and start a quake that would level L.A. The death toll would be staggering, millions trapped and dying in the radioactive rubble as the lava rose from the wounded Earth. But the arms dealers inside their Nuclear-Bacteriological-Chemical proof APC would be completely safe. So would Phoenix Force, and that offered no comfort to the grim commandos.

"Check the Geiger, see if there's any reading," Manning suggested, laying aside the empty Barrett and working the bolt on an AK-74.

"Damn right there is!" James answered checking the control board.

So they had the nuke on board. Manning sent a silent request to the universe for some backup on this, then concentrated on the present fight.

Slamming into cars in both lanes as it drove down the middle of the street, the Russian APC brushed past a school bus, then took the access ramp going to Route 405 and crossed the median to head south.

Hawkins tensed at the sudden move. The city streets had more protective traffic than the highway, so the enemy just gave up cover for speed. That had to be important, but what did it mean? The other APC had to be carrying at least one Shkval on board, possibly armed with the nuke. What was he missing here? Pulling out his pocket computer, Hawkins saw it had caught a round from the fight at the foundry and he grabbed Encizo's from his web harness.

Already keyed for the area, he pulled up a map of Los Angeles and studied the city. They were heading for the ocean, but almost any direction led to the water in L.A. What was he missing here?

A man holding a fat plastic tube stood in the top hatch of the second APC and aimed it at Phoenix Force's vehicle. Waiting until the telltale flash of a launch, Encizo roughly swerved to dodge the RPG rocket and the highway exploded behind them, showering chunks of asphalt. Thankfully, no civilians were hurt by the blast. Even the stubborn L.A. drivers knew when to get off the road, and the highway was clear for half a mile. They finally had the needed combat room, and nothing to attack with but small arms and a few grenades.

"Heads up," Manning said from the top hatch. "I just figured out where they're going. Look!"

Squinting at the horizon, Encizo cursed at the sight of large cylindrical structures rising above the city. Gasoline storage tanks! A single Shkval into those and the city would be engulfed with a radioactive firestorm. The perfect cover for their escape. Designed to be radiation proof, the BTR-80 would roll through the blaze completely unharmed while L.A. burned, the exploding gas tanks hiding the use of the nuclear weapon until it was too late. Hundreds, maybe thousands more would die of radiation poisoning before the truth was realized.

"Just like Murmansk," James snarled. "Last time they used the tactic to get into a base, now it's to get out."

"Vadas can't launch the Shkval from the highway," Hawkins told him. "It has to be at least ten blocks away or he'll also die in the fireball." Radiation proof was not the same as nuclear-explosion proof. "That APC has to reach flat ground first, so we hit them on the exit ramp. Ram them off the road and flip it over!"

Nobody mentioned that they would die, too, in such an attack.

"No good. We're not fast enough!" Encizo shot back, his leg aching from holding the gas pedal motionless on the floor. "Lighten this thing!"

Moving fast, the men began tossing anything loose out of the APC—cases of weapons, spare ammo— until the APC was bare.

"Not enough!" Encizo growled, then clenched his teeth. "More!"

"Brace yourselves!" James ordered, and flipped a switch on the control board.

In muffled bangs, a dozen explosive bolts detonated and every armored hatch blew off the APC, leaving the commandos exposed to the rushing air. Instantly, the Eighty lurched forward in renewed speed, and slowly the enemy drew closer, but still they couldn't reach the other vehicle. The gasoline storage tanks loomed before them now, and the second APC took the next exit and raced along the curved concrete ramp.

But just as the vehicle reached the street, the radar began to wildly beep and a fiery dart streaked inward from behind Phoenix Force and exploded directly on the second APC. The Russian transport vanished in a boiling fireball and came out again a few seconds later, badly dented and missing two tires. But still moving. Angling sharply, the APC plowed past some barricades and into a work site, disappearing inside the partially constructed building.

Looking skyward, Hawkins saw a police helicopter hovering nearby, a dirty-faced Jack Grimaldi standing in the side hatch holding an Armbrust rocket launcher.

"Abort! Abort! Do not shoot again! He has the nuke!" Manning shouted, slashing a thumb across his throat.

Unable to hear the words because of the radio jamming, Grimaldi understood the gesture and nodded in acceptance, lowering the launcher.

"Now it's our turn!" Encizo stated grimly, flipping down the UV visor to check the dark alley alongside the construction site. There were people about, but all of them were running away and his attack zone was clear.

"Ramming speed!" Hawkins ordered, shoving the computer into a pocket. Then he rummaged under the commander's seat and came up with a signal flare gun. In close-quarters combat, the flare gun was a soldier's best friend. That was, if the Czechs weren't expecting the trick. He would have to take that chance.

The APC diesel engines roared as Encizo killed every secondary system to give the engines more juice and the fifteen-ton war machine surged forward into the alley. Reaching the middle of the building, he twisted the steering wheel and the APC crashed straight through the decorative fieldstone wall, rocks and comcrete flying like shrapnel. But the Stony Man warrior didn't stop and kept going. Dust and boards blocked his view for a few moments, and then he saw the enemy straight ahead. The Czechs had turned their vehicle to face the smashed window, obviously expecting Phoenix Force to follow the same path. Two men were kneeling on the floor, holding primed American LAW rockets to their shoulders. More than enough firepower to remove the BTR-80 from existence.

But at the sound of the crash, the Czechs turned in shock, startled by the flank attack, and started to swing the plastic tubes of the deadly antitank weapons toward the charging APC when Hawkins stood and fired the flare gun.

The sizzling magnesium charge streaked ahead of the Eighty, radiating a blazing nimbus of light. Temporarily blinded, the Czechs launched the LAW rockets anyway and the twin firebirds went right past the Stony warriors to detonate on the fieldstone wall in hellish fury.

"Brace yourselves!" Encizo shouted, and the second APC loomed before them with frightening speed.

CHAPTER EIGHTEEN

Pacific Ocean

Time passed in silence, the pressure of the depths steadily increasing on the Stony Man team as it continued into the ocean. A school of fish swam by the men, moving in perfect unison like birds in flight. Then suddenly there was a large black shape on the bottom. For a wild moment, Lyons thought it was only a rock formation covered with seaweed, but when he got close enough he could see the seaweed was attached to a camouflage netting draped over something truly large. At first, Lyons thought it was a railroad car, then the details became clear. A submarine! Right there in the L.A. harbor basin!

A Russian diesel in American waters. It had to have arrived during a storm and run on only battery power, scraping the bottom for miles to get this close and not set off the P-3 sonar nets. Then again, the civilian traffic was so heavy on the surface—surfers, amateur divers, supertankers, speedboats, water skiing, cargo tugs—the damn thing may have simply ghosted some larger vessel going into the marina and then descended to its hiding place among the kelp and the pinnacles, harbored safely in the penumbra of the underwater cliff.

Swimming all the way down to the sandy bottom, the men slipped under the camouflage netting, pausing motionless for a few seconds as a deadly moray eel slithered by hunting for food. When it was safe once more, they rose alongside the massive steel form, unsure of what to do next.

Lyons gestured a question at Blancanales, who shrugged in response. Kicking past the two men, McCarter took the lead. Staying low as he went by the periscope of the conning tower, the former SAS commando proceeded along the aft section of the hull. Yes, he recognized this model—it was a decommissioned Soviet diesel. Even in the murky light he could still see the double row of round hatches along the hull showing where the missile launcher tubes used to be. Those would have been the first thing removed before the Russians sold the boat, but then again, these Czechs were actually making their own torpedoes. How difficult was a missile tube?

Lyons also identified the craft, and while he agreed that wasting money was poor business for any nation, selling warships just because your front-line ships were better had never made any sense to him. America and Russia had both been doing that for years, and it was finally coming back at them.

His cut ear and arm stinging badly from the salt

water, McCarter headed amidships. With the others close behind, he ignored some secured rigging lashed into place to go straight for a particular section of the decking. Using his knife blade in lieu of a wrench, McCarter got the cover off a deck grid and gently swung it aside to expose the bare hull, now with a dim outline of a rounded square visible in the metal. The emergency escape hatch!

Trying not to allow his weighted belt to tap against the hull, McCarter measured off inches from the left corner and slid his stolen knife into the thin crack around the plate, only to have the blade snap off. As it fluttered away, Lyons handed over his knife and the same thing happened. With growing apprehension, McCarter tried once more, using Blancanales's pocket Swiss Army knife, and the smaller blade slid deeper into the crack until he was soon rewarded with a solid click.

As the hatch plate came away, the wheel lock of the watertight hatch was exposed. In slow motion, Lyons slapped the Briton on the shoulder and kept watch while McCarter and Blancanales worked on rotating the wheel, every minute creak of metal sounding like a clarion call by the amplifying water. Then they heard a distinct clang. The two men barely got out of the way in time as the internal air pressure slammed the hatch aside in a great explosion of air that fluttered the camouflage netting above them. Inside was a steel chamber large enough for a single man and breathing gear.

As soon as the pressure equalized, McCarter was already swimming into the chamber and closing the top hatch. After a minute, Blancanales went next, and finally Lyons. As he cycled through the cramped airlock, the Able Team leader stepped into the warmth and light of a steel corridor to find McCarter checking an AK-74, with Blancanales tying up a guard with strips of cloth from his torn clothing. Dim overhead lights were protected by wire cages, distant voices spoke a foreign language and something heavy boomed, the vibrations quivering along the deck plates.

"What now?" Lyons whispered, scuba equipment placed aside. The deck was slippery with the water from the airlock and the excess running off their civilian clothing. "You know how to sink this tub by any chance?"

"Abso-bleeding-lutely, mate."

Pulling out his Colt .380 pistol, Blancanales shook the weapon hard to dislodge excess moisture, then jacked the slide.

"Good. Let's scuttle the ship, then kill Vadas," he growled, threading a sound suppressor onto the barrel.

"Boat," McCarter corrected automatically. "This isn't a ship."

"Yeah, whatever."

Just then, the heavy boom sounded again, the vibrations felt through their sodden shoes.

"What is that noise, the engines?" Lyons asked.

"Too slow," McCarter stated, squinting his eyes

to force a memory. "This is a diesel torpedo boat, so we must be near the...air plant, deck four, aft storage."

In a flurry of motion, the mercenary stopped pretending to be unconscious and struggled wildly against his bonds to get free. McCarter turned the AK-74 on the prisoner as Blancanales pinned his legs and Lyons slammed the man's head against the deck. The merc went instantly still, but his chest continued to rise and fall in regular breaths. He was merely unconscious, not dead.

Dragging the body into another compartment, the men found it was a storage unit filled with signal flares, emergency medical supplies, inflatable rafts, life jackets and other supplies to be used by the crew leaving through the escape hatch. But more important, a map of the submarine on the hull showed the location of other escape routes.

Rummaging through the sealed plastic boxes, the Stony Man warriors found dry clothes and quickly changed into loose, nondescript garb and canvas deck shoes with rubber soles. Lyons and Blancanales tried their com links, found the devices were still functioning and turned them off. Radio signals inside the craft would only reveal their exact position with lethal efficiency.

"Okay, which should we head for?" Blancanales asked, removing the map from its plastic frame and spreading it across a bundle of rain ponchos. "The bridge or the torpedo room?"

"Bridge," Lyons decided, smoothing back his wet hair. "Everything can be controlled from there."

Taking a flare gun from inside a hinged glass box on the bulkhead, McCarter tucked the signal device into his belt.

"Christ, the forward tubes are a long distance from the cargo bay."

"And we would have to go through the crew quarters to reach that section of the vessel," the Briton stated. "There's no other way. Submarines are designed to be defended by a handful of men against a superior number of invaders."

Lyons scowled. "How big a crew?"

"This class of sub can run with a skeleton crew of six, but normally carries a hundred hands, plus six officers."

"If it's a hundred, then we're in deep shit," Blancanales commented dryly. "But at least that's familiar territory."

Lyons gave a snort in lieu of a laugh, and then the entire vessel trembled slightly and the men felt an odd rising sensation.

"Bloody hell, they're getting under way," McCarter growled.

There were muffled noises sent along the deck as the huge vessel lifted from the sandy ocean bottom and began making headway. Time was against them now, and the three men intently returned to the map. The engine room was a good goal; kill the electric and hydraulic power and the torpedo tubes couldn't function. But the compartment was three decks down, two sections aft, sealed behind multiple blast doors to protect the forward crew in case of an explosion. The stern of the boat was a fortress. That would be difficult to take with their meager armament.

Checking for the ship's arsenal, Lyons found it in the officers' quarters. Damn, once again there was no way to reach that section of the sub without going through the bottleneck of the crew quarters, and that was a deathtrap.

"Any air vents?" Blancanales suggested, looking around the storage unit. "Or maybe crawl spaces the snipes use to reach cables?"

Surprised, McCarter eyed the infantry soldier. Snipes? So he knew the nautical slang for the grease monkeys who worked in the bowels of the great boats, the lowliest, dirtiest job in any nation's navy. Impressive. The man really was a chameleon.

"Both are useless to us," he replied. "The vent shafts are exactly a foot square to prevent travel that way, there are no crawl spaces, the perforated deck grids come up for repairs."

"Which means they could see us every foot of the way," Lyons muttered. "What if we crashed the computer in missile control?"

McCarter shook his head. "That's the auxiliary. The main computer is two rooms ahead and one level up in the main control room. One door, always guarded inside and out."

"Shit, this is well designed," Blancanales said.

"Maybe we should just open the escape hatch and flood the ship."

"Internal pumps and too many hatchways. The escape hatch is too small to allow enough flow to threaten the boat. Again, designed that way."

"What about there?" Lyons demanded, pointing at a low section of the map. "The morgue."

"That's the kitchen," Blancanales corrected, then saw he was wrong. A small section of the main food locker was designated as the ship's morgue. Probably to keep the bodies from decomposing during long periods while underwater. Grisly but efficient.

"What good is the morgue?" McCarter scowled.

"It's the most direct route to the ballast tanks," Lyons explained, going over to the rebreathers and checking the gauges. Less than an hour of service life remaining. Close, but it may be enough. "We blow open the deck with grenades, then use the rebreathers to swim through the seawater in the tanks, find the scuttling charges and rig them to blow. Then we leave through the overflow vents."

"That'll work," McCarter stated, locking the details of the map into his mind, then folding the plastic sheet and tucking it into a pocket. "If these plans are correct.

"Why shouldn't they be?" Blancanales asked, arching an eyebrow.

McCarter lifted the plastic frame to display the date in the corner. "This hasn't been updated in four years. A lot of things could have changed by now."

Damn, not good news. Outnumbered and lost in an enemy stronghold was a deadly combination. ''Any other options?'' Lyons asked, checking his revolver. ''No? Then let's get moving.''

A murmur of voices came from outside the room, and the men froze.

''I swear I heard voices in the air vent,'' a man said from the other side of the bulkhead.

''Right. Maybe it's a talking fish.'' A second voice laughed.

''Fuck you, smart-ass. Hey, the deck is wet!''

Moving at panther speed, the Stony Man team drew its weapons and threw open the compartment door. Near the escape hatch stood two men in stained fatigues with AK-74 carbines slung over their shoulders. As the mercs looked up at the noise, then clawed for their weapons, Blancanales fired his silenced pistol. Both men doubled over and slid to the deck.

Hauling the corpses into the compartment, Mc-Carter used their wet clothes to wipe up the blood, then a dry shirt to mop the deck. Searching the mercs, Lyons took the two carbines, a set of keys and a brace of grenades, both concussion. Which made sense— detonate a thermite grenade inside a submarine and the vessel would be destroyed. Passing around the fresh weapons, the former cop made damn sure the tape was tight on the arming levers of the military spheres.

Once more the men strapped on the rebreathers.

"Single file, two-yard spread, I'm on the point," McCarter said, taking command.

Knowing the man's familiarity with submarines, Lyons and Blancanales had no objections. The trio moved out into the boat, their deck shoes silent on the steel plates.

Reaching the stairs, they found a cigarette smoldering in a sand trap, but could hear nobody moving nearby. Hopefully, one of the mercs they killed had been smoking.

With the appropriated Kalashnikov chambered for instant use, McCarter walked down the stairs so he could see through the steps. Blancanales stayed close behind with the silenced .380, and Lyons covered the rear with the second AK-74 carbine. There was nobody in sight in the lower deck. The corridor was lined with oval hatchways leading to the massive storage rooms. A million useful things could be behind the hatches, but they didn't have the time to check. When the two dead men were reported missing, more mercs would arrive, heavily armed and ready for trouble. The Stony Man warriors wanted to be long gone before that happened.

The second flight of stairs was equally clear, but there came the clatter of pots and pans from the galley, along with the smell of cooking food and the rich aroma of strong coffee.

Easing a plastic mirror from his wallet around the jamb of the hatch, McCarter counted six men without weapons busy in the galley, and roughly calculated they were making enough food for twenty or so men. If the crew worked in shifts, then the vessel had a full complement of a hundred men. He relayed the news with gestures and the others nodded in comprehension.

One at a time, the commandos slipped past the open hatchway and reached the next set of stairs without being detected. But as McCarter walked backward down the companionway, he saw this lower storage area was open, not in sections, the deck packed with a multitude of boxes, crates and drums. At the far end stood the cargo elevator, and off to the side was the huge burnished door to the main freezer.

Reaching the deck, the trio started along the crates, keeping low when three mercs appeared from around a stack of crates, their arms full of wet rebreathers. From Vadas and the second Czech?

Even as he made the connection, Blancanales fired fast, and two men dropped, but the third was only wounded and he cried out a warning before being silenced forever by a whispery .380 round.

There was a crash of pots from the deck above, and footsteps mixing with excited voices. Taking cover, the Stony Man team waited until the men were halfway down the stairs and then opened fire through the gaps between the steps. On bloody legs, the cooks tumbled to the deck, losing their carbines, and then their lives. However, the chatter of the Kalashnikovs echoed along the metal corridors, spreading through the metal boat.

Going to the freezer door, McCarter found it locked with a keypad. Probably to stop pilfering by the mercs. Without an EM scanner to try a bypass, the team had no choice but to stuff a concussion grenade under the handle and pull the pin. Moving fast, the men barely made it behind a crate of canned goods when the charge detonated. The blast seemed to shake the whole boat as the door flew open with a resounding crash.

As the team charged for the bent, sagging door, alarms began to howl and shouting voices could be heard from every direction. Inside the freezer, they found racks of beef hanging from a motorized track, the walls lined with boxes full of frozen chickens, lobsters and imported sausages wrapped in big plastic bags.

"Any way to lock that door?" Lyons asked, scowling at the twisted array of crumpled steel and insulation.

McCarter grunted. "Not from this side."

"Look up. We can rig a pulley," Blancanales said, squinting at the tracks bolted to the ceiling.

They operated as a team, Lyons lifting a frozen carcass off its hanging hook, while McCarter used the control box to lower the chain. Blancanales attached the hook to the broken door, then McCarter winched the chain tight, pulling the metal door inward until the insulated frame groaned from the pressure.

"That wouldn't hold for long," Lyons stated, his breath fogging from the cold as he used a butcher's apron from a carving table to wipe the icy blood off his hands.

"Long enough," Blancanales replied past chattering teeth, moving among the hanging sides of beef heading deep into the freezer.

In the far rear was a second door, but the designation plaque had been removed, and when the men opened the compartment, inside was only thumping machinery, huge pipes, racks of tools, pressure patches, countless metered levers and pressure gauges.

"Those Czech sons of bitches did make some modifications to the boat," McCarter said, staring at the housing. "This is a fuel pump pressure screen. We're not over the saltwater ballast tanks, but an eigthy-thousand-gallon fuel tank!"

"Any access to the scuttling charges?" Lyons asked hopefully, flexing his hands against the frigid air of the meat locker.

"No, but if we use a grenade here, the entire boat blows."

"I'm not ready to go down that road yet," Blancanales said, shifting his grip on the cold assault rifle.

Suddenly, there was a hard pounding on the distant freezer door, and somebody fired a Kalashnikov through the blast hole, the spray of rounds jiggling the hanging sides of beef in a grotesque pantomime of life.

"Okay, new plan," Lyons said, shutting the door of the pumping room and grabbing a crescent wrench from a rack of tools.

CHAPTER NINETEEN

Carson City Fuel Depot, South Los Angeles

The members of Phoenix Force braced themselves, and a heartbeat later the APC slammed into the side of the enemy transport.

Everything loose in the vehicle was thrown free, pencils, scraps of paper and spent brass filled the interior of the machine as the commandos almost burst free from the seat harnesses. The ringing crash was deafening inside the machine, metal crunching and twisting, but they still vaguely heard the headlights smash, a man scream in terrible pain.

Grinding gears, Encizo pulled the big brute backward to see that one of the mercs had been crushed between the two Eighties, then he threw the tandem diesels into gear and rammed the second APC again, forcing it ahead of them like a shield. Tires blew and the Russian transport began to slide sideways across the construction site. Encizo knew that if the other driver had been wearing his harness, the man would only be stunned for a few moments and he had to seize the advantage. As if by sheer force of will, he shouted a roar at the vibrating diesel, trying to make it go faster.

Ceiling fixtures exploded in fluorescent glass showers, conduits were crumpled, iron scaffolding was smashed aside. The heavy metal frames fell on top of the wrestling machines and bounced off the Russian armor, sounding like the end of the world to the commandos inside the bucking, shaking, roaring war wagons.

"Time to die," James muttered, his words echoing strangely in their ears over his throat mike. The jamming was gone, the com link was back!

The men braced themselves as well as possible, and the APC violently slammed to a dead halt against the opposite fieldstone wall. Even before they had recovered, Encizo threw the grinding transmission into reverse, gained a few yards and rammed the wounded APC again and again, buckling the side armor until diesel fuel and hydraulic fluids started pooling around the damaged transport.

"Enough," Hawkins shouted, throwing open the roof hatch.

As the Cuban braked the crumpled vehicle, Phoenix Force piled from the APC on shaky legs, but hands on weapons.

They were in the corner of the building. Debris covered the floor, and most of the two walls and ceiling were gone so that they could see up three flights. The second APC was buckled in the middle, red blood dribbling from the gun ports, the chassis bent slightly around an exposed main support beam in the very corner junction.

Savagely, Hawkins grinned for a split second as he started for the trapped men. Damn, he should have thought of this trick himself. Trained in demolitions, he knew how to bring down a building, and the one point where a soldier never placed a charge was in the far corners. That was where the internal steel frame would be anchored its strongest, sunk deep in granite and concrete. The worst location to explode a bomb, but the perfect spot to smash an APC.

His AK-74 at the ready, Manning reached the vehicle first and shoved his gun barrel through the firing port and let loose a long burst, angling it around. There came the meaty thwack of lead hitting flesh, but no screams. Then a movement at the rear of the vehicle caught their attention, and the rest of the team cut loose as the aft armor plate dropped away, forming a ramp to the dirty floor.

What the hell? Hawkins couldn't believe his eyes. No configuration of the Russian BTR-80 had a rear hatch. But then he saw that the edges were shiny smooth, cut with lasers or acetylene torches then filed smooth. It was a modification done at the foundry, and he could guess why. Firing steadily, Hawkins moved around the smashed APC and stitched Sergei Zofchak as he threw an arming switch. The man staggered from the 9 mm rounds and dropped, but a low rumble started to build into controlled thunder and a hellish light filled the interior.

The light from inside the APC got ever brighter, tendrils of flame writhing from the gunports and cracks, as two huge objects began to slide from the rear of the APC, scraping noisily along the metal ramp—black tubes with flat-head armor crowns.

"Shkvals!" James yelled, strafing the torpedoes with his MP-5 machine gun.

The team raked the hulls of the torpedoes with their weapon until the Shkvals reached the floor and their fiery exhaust filled the area with heat and light, forcing the men away. The sharply defined flames extended for yards as the rocket motors shoved each massive weapon forward, slowly increasing in speed.

Maintaining fire, Phoenix Force hit the torpedoes a hundred times with no damage done, until Hawkins threw his thermite grenade. The searing fireball engulfed both torpedoes and the closer one detonated, the blast seeming to shake the world.

As the Stony Man warriors struggled back to their feet, they saw one Shkval lying in a thousand pieces, its internal fuel tanks blown from the heat of the thermite. But the other was still moving, scraping along the city street throwing out a fountain of sparks.

Clambering inside the Russian APC, Encizo hunted for any more of the rocket launchers, while Manning checked in the rubble outside. Both men found the weapons, smashed and completely useless.

"I found a launcher but no rocket," Manning reported.

Excitedly, Encizo held up a pointed object. "One rocket, no launcher."

Taking the projectile, Manning loaded the RPG and went to the hole in the wall. The Shkval could be seen fishtailing along the street, almost six blocks away. Almost at the range of the RPG, and nearly far away enough to arm the nuke. Shit!

Nobody spoke, not even to pray, as Manning assumed a firing stance and leveled the weapon. Closing his mind to all distractions, the sniper held a breath, aimed and fired.

The 40 mm rocket blasted away, streaking down the street to slam up the flaming nozzle of the Shkval. The torpedo instantly lifted into the air, spinning then detonating in a staggering explosion, shattering windows and flipping over nearby cars. For a split second, Phoenix Force thought the nuke had detonated. But then the wreckage of the destroyed Shkval slammed back onto the pavement with a resounding crash, the tubular body split from stem to stern.

In spite of the amazing hit, the Stony Man warriors stood solemn and pensive. The city was saved; now they had to find out if they had died doing the job.

With a pensive expression, James lurched back to the smashed APC and checked the control board. "All clear." He sighed in relief. "No radiation detected," James announced with a wide smile, poking his head out of the BTR-80 hatch. "The sphere didn't rupture. We're okay!"

Now the men relaxed their shoulders and allowed broad smiles to cross their weary faces.

"Beautiful shot there!" Grimaldi said over the com link. "Now get moving! The National Guard is already on the way with a decontamination unit to recover the Shkvals. I'll stand watch until the Guard arrives."

"Roger," Hawkins replied, casting away his weapon, "out."

Tossing away their weapons and web harnesses, Phoenix Force stripped off their battle gear and slipped outside in only their civilian clothing to mingle with the growing crowd even as the police and fire department sirens began to howl in the distance.

Main Bridge, Varyag

"THERE'S A WHAT ON D deck?" Vadas demanded, looking up from the chart table. The instrument panels edging the ceiling of the submarine bridge cast a rainbow of hues across his gnarled features, giving the soldier a demonic appearance.

"Some sort of firefight," Bezdek replied, holding one side of a headphone to his ear. Seated at the diving controls, he was handling several chores at the same time. As a precaution against any treachery from the German mercenaries, the Czech team had made sure none of the hired men knew anything about operating a submarine.

"A mutiny?" Vadas demanded, pulling out his .44 AutoMag and jacking the slide to chamber a round.

Setting the computer to handle the submarine for a while, Bezdek frowned. "No, six, eight mercs dead. It is three big men, armed with AK-74 carbines."

"How the hell did they get on board?" Vadas demanded. "Has the hull been breached?"

"Negative, none of the security sensors have been tripped. Maybe they stowed away inside the last crate of Shkvals we brought aboard last night."

That made sense. How else could anybody have gotten inside the *Varyag?* But this wasn't good. The sub was still well within the territorial waters of the U.S., dangerously near their Coronado Navy Base with its fleet of warships. Studying the chart of the undersea canyon they were following, Vadas saw no clear avenue of transit and made a decision.

"Prepare the Shkvals. Use four that we already have loaded into the forward tubes. Keep the others as reserve. Set the internal computer of the Shkvals to our GPD setting and launch immediately. We will use the distraction of San Offrey as a cover, and sail through the radioactive blast zone safely in deep water."

The missile carriers on the surface wouldn't be in any condition to threaten the *Varyag,* and the Czechs could easily destroy anything ahead of them underwater with the remaining two forward Shkvals, with the four in the rear tubes as backup for any pursuing American subs.

Without comment, Bezdek stiffly went to the weapons station, linked to the torpedo room feed and downloaded the coordinates into the miniprocessor of the weapons.

"Done," he replied, locking the instructions under a cipher keyword. Almost immediately, red lights on the status board turned yellow, then green and finally white as the four Shkval torpedoes automatically hard-fired. Now there was no stopping the destruction of the West Coast.

"Now let's kill the intruders," Vadas growled, going to an arms locker and taking out a KEDR subgun. "We shall handle this minor matter ourselves."

"With pleasure." Bezdek grinned, seizing a machine pistol. Slapping in a curved clip, he snapped the bolt and slung the subgun over a shoulder as he headed for the brass pole that led to the wardroom three decks below. From there they could grab the next fire pole and reach D deck in half the time spent using the elevators.

But as they approached the pole, the elevator doors exploded, the concussion slamming both men painfully to the deck and setting off a dozen Klaxons.

The ceiling ventilation fans fought to draw off the billowing cloud of smoke as the men struggled to recover from the effects of the blast. From the deck, Vadas saw three men drop through the ceiling of the elevator into the cage—three big men covered with slimy diesel fuel and holding automatic weapons covered with plastic freezer bags.

The truth hit Vadas like a bullet between the eyes. So that's what the intruders had been doing on D deck—finding a pump room to gain access to the fuel lines and swim up to reach the main elevator shaft! Good God, who was invading his vessel? Not the CIA or the FBI. These big men had to be Navy SEALs. Nobody else would have dared such a hideously dangerous stunt. The very thought made the man shudder.

Forcing himself to stand behind the chart table, Vadas swung up his KEDR subgun and took aim. Well, he had killed Navy SEALs before, and had no doubt that he could do so again this day. Bravery didn't make them bulletproof.

Then he realized that the plastic-wrapped guns were merely for effect. Covered with fuel, the SEALs couldn't use the weapons without setting themselves ablaze. But the Czechs were under no such handicap.

Firing their KEDR subguns, the Czechs riddled the two men in front. They staggered under the bullets, but didn't fall. Bulletproof vests, eh? Dropping the KEDR, Vadas started to draw his .44 AutoMag when the man safely behind the front two SEALs made a throwing gesture and something landed in the middle of the bridge.

The grenade landed between Vadas and Bezdek, both men jerking away as they prepared to dive for cover. Then they saw that charge wasn't primed, the pin in place, handle taped firmly to the sphere. A trick!

Diving over the chart table, Carl Lyons tackled Vadas, knocking the huge silver gun out of his grip. The Czech flowed with the strike and spun to ram a stiff-fingered hand directly at Lyons's kidneys. Agony erupted through half his body, but Lyons fought through the red haze and rammed a thumb directly into his adversary's left eye. The orb burst under the pressure and the man recoiled, howling from the terrible pain.

Hands, knees, elbows flashing, McCarter was trading lightning-fast blows with the second man, so Blancanales attacked from the rear, chopping the man across the back of the neck with the flat of his hand, and felt the bones snap. Twitching uncontrollably, Bezdek slumped to the deck, dead long before his body accepted the fact.

Screaming obscenities in Czech, Vadas pulled a flat black handle from his belt, aimed and pressed the firing stud. The spring-loaded knife launched the blade out of the handle, and Lyons turned just in time to take the steel in his shoulder instead of the chest. McCarter dove across the deck and came up with both hands together, driving the mass of bone and sinew directly into the face of the enemy. His jaw cracking from the blow, Vadas reeled, spitting teeth and blood, then kicked sideways, catching the Briton exactly in the solar plexus. Unable to breathe, the Phoenix Force commander doubled over, then threw himself forward and butted the Czech hard, slamming his spine hard against the metal edge of the anchored chart table.

Half blind and pinned in place, Vadas lifted both hands high for a killing blow when Lyons slashed the man across the throat with the bare knife blade. Gushing blood, the huge former soldier grabbed his throat, and Blancanales rapped his temple with a knuckled fist. Then McCarter rose, grabbed the Czech, turned and pivoted, flipping him over his hip.

Twisting as he fell, Jozsef Vadas crashed to the deck with a loud crack and a broken neck. Incredibly, the man tried once more to rise, then collapsed and went still.

Not trusting the big Czech, Lyons limped over to the body, knelt in the blood and slit his throat from ear to ear with the knife blade. Their blood mingled from the act, but when the ex-cop stood there were only three men alive on the bridge.

"K-kill those a-alarms," McCarter panted, leaning on the chart table. But glancing at the navigational maps, he went pale.

"San Offrey," he said in a whisper. "The bastards have the nuclear power plant targeted for a strike."

The others knew what the fallout damage would be from such an attack and limped over to the weapons board.

"Four Shkvals are already on their way," Blancanales said, studying the computer monitor. His Russian was poor, but the graphics were plainly visible.

"Where's the abort button! Find it fast!"

"Here," Lyons said, holding a fistful of wires and smashed transistors. "It got busted in the fight."

Standing on the bridge of the Russian torpedo boat, the Stony Man warriors remained silent. There was nothing to say. The prime minister of England, several presidents and most of California were doomed, and there was nothing they could do about the situation.

Coronado Navy Base, CINCPACFLT HQ

DEEP UNDERGROUND in a concrete bunker, a double bank of sonar operators watched the western coast of the United States for any possible enemy activity. The conversations were hushed, and no music played to ease the long, boring shift. The sonar men and woman plied their trade with their ears alone, and any distraction was tantamount to treason in their opinion.

Then six perked their heads up at the same moment with puzzled expressions.

"Duty officer, hot noise in the water," a sonar operator crisply reported over his throat mike. "We have a live fish."

"Confirm that," a voice snapped in their headphones.

"Aye, sir. We have confirmation," another added. "Ident is Shkval."

"Course!" the duty officer demanded, an alarm already howling in the background.

"Due west—no, south. They're turning toward the

coast,'' the first sailor said slowly. ''But there are no ships in sight in that direction.''

''San Offrey!'' another cried. ''They're trying to make a Chernobyl meltdown!''

''Alert, we have a Broken Glass,'' the duty officer said over the PA system. ''This is not a drill. Repeat, we have a code Broken Glass. Eastside batteries fire all available missiles at the Shkvals. I want a god-damn wall of fire between those things and the nuclear plant!''

''Too late,'' a sonar operator whispered, and another nodded in agreement. It took four minutes to launch, and the torpedoes would strike the beachfront power plant in three and a half. There was nothing anybody could do to save California.

Bridge, Varyag

''TIME TO IMPACT?'' Lyons demanded, holding his aching side.

Schwarz would have been able to read the sonar screen, but Blancanales did his best. Hopefully, his friend had gotten out of the foundry in time.

''Two minutes,'' he reported. ''Sonar has them a mile to sea starting on primary run.''

''They fired blind,'' McCarter said aloud, ''with the sub pointing in the wrong direction. The Shkvals were zoning in on the target, but they had lost minutes getting realigned.''

''Are they set for impact or range?''

Blancanales raised his hands. "Unknown!"

"Then we set those two for countermeasure," Lyons commanded. "Let's see if a Shkval can take out a Shkval."

Moving as fast as possible, Blancanales used fifty irreplaceable seconds setting the commands and hitting the launch button.

Nervously, the men watched as the lights on the weapons board flashed down to white and the rocket torpedoes launched. Hardly daring to breathe, they listened to the escalating pings of the sonar as the weapons locked on each other, the outcome completely unknown.

THE ALARMS WERE howling at the San Offrey nuclear plant, red lights flashing as the control-room crew did its best to scram the core without creating the very kind of meltdown they were fighting to avoid.

Then a tremendous explosion tore apart the ocean about a hundred yards from the sandy beach, closely followed by several more, the blasts overlapping one another so that an accurate count was impossible.

"What happened?" a technician asked, staring out the wide windows facing the Pacific Ocean.

"Damned if I know," a woman whispered, licking dry lips.

Tense moments became minutes, then a phone rang and the chief technician answered it with shaking hands.

"They stopped them!" he cried, waving the receiver. "A Navy sub blew the torpedoes out of the water!"

The control-room crew broke into wild cheering, more than a few openly weeping in relief. The alarms continued to howl for a few more minutes, then abruptly cut off, a blessed peace filling the power plant.

Out at sea, the ripples from the titanic blasts were already fading across the surface, the sea cleansing the wound until there was no sign of the brief struggle that had violently ripped it apart only heartbeats earlier.

EPILOGUE

Arlington National Cemetery, Washington, D.C.

The patchy clouds of gray were breaking apart in the sky, admitting a wealth of sunlight on the military graveyard.

Marching to a slow drumbeat, the Third United States Infantry was moving alongside the line of horse-drawn carts holding the flag-draped coffins of the sailors from New London and Pearl Harbor.

Situated on a low hill, the columned front of the Curtis-Lee Mansion overlooked the solemn procession on the gravel road winding through the wide green fields sectioned off by long, neat rows of simple white headstones. The soldiers of America were laid to rest here, along with a small handful of citizens who had performed some extraordinary service to the nation.

"Pre-sent arms!" a color sergeant shouted, snapping a hand to his saber.

Wearing sharply creased Dress A uniforms, seven U.S. Marines smartly brought their Browning bolt-action rifles into position with machine perfection and dutifully fired three times, giving the honored dead a full twenty-one gun salute, the ancient naval tradition having been adopted by every branch of the service.

There were no reporters allowed at the funeral service, only the families of the deceased, the President, his bodyguards and a small group of somber men and women.

"They fought the good fight," the President said, bowing his head.

"They stayed the course, they kept the faith," Brognola finished the quote. The quotation was a favorite of most soldiers across the world. Far too many times Brognola had heard the words as another friend was laid in the ground, and he knew that he would hear it again in the future. Perhaps one day to have those words said over his own coffin. The thought wasn't depressing, but oddly comforting, the circle of life continuing.

"A twenty-one-gun salute and a folded flag to your nearest relative," Barbara Price said. "That's not much of a reward for doing your duty."

"More than enough," McCarter said as he threw a salute to the line of coffins as they began to cycle downward into the ground on the silent hydraulic frames.

The soldier was sore and badly bruised, but felt honor bound to attend the service. Carl Lyons was in the hospital recuperating from his wounds, along with Gadgets Schwarz, who had stopped the Shkvals from launching at Los Angeles, and escaped from the exploding foundry at the cost of a broken arm. Actually, he was looking forward to the hospital stay; it would give him a chance to work on another magazine article.

On the swing side, Rosario and Toni Blancanales had salvaged a lot of the illicit cash from the Red Dagger team and set up a freelance foundation run by the homeless to hire the homeless and repair confiscated crack houses to be sold. The profits would be used to do it all again. Everybody came out on top in that deal. A small ray of sunlight amid all of the bloodshed. But that was how battles were won, one step at a time.

"Any decision about San Offrey?" Brognola asked pointedly.

Holding a hat in both hands, the President nodded. "The Army Corps of Engineers is already laying the foundation to erect a concrete seawall between San Offrey plant and the beach. Nothing short of a nuke will get through it—I've seen to that. We may make mistakes, but not twice in a row. And repairs are already under way for all of the other damage done by those damn torpedoes."

"Good," Price said, passing the politician a computer disk. "Here, I wanted to give this to you personally. We retrieved it from the bodies of Vadas and Zofchak. It's a complete technical manual on the Shkvals."

With the wind from the nearby Potomac River ruffling his hair, the Man glanced at the disk, the cause of so much destruction and death.

"I'll push a crash program through Congress to start building countermeasures," he said grimly, tucking away the disk. "Those damn things will never again be a threat to the world."

While the sad strains of taps was played for the fallen heroes, the small group stayed until the very end of the mass funeral, then turned and started their separate ways. Although America won an important battle, the war against terrorism raged on.

But the soldiers of Stony Man stood ready.

Readers won't want to miss this exciting new title in the SuperBolan® series!

DON PENDLETON's

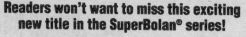

MACK BOLAN®

Sleepers

A decades-old KGB campaign involving sleeper assassins planted in each of the fifty-one American states has been activated by a dedicated Soviet hard-liner whose vision demands a long overdue day of reckoning. Burke Barnum is a traitor to his American government, but he's Mack Bolan's last hope for nailing Jasha Seriozha and his Soviet moles. With his prisoner in tow and a beautiful Russian agent riding shotgun, the trio races to defuse these human time bombs—before everyone's luck runs out.

Available in January 2003 at your favorite retail outlet.

Or order your copy now by sending your name, address, zip or postal code, along with a check or money order (please do not send cash) for $6.50 for each book ordered ($7.99 in Canada), plus 75¢ postage and handling ($1.00 in Canada), payable to Gold Eagle Books, to:

In the U.S.

Gold Eagle Books
3010 Walden Avenue
P.O. Box 9077
Buffalo, NY 14269-9077

In Canada

Gold Eagle Books
P.O. Box 636
Fort Erie, Ontario
L2A 5X3

Please specify book title with your order.
Canadian residents add applicable federal and provincial taxes.

GOLD EAGLE

GSB88

James Axler
Outlanders®

EQUINOX ZERO

As magistrate-turned-rebel Kane, fellow warrior Grant and archivist Brigid Baptiste face uncertainty in their own ranks, an ancient foe resurfaces in the company of Viking warriors—harnessing ancient prophecies of Ragnarok, the final conflict of fire and ice, to bring his own mad vision of a new apocalypse. To save what's left of the future, Kane's new battlefield is the kingdom of Antarctica, where legend and lore have taken on mythic and deadly proportions.

In the Outlands, the shocking truth is humanity's last hope.

Or order your copy now by sending your name, address, zip or postal code, along with a check or money order (please do not send cash) for $6.50 for each book ordered ($7.99 in Canada), plus 75¢ postage and handling ($1.00 in Canada), payable to Gold Eagle Books, to:

In the U.S.
Gold Eagle Books
3010 Walden Avenue
P.O. Box 9077
Buffalo, NY 14269-9077

In Canada
Gold Eagle Books
P.O. Box 636
Fort Erie, Ontario
L2A 5X3

Please specify book title with your order.
Canadian residents add applicable federal and provincial taxes.

GOUT24

Readers won't want to miss this exciting new title in the SuperBolan® series!

DON PENDLETON's

MACK BOLAN®
CAGED

A desperate cry for help draws Mack Bolan into a world where educated, attractive foreign women are kidnapped and forced to work in America's top companies as blackmailed industrial spies. Mack Bolan and a fellow Stony Man warrior must work together to smash the international slavery ring and end the human misery.

Available in November 2002 at your favorite retail outlet.

Or order your copy now by sending your name, address, zip or postal code, along with a check or money order (please do not send cash) for $6.50 for each book ordered ($7.99 in Canada), plus 75¢ postage and handling ($1.00 in Canada), payable to Gold Eagle Books, to:

In the U.S.	In Canada
Gold Eagle Books	Gold Eagle Books
3010 Walden Avenue	P.O. Box 636
P.O. Box 9077	Fort Erie, Ontario
Buffalo, NY 14269-9077	L2A 5X3

Please specify book title with your order.
Canadian residents add applicable federal and provincial taxes.

GOLD EAGLE

GSB87

DEATH LANDS®

Destiny's Truth

Available in
December 2002
at your favorite retail outlet.

JAMES AXLER

DEATH LANDS

Destiny's Truth

Emerging from a gateway in New England, Ryan Cawdor and his band of wayfaring survivalists ally themselves with a group of women warriors who join their quest to locate the Illuminated Ones, a mysterious pre-dark sect who may possess secret knowledge of Deathlands. Yet their pursuit becomes treacherous, for their quarry has unleashed a deadly plague in a twisted plot to cleanse the earth. As Ryan's group falls victim, time is running out—for the intrepid survivors…and for humanity itself.

Or order your copy now by sending your name, address, zip or postal code, along with a check or money order (please do not send cash) for $6.50 for each book ordered ($7.99 in Canada), plus 75¢ postage and handling ($1.00 in Canada), payable to Gold Eagle Books, to:

In the U.S.
Gold Eagle Books
3010 Walden Ave.
P.O. Box 9077
Buffalo, NY 14269-9077

In Canada
Gold Eagle Books
P.O. Box 636
Fort Erie, Ontario
L2A 5X3

Please specify book title with order.
Canadian residents add applicable federal and provincial taxes.

GDL60

THE Destroyer™

WASTE NOT, WANT NOT

Mayana—a South American country known only for a mass cult suicide—is poised to become the salvation of a trash-choked globe. A revolutionary device, the Vaporizer, can turn garbage into thin air and trash into cash for the beleaguered nation. But with the President scheduled to attend a global environmental summit in Mayana, Dr. Harold Smith smells trouble—and dispatches Remo and Chiun to the scene to pose as scientists.

Available in January 2003 at your favorite retail outlet.

Or order your copy now by sending your name, address, zip or postal code, along with a check or money order (please do not send cash) for $6.50 for each book ordered ($7.99 in Canada), plus 75¢ postage and handling ($1.00 in Canada), payable to Gold Eagle Books, to:

In the U.S.	**In Canada**
Gold Eagle Books	Gold Eagle Books
3010 Walden Avenue	P.O. Box 636
P.O. Box 9077	Fort Erie, Ontario
Buffalo, NY 14269-9077	L2A 5X3

GOLD EAGLE

Please specify book title with your order.
Canadian residents add applicable federal and provincial taxes.

GDEST130

DEATH LANDS®

JAMES AXLER

Skydark Spawn

Skydark Spawn

*Available in
March 2003
at your favorite retail outlet.*

In the relatively untouched area of what was once Niagara
Falls, Ryan and his fellow wayfarers find the pastoral
farmland under the despotic control of a twisted baron and
his slave-breeding farm. Ryan, Mildred and Krysty are
captured by the baron's sec men and pawned into the cruel
frenzy of their leader's grotesque desires. JB, Jak and Doc
enlist the aid of outlanders to organize a counterstrike—but
rescue may come too late for them all.

Or order your copy now by sending your name, address, zip or postal code, along with a
check or money order (please do not send cash) for $6.50 for each book ordered ($7.99 in
Canada), plus 75¢ postage and handling ($1.00 in Canada), payable to Gold Eagle Books, to:

In the U.S.	In Canada
Gold Eagle Books	Gold Eagle Books
3010 Walden Ave.	P.O. Box 636
P.O. Box 9077	Fort Erie, Ontario
Buffalo, NY 14269-9077	L2A 5X3

Please specify book title with order.
Canadian residents add applicable federal and provincial taxes.

GDL61